Urban Legend
Murder at the House of Blue Lights

By

Garry D. Ledbetter

ISBN-10: 1475133731
ISBN-13: 978-1475133738

Cover design by Karen A. Phillips www.phillipscovers.com

This book is dedicated to Skiles Geraci the Great
Granddaughter of Skiles Test

Introduction

A dead wife in a glass casket, blue lights illuminating the countryside, 150 cats, vicious dogs, a pet cemetery, and an underground tunnel. Yes, I'm talking about the most famous urban legend in Indiana, The House of Blue Lights.

Yes, it was a real place! It was located on the northeast side of Indianapolis. It was the home of Skiles Test from 1913 until his death in 1964.

Most of the buildings including the house remained on the property after his death until they were demolished in 1978. At that time the property became the Skiles Test Nature Park.

Even today, nearly 50 years after his death there are TV documentaries, Radio shows, and Newspaper articles about the legend. Links to these along with pictures and stories can be found on the official web site set up by the Test family at http://houseofbluelights.com

This novel is based on that legend. It involves intrigue, mystery and murder surrounded by a romantic passion for life at the highest level of sexual sensuality.

Follow the main characters as they search from past decades to the present looking for clues as to the names of the ruthlessly murdered bodies and who killed them.

Even though part of the book is fiction the story delves into a lot of truths concerning the actual legend. Whenever possible real names, places, and events were weaved into the story line. An example of these truths is there was a secret phone line installed by the FBI and a secret post office box. There was also a dead body found on the property in 1963 as well as little things like a speaker grill turned into an alcohol hideaway, and a sundial with a poem.

The animal names and stories, farm buildings and area locations are factual.

Although some names were changed or not used the pictures in this book and on the web site are actual photos of people and places from the property. The web site contains actual photos of the underground tunnel, the garage, and other house pictures.

Music was also a big part of life at the farm. Skiles had purchased a huge jukebox and had collected thousands of records, thus you will find references to songs throughout the novel. These songs give some insight as to the personality of some of the characters. I encourage you to visit the website listed above and click on the tab "Novel". There you will find links to the songs referenced in this book.

Another link you might find interesting is the one called Chucks Toyland. This takes you to a section maintained by Charles Test, the great nephew of Skiles Test. This site has a lot of history in it and links to other books about the legend. You will find this link under the tab "links".

Prologue

The Legend, Circa 1955

It was a clear night as we turned off Shadeland Avenue onto Fall Creek Road. I could see the stars from the back seat of Mike's convertible. We had the top down for two reasons. One it was a warm summer night and two was that we thought we might need to make a fast getaway. It's much faster to jump into a car with no top than to stop and open the doors when you are in a hurry.

As we turned onto Johnson Road I could feel the hairs on the back of my neck stand up as I thought about what we were about to embark upon.

There were four of us that night. Wayne, Carol, myself, and of course Mike since it was his car. I had been here before with other friends but we had always "chickened" out at the last minute. This night, however was different. Wayne was a real go-getter and would never back down from a dare. In addition we had just been to the "Haunted Bridge" the night before and even though we were scared we still made it all the way to the bridge.

The rumours about the Haunted Bridge in Avon may or may not have been true about the lady ghost at midnight but we left there at 10 pm so I really don't know.

As we rounded the curve the headlight beams cast a dim light against the tall gate guarding the entrance to the drive that led to the house. The gate looked to be about twelve to fifteen feet tall. I was never one to be exact on measurements but I know it was really high.

It was a gray metal type gate that was hinged on both sides and closed in the middle of the drive. There was a hole in the pavement where the locking rod rested.

If we were really going through with this we would have to find a shorter fence. There was no way we could climb that gate.

We drove about a quarter of a mile past the gate and pulled off into this little grassy lane. It was a short lane that only ran about the length of the car. It looked like a wide path that could have been used as an entrance to a pasture. We jumped out of the car and followed the road back down to the gate. There we found a fence that ran up a steep hill. The trees and brush were dense but with the help of flashlights we found a place where the fence was partially down. One by one we went through the fence. Wayne was out in front, then Mike, then Carol and me. Once through the fence we made our way back toward the gate. We figured it would be much easier to walk up the lane than go through the woods.

As what seemed like a mile going up this steep lane we saw a blue haze off to the right just ahead of us. A few yards later we saw a building that was blocking part of the blue haze. We moved off the lane and went up along side the building. It was a steep climb but when we reached the top we discovered the reason for the blue haze.

There was a magnificent swimming pool with blue lights under glass all around the pool. There were no other lights visible near the pool but not far from it we saw more lights surrounding a house. We made our way toward the brightest part of the house which was made of all glass. The brightness was almost blinding but as we neared the house we all saw him at once and we stopped dead in our tracks.

The man didn't seem to be moving. He just sat there in front of an open glass casket. His hands were grasping the edge of the casket as if they were glued to it. His face was stern looking yet sad and at his side he had a shotgun and a dog. The dog was not glued to anything and he saw us!

Wayne shouted, "Scatter." and we did.

All we heard as we ran was a door slam, a shotgun being fired, dogs barking and the sound of our feet breaking every twig in our path. Wayne and Carol headed toward the right side of the pool, Mike took the walk that led straight to the pool and I headed into the woods on the left side of the pool. I heard Mike yell "The dog has me" as he jumped into the pool. More shots were fired; Wayne yelled, "I'm hit." Carol said, "They are coming out of the tunnels, God help us".

What seemed like minutes since Carol had yelled God help us but probably was only seconds I had made it past the left side of the pool. I turned to see if anyone or thing was behind me and that's when I tripped over something and fell.

It suddenly became quiet. I looked up and saw this blue mist rolling toward me like fog. I clicked on my flashlight and saw what I had stumbled over. It was a small tombstone, however there was not just one tombstone, there were hundreds of them. The one in front of me said "Kitty Joe". I stumbled to my feet and tried to move but something had me...

Skiles Test, his first wife, and the first blue lights.

South view of the house early 50's

Pool house and pool early 50's

Skiles and his Daughter

Time clock room and milk barn 1963

Farm Workers during the Sixties

Garry Ledbetter

Allen Hefley

Charles Lockhart

Tom Brinkman

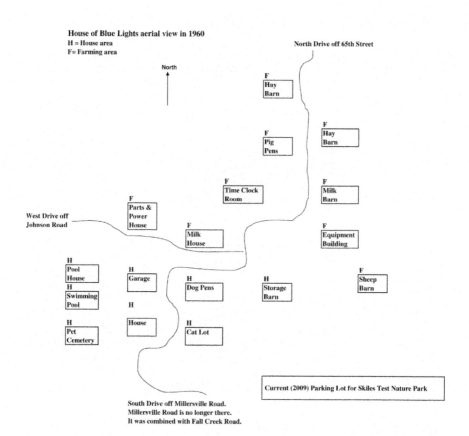

House of Blue Lights aerial view in 1960
H = House area
F= Farming area

North Drive off 65th Street

North

F
Hay
Barn

F
Hay
Barn

F
Pig
Pens

F
Time Clock
Room

F
Milk
Barn

F
Parts &
Power
House

West Drive off
Johnson Road

F
Milk
House

F
Equipment
Building

H
Pool
House

H
Garage

H
Dog Pens

H
Storage
Barn

F
Sheep
Barn

H
Swimming
Pool

H

H
Pet
Cemetery

H
House

H
Cat Lot

Current (2009) Parking Lot for Skiles Test Nature Park

South Drive off Millersville Road.
Millersville Road is no longer there.
It was combined with Fall Creek Road.

Cast of *Main* Characters
Present Day

Brian Fallon – Newspaper Reporter – Indianapolis Papers
Jack Daring – Editor and Brian's boss
Paul Langley – District Attorney
Amanda Steele – Local TV News Reporter
Laura Needham – Amanda's college friend
Jeff Needham Jr. – Laura's dad
Troy Bennett – Coroner
Chip Reynolds – Police Detective
Preston Hammond – Crown Hill funeral director
Bruce Bowser – Lucy Gordon's attorney

Past Day
Skiles Test – Himself
Madeline Harrow Test – Skiles's wife
Dan Langford – Madeline Test's Doctor
Dr. Timothy Franklin – Colleague of Dan Langford
Kelly Test – Daughter of Skiles Test
Ralph Castle – Kelly's physiatrist
Bonnie Hanover – Kelly's mother
Charles and Gladys Hanover – Bonnie's parents
Diane Cummings – Kelly's friend from college
Curtis Tompkins – Acquaintance of Kelly Test from Bahamas
Doug Raines – Farm worker
Daniel Raines – Doug's brother
Kathy Kistner – Kelly's nanny
Jim Tyler – Farm worker
Tom Tyler – Jim Tyler's son
Ned Tyler – Jim's father and Tom's grandfather
Larry Thomas – Skiles's Private Detective
Jeff Needham – FBI agent
Frank Wayne – Skiles's Veterinarian
Jack Test – Skiles's cousin
Louise Buckner – Skiles's House maid
Emma Jones – Skiles's Cook
Lucy Gordon – Skiles's secretary
Keith Wiley – Skiles's Timekeeper

Chapter 1
Present Day
The Discovery

"Hey Bowling, did you know you're burning daylight? Let's get started, I want to hear those diesel engines humming and smell that diesel smoke. We have nine more homes to complete by August or we could lose our contract with the state." "Not to worry Tony," said Joe as he drank his last drink of morning coffee and headed for the backhoe. "I'll have that first one dug before you can survey the next group."

No matter what Joe said Tony Castrol still worried. He had been the foreman with Avalon homes for one year. Avalon was a start up company with few resources and capital.

Homebuilders like Avalon; unless they were run by huge corporations didn't last long in today's market. After all they had only been around for three years and had been near bankruptcy just prior to getting this contract.

The contract consisted of building an entire housing complex in an old nature park. The complex would consist of several upscale homes complete with a community pool and playground.

Tony was still puzzled as to how Avalon won the contract. There were other more prominent builders with much more experience and knowledge than Avalon. It was his guess that Avalon won by underbidding and he would end up having to take shortcuts to make any money. But that was a problem for another day. Right now he needed to be making more progress than he had so far.

Tony's main concern was missing out on what he called his "Golden Opportunity." This was his chance not only to make a name for himself but also to make enough money to buy a stake in Avalon. After all he had been building houses for ten years and this could be his last chance to break into the big time.

Just as Tony was about to get into his truck he noticed that Joe had stopped digging. Joe was off the backhoe and was standing quietly looking at the hole he had dug. Tony walked toward Joe and said, "What's wrong Joe?" Joe didn't answer he just stood there.

Joe Bowling was a very mild and timid man and very easy to scare. All of his friends said that during his time in the military he was around a lot of explosives and that made him very jumpy. Even today if you sneaked up behind him and said boo, it would startle him.

"Joe, what is it? Are you okay?" Joe still didn't answer; he just stood there pointing at the hole. Then Tony saw what had spooked him.

Beneath the dirt the corner of something was showing. That something was some type of glass enclosure. The enclosure looked about the size of a casket and something was buried in it!

Brian Fallon thought it was going to be just another Monday as he climbed the stairs up to the third floor. He never used the elevator; he liked exercise, whether it was at the gym or stairs. The body was made to move and he wanted to be sure he moved as much as he could when he could. The stairs ran along the east end of the building. There were windows at all levels with rusted frames and missing caulk. The view out the window wasn't much better; it was just a parking lot.

Once he reached the door he knew the routine. He would go by the coffee machine for some fuel, grab a donut, one of his weaknesses, and stroll on over to his desk. On the way he would say good morning to all the other workers at the newspaper. Once he reached his desk he would have to clean it off. He tried to keep everything neat and organized but on weekends some of the staff would use it and leave their trash.

He never had any reason to believe there would be anything different to work on this Monday than any other Monday. He was sure all his assignments today would just be the typical city news of the day. Typical news was okay he guessed. It wasn't that he hated doing just the normal daily stuff but it had been a long time since he had a "great" story to write about. He knew nothing had happened over the weekend that was special for him.

His fear in life was that he would be stuck in the same old routine that every reporter ends up in. Reporting was a good start but there had to be more to life. There had to be something exciting happen. If it wasn't a good story then it had to be something personal. It had to be something that made life fun everyday and something you looked forward to when you got up in the morning.

He had been lucky and was hired just out of college as a junior reporter. After a couple of years he had already moved up a position due in part to his aggressiveness. He was not an aggressive person, just aggressive in his reporting. If you had a story that needed lots of background work he was your man. He would dig until he found all the facts and the real truth. He didn't care about your politics, your community stature, or anything else. He cared about one thing and that was the truth and did whatever it took to get it.

Brian had turned twenty-five on January 5th. He was six feet tall with natural dark hair and rugged looks. Even though he was rugged looking with a deep masculine voice he was still quite handsome. His voice seemed to be his most striking feature. Everyone always told him it was very masculine and sexy. He also had a great sense of humor and loved little one line jokes.

He was clean-shaven at this time, but had grown some facial hair in the past. He thought it made him look too much like a mountain man so he shaved it off.

His hair was cut to a normal length just above the ears and he just let it fall where it wanted to. He dressed with what you would call a "preppy look".

He always took pride in his appearance with clean and pressed pants and shirt. He occasionally wore a sport jacket but rarely wore a necktie. He didn't like them. He always said that the guy who invented them should be hung with one. He preferred the open neck look and it was much more comfortable.

"Brian, in my office now," yelled Jack! It wasn't a bad yell, after all Jack liked Brian. Brian reminded him of himself years ago.

Jack started in the same junior reporter position that Brian had but it had taken more years than he would like to admit to get where he was today. As the top editor Jack Daring had several reporters working for him but Brian was his favorite. He didn't know why but he just liked the guy.

Jack was a small frame person with a receding hairline. He had begun losing his hair about the same time that he started to gain weight. Being five foot and four inches tall didn't help his appearance either. When you're short and fat, you look worse than if you were tall and fat or at least that was his opinion.

"What's up Jack," asked Brian? "Close the door, have a seat, and let's talk," said Jack in a jittery voice.

Brian noticed right away that Jack was not his usual self. He was jumping around like a nervous kid. Jack was not always calm, as you would expect from an editor, but this was behavior Brian had not seen before.

"Brian, I'm going to be quick and to the point with this," he said. "Knowing you I know you will investigate this until you have all the facts and the truth." "You can count on that," said Brian, "but why are you so jumpy?"

"You would be jumpy to if you knew what I know," said Jack. "Or let me put it another way. If you knew what I always thought I knew and now I found out that maybe I really didn't know." "You are not making sense," said Brian. "I know, I know;" said Jack, "so let me tell you what's going on."

"Are you familiar with the urban legend about the house of blue lights," asked Jack? "I'm no expert on it but I have heard of it," said Brian. "I believe it was about a man named Test who kept his dead wife in a glass casket. I read an article on it years ago but never gave it much thought."

"Well," said Jack, "the property where the house was is now the site of a new housing development. When Skiles Test died his will stated that after a certain period of time and other stipulations the land was to be made into a nature park. Then if the costs to maintain it became unfeasible for the city they were to turn it over to a charity such as the Boy Scouts. Now, I don't know all the details but the city ran out of money to maintain the park. But instead of donating it to a charity they opened it up for bids for development. To make a long story short there was a court battle over the whole

---

4

thing and the charities lost. We ran the story on it but it was just prior to you coming here so I doubt if you would know anything about it."

"You are correct, I didn't know anything about all that stuff," said Brian.

"Anyway," said Jack. "The city sold it to a developer and they got tied up in court with environmentalists. The environmentalists lost and now they are building houses."

"Do you know where the area is," asked Jack? "Yes, I have driven by there before," said Brian. "I think the last time I was out that way the old Nature Park sign was still there but the place had been taken over by nature, No pun intended!"

"Well," said Jack, "you need to get out there and I'll send a camera crew to meet you. What I thought was just an urban legend has turned out to be a little more. They just dug up a glass casket and there is something in it!"

Chapter 2
Present Day
The Scene

It was a beautiful spring day as Brian drove to the site. The trees had bloomed about 2 weeks ago and there were a few colorful blossoms remaining but most of the trees were green with leaves by now. Birds were chirping and you could still smell spring in the air. It was late April and the weather had been good for Indianapolis in the springtime. Most years it rains the entire month of April and sometimes into May.

Brian had taken I 70 to I 465 to the Shadeland Avenue exit. Shadeland Avenue, Johnson Road, Fall Creek Road, and 65th Street bordered the area surrounding the old park. The trip took about thirty minutes once he pulled out of the parking lot. If he had been driving what he wanted he may have made it in a lot less time. He was currently driving a 2010 Chevrolet Equinox. It was on okay car. The gas mileage was good and for his purpose it was fine. It had enough storage for all his work stuff and enough cup holders for his cherry cokes. Cherry cokes were also a weakness for Brian along with the donuts. He had found the best ones were at Steak n Shake. He loved to go there for the cokes but hated the service. He had been to several and he always had lousy service. On two different occasions he gotten up and walked out because they never waited on him.

Brian's choice of cars was the 1970 Chevelle SS. Chevelles were another weakness along with most old cars. They didn't come with cup holders back then but they sure came with horsepower and a lot classier look than the current crop. All cars looked the same now days.

One of his dreams was to buy a big house with three bedrooms and a ten-car garage. With that he could have room for a Chevelle along with other classics.

His love for cars came from his father. His father was still driving a 65 Chevy Impala Super Sport with the last of the 409 Engines in it. Brian's grandfather had bought it new and passed it down to his dad.

His father and mother were still living but both his grandparents had passed. His family had always been very close and tight knit. Brian was an only child and grew up in a happy home. The only trauma he had suffered so far in his life was the loss of his grandparents. He was very close to both of them but especially his granddad. His grandfather, his dad, and he would spend hours and sometimes days either working on old cars or going to car events. They all three shared that common interest. Brian grew up with the smell of grease on him and gasoline flowing through his veins. However, he didn't quite fit that mold anymore of grease and gasoline. During college he had become *preppy* and wanted to keep his nails clean. He still loved the cars but no more grease. He still washed and waxed them but the dirty work was left to the professionals.

As Brian neared the area, he was trying to remember the article he had read many years ago about this place. He was born in Indiana and even grew up not far from here but the legend was so old and almost all who knew anything about it had died. He had run across the article while researching property rights for a college project. All he could remember was what he had told Jack.

He wished now he had paid more attention to the article but he was never one for that type of stuff. He considered himself "grounded" and liked what was real and could be proven, not some wild story that had been passed down and added to over the years. He could only imagine the kind of freaks this sort of thing would bring out of the woodwork. There would be paranormal people crawling all over the property trying to talk to the dead. There would be environmental loons saying we shouldn't be building houses over sacred ground. It would just go on and on.

The police had Fall Creek road blocked at Shadeland on one end and at the parkway on the other because Brian couldn't see any traffic coming eastbound. He showed his press pass and they let him through but he had to park along Fall Creek. He would have to walk almost a half-mile up the hill.

He ran into the camera crew as he neared the top of the hill where they had roped off the area. They could see the hole but were still too far away to see what was in it. One of the other reporters told Brian they had moved all the dirt from the glass container but were waiting on the coroner and forensics before lifting it out.

"Hello Brian, imagine finding you here." "Ah, a familiar voice," Brian said as he turned to face Amanda.

Amanda Steele worked for a local TV station as a reporter. Brian had met her last week during a charity fundraiser. He was glad she was there. He had thought about her a lot since the event. She was a very attractive woman. Brian wasn't good with guessing height but she was shorter than him. He figured she must be around five foot eight inches.

She had gorgeous black hair. It was so shiny it looked like she used car wax on it. Brian couldn't figure out why she was a reporter. She would have been more suited as a model or soap opera star. However, it didn't matter to him what she did, she just looked good which was another one of his weaknesses. He loved to look at women.

He figured if he had a 70 Chevelle, a box of donuts, a cherry coke, some old songs playing, yet another weakness, and a pretty girl to look at he would be as happy as a coon in a corn patch as his grandfather used to say.

"How are you Brian," she asked as she moved closer to him? She liked Brian, probably too much for someone she had just met. Her life had been filled with one fling after another since she graduated from college. Not that she played the field a lot; she just seemed to attract the wrong kind of guys.

—

8

Most all guys wanted one thing and she found her looks to be intimidating to the "other type of guy" whatever that meant. It was just she couldn't seem to attract the sincere ones and so after bouncing around trying to find the "right" guy, she gave up and left town.

She was from Ohio and had graduated from Ohio State. A college girlfriend of hers, Laura Needham, was from Indy so she invited her to visit; she liked the town and stayed.

She had been in Indy for about a month and landed this job with the TV station. It was a good break and she was lucky to get the job without any experience.

She had moved in with Laura on a temporary basis. Laura had a nice Condo in the Fishers area, which was a horrible drive to work, but you take what you get.

Laura was currently "between jobs" but her father was wealthy so she had no worries. She was between jobs because of the same problem Amanda had. Too many men wanting the same thing and Laura was not willing to give it. She had worked a couple of places but didn't want to put up with the sexual harassment. She was like Amanda, very attractive but with red hair.

"I'm fine," said Brian as he held out his hand to help her navigate the terrain near the hole.

"So do you know anything about the legend," she asked? "Only what I read years ago from a small article. How about you Amanda, do you know anything?" "Yes, my roommate Laura grew up here. While we were in college she talked about this place a lot. It seems her grandfather and dad knew some of the people who worked here before it became a nature park."

"Aren't you from Indiana Brian?" "I am," he said. "I have lived around here all my life except when I went to college at IU. As you probably know it's down the road in Bloomington." "Yes, I do know that," she said. "Laura and I came over to a ball game once. We both attended Ohio State."

The coroner and forensics team were there now. After several minutes of inspecting the area, taking pictures, and doing what they normally do they released the container so it could be

—

brought up. Tony had provided a crane and was operating it himself. Joe had been filled with terror because of what he saw in the glass casket and was long gone.

"You know," said Amanda, "there was a pet cemetery here on the property somewhere. Maybe it's just a bunch of animals they buried all at one time. I understand there was a fire here once and quite a few cats were lost. That would explain it if they just lumped them all together."

"Well, we'll know soon," said Brian, "it's almost out of the hole."

"What a minute," said Brian. "I don't believe those are animals unless they have 4 feet and 2 human heads! I can't see for all the dirt but is it one body with 2 heads or 2 bodies?" "And look at that casket or whatever it is. It looks more like some kind of weird fish tank," said Amanda.

It did look similar to a fish tank even though it was about the size of a casket, just slightly larger. It had metal terminals at both ends that were bolted to the glass. They looked to be around one foot in length and were attached to wires that ran the length of the tank. The glass looked very thick or could even be several layers of glass to make it strong. There was a lid on it but it was not made of glass. It was made of medal and fit down over the casket.

"I'm going to go over there and ask one of the forensics guys a question," said Amanda. "I'll go with you," said Brian.

"When do you think we can get some information about what's in that casket," asked Amanda? "We'll know some preliminary information late this afternoon if there is no problem with getting in there without doing any damage," he said. "Since there are so many of you press people here we will just hold a small press conference. For now we are going to load the thing up and get it to the lab."

"Amanda, what does the rest of your day look like," asked Brian? "I have some free time," she said, "what did you have in mind?" "I thought you could bring me up to speed about this urban legend over lunch," said Brian. "I can do that," she said, "but I'll need a ride. I rode with the camera guys."

"Is this a new car," asked Amanda as Brian opened the door for her. Brian was always taught to open the door for all women. It didn't matter whether it was his grandmother or a young lady. If it was a woman you opened the door. "It's not new, I've had it almost two years," he said. "It's so clean, you must wash it all the time," she said. "It's a little dirty; it just looks clean because it's white,"

Actually Brian did wash it quite often. He hated dirty cars especially inside. If fact he hated anything dirty. He was meticulous about everything from his personal appearance to how he kept his closet. He always remembered two things he learned early in life. He had a fifth grade teacher named Mr. Moon. He told Brian that you could always tell a man by how he kept his closet and one thing people judge you by was how your fingernails looked.

Brian drove north on Shadeland toward the Castleton area. Castleton was about two miles up the road. It used to be a very small town until they built the shopping mall. It used to have one small grocery store, a two-chair barbershop; a grain elevator (owned by Skiles Test) a grade school and a church. Now there was every kind of strip mall, hotel, and restaurant you could think of.

"There's the Olive Garden," said Amanda. "Would you mind if we eat there?" "Not at all," he said. "That will be fine."

Chapter 3
Present Day
The Urban Legend

"Could I get you folks something to drink while you look at the menu," said the waitress? "I'll have sweet tea," said Brian. "I'll have the same," said Amanda, "and I'm ready to order." I'll have the grilled chicken flatbread." "That sounds good, make it two," said Brian. "Are you always that easy to please," she asked? "I'm not hard to please when it comes to eating," said Brian. "I like most things but I also like to keep it simple. I'm just as happy with a bowl of cereal or can of soup for dinner as I would be with a full course meal."

"Okay, tell me what you know about this urban legend Amanda." "Okay" she said. "Let's start at the beginning as I know it.

There was a man named Skiles Test. He grew up in Indianapolis in the part of town called Woodruff place."

"I've been there," said Brian, "they have an annual flea market down there every September. I never buy anything I just like the scenery. I like the median and the fountains and I love the old houses, especially the ones that have been renovated."

"I like all that sort of stuff to, and did you know the house

Skiles Test grew up in is still there? They have restored it to almost how it was when he lived there. If you have a house in that area you must follow the covenants and rules on how you keep the property when you restore the homes. It's not any type of historical place with a 'Skiles Test lived here sign' but just a house someone lives in." "I didn't know that," he said. "I've probably walked by it several times though."

"Anyway," she said. "After he graduated from High School he attended college. I don't know which one, but he majored in Engineering. After college he met and married his wife. I think her name was Madeline and she worked as a designer and model at L.S. Ayres."

"In case you don't know Ayres was an upscale department store chain." "Oh, I know about Ayres," said Brian. "It was very big back in the old days." "Old days," she said. "Do you consider the early nineties the old days? I think that's when they went out of business." "I don't know," said Brian, "I think it depends on the day whether I consider it the old days or not."

"Okay," Amanda said. "Anyway soon after he married Madeline he bought all this property that includes the area where the casket was found."

"I'm sorry, but let me stop you for a minute," said Brian. "Where did Skiles work? I'm sure it took a lot of money to buy all that property."

"You don't want to miss any of the details do you," she asked? "Details are very important to me," he said. "When you said he bought all the property that question popped into my mind, that's just the way I am." "He was a business man," said Amanda. "He inherited several businesses from his father at an early age. I don't know what they were; Laura never mentioned their names except one. That one was the racecar business. She didn't know too much about his involvement in the business, but his father owned part of a car that won the Indy 500 in 1912. I think the car was number 8."

"Oh, our lunch is here, that was quick," said Amanda. "Can you talk and eat at the same time," asked Brian? "Only when the mouth is full," she said with a smile.

After a small break in the conversation for eating and a restroom break for Amanda she continued her story.

"When Skiles and Madeline first moved in all that was there was a small house and an out building. Over time they started expanding and with all that acreage I guess they starting farming. With the farm he hired workers and I think she said he built them tenant houses. Now, don't take all this stuff I'm telling you as gospel, she said. She told me a lot of stuff but I didn't pay too much attention to anything but the legend. I'm just throwing in bits and pieces of things I remember she told me."

"Don't worry," said Brian. "I don't take anything as gospel until I have all the facts, but so far you have given me a lot of detail. It's apparent Laura's grandfather and father told her quite a bit."

"So what about the blue lights," he asked. "Laura said Skiles loved blue lights and he strung some up on the house the first Christmas they were there. After that every time he added to the place he added blue lights. Eventually they were everywhere. He had them all around the swimming pool and down all of his driveways."

"He had his own railroad around the property, he had underground tunnels, and he made his own electricity. And listen to this! He had several dogs and over 150 cats! He built houses for them and he even had a pet cemetery as I mentioned back at the site. How scary is that Brian, huh how scary is that?" "Pretty scary if it were the truth and you were a wimpy little girl," said Brian. "Wimpy," she said. "You will pay for that at some point in the future. Anyway, Laura says she thinks he was very eccentric according to what her dad said."

"So, aside from knowing people who worked for him did Laura's dad or Grandfather know Skiles," asked Brian? "No, I don't think so; she never said anything about that."

"I have an idea," said Brian. "How about asking Laura to set up an interview with her dad? Maybe he could tell us if any of the workers he knew are still alive." "Okay," she said. "I'll see what I can do."

"So where did the rumor come from about the glass casket," asked Brian? "I'm getting to that," said Amanda.

"Laura told me that Skiles's wife became sick and never recovered. She said Skiles hired a doctor full time to come out to the house. It was rumored he spent several hours there every day. Laura said they never told her what was wrong with Madeline and she passed away around 1945 or 1946."

"Laura said no one knew when the rumor about his dead wife started. It started sometime after Madeline died of course but no one knows why. It was thought that Skiles was so distraught over losing his wife he had a glass casket made for her. He placed her in the sunroom, placed blue lights around her, and sat every night guarding her. He had dogs by his side and a shotgun to ward off anyone who came around."

"Laura said she heard part of the rumor was true but didn't know what part." "I'm not sure any of it's true," said Brian. "I don't know either," said Amanda. "I know from what Laura told me the guy sounded pretty out there so maybe he went off the deep end when she died."

"I also know there were a lot of kids that used to sneak onto the property at night. Laura said all the kids from the local high schools would go out there on weekends but most of the time they would get run off by shotgun shots or barking dogs."

"Well, I for one am skeptical," said Brian. "Some man sitting by a casket with dogs and a shotgun seems a little far out. It looks like I have a lot of research to do." "While you are researching you might research what happened to the web site," said Amanda. "What do you mean," asked Brian?

"All I know," she said is there used to be a web site called 'the house of blue lights' and it had stories and pictures on it. I used to go there all the time looking for new postings but one day it was gone." "That is interesting, said Brian." "I'll check with my boss and see if he knows about the web site. I also have a friend that may be able to find out what happened to it."

Chapter 4
1933
Skiles and Madeline

Skiles liked this car! It was the first convertible he had bought. A customer had traded it in at the dealership he owned. It was a 1929 standard six series 422 convertible coupe with 15,000 miles on it.

He had purchased the car for his wife Madeline. She did not like driving the bigger business sedans that Skiles drove. Of course with Skiles being a businessman he had to project a professional appearance and a convertible just didn't fit the bill.

It was a beautiful summer day as he drove out Millersville road toward his home. The temperature had peaked at eighty-six degrees around 3:00 p.m. It was a perfect day to put the top down and Skiles loved the feel of the wind as it sliced around the windshield and gently touched the side of his face.

Skiles wasn't a tall man; he stood five feet and 5 inches tall. His hair was hard to define other than the dark color. Sometimes it appeared wispy and other times it looked thicker. His face was curved with a slight dimple on his right side when he smiled.

He was dressed in a blue suit but he had loosened his tie after he left the dealership. He didn't like ties all that well but he did like to dress professionally. His father taught him at a young age that appearance was important to success. Even around the house and on weekends he always wore a white shirt.

Skiles was lucky to be only   twenty-three and have so much. Everything he had of course came from his father. His father had gotten sick when Skiles was twenty. He had to drop out of college early to take care of him and run the businesses. Of course that was not hard for him. His dad had been tutoring him for years, teaching him what he needed to know, how to act, and dress.

His dad, Charles Test was born in 1856 in Richmond, Indiana. Charles met his wife Mary Elizabeth there in 1888 and they soon moved to Indianapolis. This was a time in the country, after the end of the Industrial Revolution around 1870, where opportunities were abundant for smart businessmen such as Charles. As a result Charles started associating himself with other businessmen. He got involved with a group of investors and a man named Newby. They sponsored a car in the 500 each year and won the race once.

Charles also became involved in banking. Of course he was no stranger to banking. His father was a banker and with that knowledge, a little money, and the right connections Charles could do no wrong except for one. He got sick earlier in life than he had expected to. Skiles was an only child and luckily for him his father's good health lasted until he was grown. His dad was still living at this time but couldn't do much. The recent stroke he had suffered left him almost paralyzed. His wife Mary took care of him and Skiles hired a live in maid to help her.

After his father became ill, Skiles dropped out of college. He had been going to engineering school at Purdue. Schooling was a formality for Skiles. Even though he learned a lot at school Skiles had been building things from an early age so the lack of an actual degree didn't slow him down any.

It had been three months since Skiles left college when he met his future wife Madeline Harrow. They met during a shopping trip Skiles was on. He didn't love shopping but he didn't mind it either and this trip was necessary. His wardrobe needed a fresh look if he was to maintain the businesses he had received from his father. Skiles shopped for his clothing exclusively at L.S. Ayres.

Ayres was an upscale department store located in downtown Indianapolis. It was host to the famous Ayres Tea Room. The Tea Room was started in 1905 and became the place to go for high society. It was a magnificent place that served famous dishes on fine China. It was decorated with the latest fashions in draperies and carpet.

Skiles was attracted at first sight when he saw Madeline. He

17

was coming from the men's department where he had just purchased a suit. As he was leaving he had to pass by the women's department to reach the nearest exit. As he casually strolled along he kept glancing from left to right with no particular thing in mind when he saw her.

Madeline had just dressed a mannequin in the upcoming season's dress and was walking toward the aisle. Just as Skiles glanced her way she looked forward and saw him. Skiles had stopped by a display and was pretending to be interested in a sweater.

"May I help you sir," she said to Skiles? "Well," he said. "I don't know I just saw this sweater here and stopped to look at it." "Is it for your wife," she asked? "Oh, no, I'm not married," he said. "I just like the color blue, it's my favorite."

"I'm glad you like it," Madeline said. "I helped design it." "Are you serious," said Skiles? "Yes," she said. "I am a model and part time designer for Ayres." "Do you do anything in men's clothing," asked Skiles. "Not really," she said "but I am familiar with most of the styles and colors, is there anything I can help you with?"

"Well," said Skiles. "I just bought this suit and I could use a matching shirt and tie." "Oh, I'll be glad to help you with that, "she said. "Follow me."

Following her wasn't hard for Skiles. She was very pleasing to the senses. She was just a little shorter than him with curly blonde hair. It was a medium length and had bangs that stopped about an inch above her eyes. Skiles thought she fit the modeling part exceptionally well. She looked like one of those models you would see in magazines. In fact Skiles thought perhaps she was in them, he had never paid much attention.

As they walked toward the men's department Madeline wondered what he was thinking. He was behind her and she guessed he was looking at her butt, since that was what most men do. Madeline wasn't the kind that flaunted her body and she thought men should be just as interested in the person as the body.

Her designs always reflected that philosophy. She had the natural ability to know how give a pleasant feminine look to her designs and yet attain just enough room for imagination.

"Let me see here," she said. "I think this shirt would make a nice contrast if we can find a tie to match. I'm guessing you are about a fourteen," she said. "Yes," he said "and my length is thirty two." "Here is the perfect tie," she said. "It has a hint of dark blue and would go perfect with the shirt. What do you think?"

Skiles liked the tie and the shirt was okay it just wasn't white which is what he preferred. However he thought maybe it wouldn't hurt to have one off color shirt in his wardrobe and he didn't want to offend her.

"I think I'll take them," he said "and I want to thank you very much for the help." "You are very welcome," she said. "Is there anything else I can do for you," she asked? "Yes," said Skiles "have lunch with me."

As soon as he said it, he wished he hadn't. His face turned red and he said, "I'm sorry, I know you don't know me; I just lost my senses for a minute." "Come on," she said, "I'm hungry."

Could it be this simple Madeline thought, as they walked toward the Tea Room? Come to work one day and out of the blue meet the man of your dreams. She had an attraction to this man when she first saw him. He seemed to have a gentle way about him that personified what she wanted in a man.

It was a short engagement. They were so compatible in everything. They both liked quiet times as well as parties. They were both born in 1910 in Indianapolis but at different hospitals. Madeline had grown up on the west side of town and Skiles the east. Neither of them had what you would call a best friend. They all knew a lot of people but there was no one special they spent a lot of time with.

During the first few months of their marriage Madeline moved into the house on Woodruff place where Skiles lived with his parents. When springtime came Skiles purchased the 700 acres

---

where they now lived. The property was heavily wooded and hilly in areas but included several acres of flat farmland. There was a small "honeymoon" cottage and an out building on the property. During the first two years they began adding to the cottage by making it a two-story house with a basement. The basement had several rooms sectioned off. Some had dirt floors and some were cement.

Most of the basement was used for storage of magazines, furniture, and other household items. Skiles bought everything he needed in bulk. If he needed a bottle of ketchup, he bought a case.

In one end Skiles had a wine room. Near that room, he had an exit built that came out upstairs just below his bathroom window. The exit was made of two large folding metal doors that resembled the entrance to a root cellar.

There were also other entrances to the basement via tunnels and of course the stairs that led up to the kitchen area.

The main level had a glass sunroom, living room, piano room, kitchen, dinning room, a large entry area and 2 large bedrooms with full baths. The upstairs had 4 bedrooms and two bathrooms.

They converted the out building to a garage and had started on the pool and pool house.

In addition he had recently started farming. Farming for him was just another business and with all the land it seemed like a good idea. Of course he didn't do any of the farming himself, he hired a few workers, bought some equipment and off the business went. In fact Skiles didn't do much labor at all. With taking care of his dad, running all his businesses and having a wife and farm there just wasn't much time.

Yes, he was a lucky man at age 23 but little did he know at the time that something was going to happen in a few years that would shake the very foundation of his life.

"Madeline, where are you? I'm home," said Skiles. "I'm in the basement," she said. "I was looking for that wine you bought last month." "It's in the far left corner of the wine room," he said. "Oh I see it. I thought we would have it for dinner."

"Say did you bring my car home," she asked. "Yes I did," he said. "Great, I want to take it for a drive before dinner."

"Oh, Skiles it's so beautiful. I always wanted a convertible. I'll be back in a few minutes Watch for cats while I back up please? You know we are getting so many cats here we are going to have to get a kennel license," she said. "I know," said Skiles, "but I love animals and people keep dumping them down on the road and they find their way up here. I have been thinking about building a little cat park for them."

"Okay, you are clear to back out, be careful."

Once clear of the house Madeline headed down the north lane. There were three lanes that led up to the house, but the north one had the longest straight area where she could open the throttle up for at least half a mile.

Madeline was in the prime of her life. She loved Skiles and her home. She joked about the cats but she loved them. She was like Skiles in that respect. In fact they had talked about getting a couple of dogs. Maybe she would surprise him with a couple of puppies for his birthday.

As she turned the corner near the end of the lane she had to slam on her brakes. There in front of her was Frank. Frank Wayne was the vet who took care of all the animals for the farm. Had he been a few seconds earlier they would have met on the corner and wrecked.

"Gee Madeline we almost ran into each other," said Frank as he got out of his car and walked toward her. "You should have Skiles clear out some of these bushes so we can see around the corner." "I'll mention that to him," Madeline said as she pulled down on her dress trying to cover most of her legs. She was wearing a pale blue printed dress, which showed quite a bit of her legs. This was one of the new dresses she had helped design and was shorter than most styles of the day. Had it been anyone else she may not have noticed but she had Frank figured out. He always had that come on look in his eyes and you could feel them crawling all over your body. Every time you saw him he would always give you the once over and if you had a low cut dress on he never looked at

---

your face.

"What are you doing here so late Mr. Wayne," she asked? "I'm going to meet Ned," he said "and please call me Frank. After all we have known each other for quite a while now. Ned and I are going to check out a cow that is due soon. Ned says she has been acting funny."

Ned Tyler was the foreman in charge of the farm animals. It was his job to see that whatever the animals needed was provided in an efficient manner.

"Say, is this a new car," asked Frank? "Yes," she said, "Skiles just brought it home today." "Nice," Frank said, "can I get in and check out the seats?" "Not now Frank, maybe next time. I have to get back, Skiles is waiting for me." "Okay," he said, "let me back up and I'll get out of your way."

As Madeline returned to the house Skiles was waiting for her by the garage. "How was your drive," he said? "It was good except I ran into Frank. He said he was meeting Ned to look at some cow. You know I don't care much for Frank; he is always staring at me." "I know dear," said Skiles, but Frank is the best vet around and I'm sure he would never try anything."

Chapter 5
Late 30's, Early 40's
Loss and Change

Skiles knew it was coming he just wasn't prepared for it and didn't know it would be this soon. He had been called to the hospital early in the morning and by noon his father had passed away.

It was a simple funeral with a few friends in attendance. Charles had purchased a large area of plots at Crown Hill cemetery. There was enough room for twenty graves and he had it plotted out for future generations of his family. Skiles would be put at the foot of his father's grave and then his children at the foot of his and so on. Charles had even planned the headstones. They were all to be the same size and material so the entire area would have the same theme.

A few days after the funeral Skiles returned to the cemetery. In remembrance of his father he planted a Ginkgo tree a few yards from the grave sites. There was a huge Ginkgo tree in the front yard where he grew up on Woodruff Place that his father had planted. After returning from the cemetery, he and Madeline also planted a Ginkgo in their front yard.

Skiles wasn't sure what to do with his mother. He wanted her to move in with him and Madeline but she insisted on staying in the house.

"Mother," he said, "this house is just too big. It has all these bedrooms, a carriage house, and an acre of land. Why don't you come live with Madeline and me? We have plenty of room."

"Skiles dear," Mary said. "I am not your responsibility. I would never intrude on you, I just don't believe in that. Instead let's keep the maid to help me take care of the place along with the gardener. I'll be fine just come and see me once in a while." Skiles agreed because once his mother she had made up her mind no one could change it.

The next few years brought a lot of changes to the farm. "The farm" became the new name for their home. The cats just kept on coming and those that came soon had babies.

They built a cat lot complete with a drinking pool, individual heated cathouses and a large heated gathering house where they could hang out with the cats.

Of course with birth comes death. They sectioned off an area a few yards west of the house and made a pet cemetery. When an animal died they would build a wooden box for it and if it had a name they would make a headstone.

They acquired several dogs and built nice pens and houses for them.

They finished the pool. It was a one of a kind in the state. It was Olympic size and heated by a solar system that Skiles had designed. It had a glass enclosure all around it with blue lights. There was a diving complex at the west end that included four diving boards and a trapeze.

The pool house was a four story building. It had an elevator, a kitchen, bathrooms, changing rooms, and a small sun deck on the roof. There was a fireplace on the main floor and the house itself was made from brick, glass, and had a lot of marble throughout.

Skiles loved blue lights. Every year at Christmas time he would decorate all the trees and buildings with blue lights. He even strung them down the south lane that led to Millersville road. At nighttime the entire area looked like an airport. In fact the FAA asked him to turn the lane lights off because it resembled an airport runway.

At the front of the house were two doors. There was a brick patio between them and they had planted several trees and bushes along the edge of it. The trees were the small decorative type that never grew very large.

The entire house was covered with white glass and there were lightning rods on the roof. Skiles was a big fan of lightning rods. He had them installed on all his buildings and tenant houses.

The living room also had a lot of the same marble that was in the pool house. Skiles also used a lot of glass and mirrors in the house. These helped fuel the legend of the house because they would reflect the blue lights. This was not done intentionally it just happened.

The kitchen had a high ceiling and the walls were covered with the same white glass as the outside of the house. Skiles also had all the latest appliances.

Off the west wall was an opening to the master bedroom. At the north end of the bedroom was the master bath. Skiles liked blue but he also liked bright colors. The bath was done in maroon with black and red accents.

Even though he dropped out of engineering school early Skiles was a smart man. Aside from the pools solar heating system, he designed and built a small miniature railroad around his property, and even made the first electric bug zapper and installed it on his back door.

He didn't like the winter weather in Indiana so he built underground tunnels to travel between the house, garage, cat lot, and pool house.

He built a powerhouse and created his own electricity. It consisted of three diesel engines hooked to generators. He had a huge tank placed behind the powerhouse where the diesel fuel was stored. The tank resembled one you would find underground at a gas station. Skiles did nothing small. Everything he did was done in a big way.

With all these additions came more workers and the need

for homes. Skiles built "tenant houses" around his property on Johnson road and 65th street. He let his workers live there for free.

Skiles was a generous man. He did not pay a high wage but he did provide free housing, electricity, water, heat, gasoline, milk, and half a hog and cow every year. In addition all who worked for him would get generous Christmas bonuses every year.

Entertaining was a priority at the farm. Summer time was especially popular with the pool but even in the wintertime Skiles would have parties in the pool house. He of course invited all his family. He had no brothers or sisters but he did have lots of cousins and of course they had friends. There were adult parties with drinking and dancing and occasional kid parties where they would get to ride on the railroad, and watch the cows get milked.

Skiles even held parties for the soldiers stationed at nearby Ft. Harrison. Skiles was very patriotic. He was exempt from the war because he provided a need for the country. He owned a chain company that made chains for the army tanks. He was sorry that he couldn't serve along side the guys and wanted to do anything he could to provide relief for them.

The entire farm had become a very festive place. Even though the farm was festive, Skiles again had to face tragedy. His mother passed away just one month before Christmas in 1942. He had been with her just two days prior to that and she had seemed just fine. The doctor said she had a heart attack and passed in her sleep. Skiles was glad she had not suffered.

Skiles laid his mother to rest next to his father at Crown Hill. It was a chilly day in November for the funeral but it was sunny which helped take away some of his sadness. He loved his parents very much and always tried to be a part of their lives. Losing them was natural but the loss hurt him deeply.

After the funeral Skiles put his boyhood home up for sale and within one month it had been sold. Skiles offered positions at the farm to the gardener and maid he had employed for his mother. Both thanked him for his generosity but declined.

Chapter 6
1944
Madeline and Frank

It was Christmas time 1944. Madeline had bought a Myna bird for Skiles and wanted to keep it a secret. Not wanting to keep it in the house she called Frank to see if he could take care of it for her. Frank agreed and told her to bring it to his house. Madeline remembered how Frank was and hated to go there alone but she had no choice if she wanted to keep the bird a secret.

Frank lived a couple of miles from the farm. He had a modest house for a vet and lived alone. He had been married for a while but his wife had moved on.

"Come on in," said Frank. "Thanks Frank, I appreciate you doing this." "I'm happy to do it he said although I don't know a lot about Myna birds their bodies can't be much different from a sparrow or pigeon.

Speaking of bodies Madeline I don't think I have ever made it a secret that I'm very attracted to you." "I know Frank and I have always ignored the glances. It's not that you aren't a good looking guy, it's just I'm married and I love Skiles." "I know," said Frank. "I respect that and I know I've been a little too forward at times. I never meant any harm, it's just when you like someone it's hard to hide those feelings." "But Frank, you don't even know me that well, I think it's just a sex thing that most guys have." "Well," he said. "Maybe part of it is sexual but I know you are a nice person, I can just tell. You are classy and you carry yourself well."

"Say, forgive my manners," he said. "Would you like something to drink?" "I can't stay long," she said. "Oh, just one drink won't take long it gets lonely here." "Okay," she said, "I'll have a scotch and soda and then I need to go."

Frank brought her the drink and sat down next to her on the couch. As they talked she began to understand Frank a little better. He wasn't that bad of a guy down deep, he was just lonely and when he liked someone he didn't hide the feelings.

Frank was also a decent looking man. She didn't think he was a great looking guy, as she had told him or that he probably thought he was. He was very tall, over six feet. His hair was a light brown, almost a cross between blonde and brown. He had a small "beer belly" on him but he was still in decent shape. He looked to be somewhere in his forties but she didn't know where. His hands were large and rough looking, as you would expect from a veterinarian.

"Another drink he asked?" "Just one more," she said, "then I must go."

As they finished the last drink Frank slowly put his arm around her. "What are you doing," she asked? "Look Madeline," he said. "I may never get another chance to spend a few precious moments with you and what does it hurt. It means so much to me just to touch you. I promise I will stop whenever you say but could I just touch your breast."

Madeline thought for a minute and told herself that maybe it wouldn't hurt just this one time. She wasn't sure if it was the alcohol thinking for her or she was beginning to like the guy. "Okay," she said, "but you promised to stop when I tell you to."

Madeline was wearing a blouse with one button undone. Frank slowly began to unbutton the remaining buttons exposing her bra. He then gently lifted her bra up exposing her breasts. As he began to rub them Madeline slowly closed her eyes. She wasn't sure what was going on inside her. No one other than Skiles had ever touched her there. What she knew was that it felt good. Then Frank did something she had not expected. He began to kiss them. She wanted to tell him to stop but the words would not come. He then began rubbing her leg underneath her skirt. As his hand touched her panties she experienced a warm feeling running through her body. Could she really be doing this she thought? As Frank worked his hand inside she realized she could not.

"Please stop," she said. Frank did as she requested. He said, "I'm sorry if I hurt you in any way Madeline." "You were fine Frank, another time, another place, another circumstance maybe I would not have stopped you."

Madeline fixed her clothes, thanked Frank again for taking the bird and left.

On her way home she still wasn't sure what she was feeling. Had she just betrayed her husband? Would she have done it had not she been drinking? She had no answers just fears. Fears that it felt too good not to do it again.

Christmas morning came early for Skiles. He was always an early riser. By the time Madeline was up he had made her a breakfast of coffee, eggs, and bacon. He was not a cook by any means and during the week they had a cook who prepared most of their meals. But on weekends the first one up fixed the meal and most of the time it was Skiles.

It was a crisp morning with a new blanket of snow on the ground. It was the first white Christmas since 1940. The last three had brought cold and rain but this one was beautiful. The snow was wet and heavy and piled up on the tree branches. It was a perfect picture of nature that Norman Rockwell would have been proud of.

"Let's hurry and eat," she said. "I want to get to the presents. I just know you bought me that diamond necklace I wanted." "How do you know that," said Skiles? "I just know you," she said. About that time there was a knock on the door. "Who could that be," said Skiles. "Oh, it's Frank," said Madeline, "and guess what? He has a package with him. Let's open the door and see what it is," she said.

"Merry Christmas to all," said Frank. "Skiles this is for you. Madeline gave it to me to keep for her so Christmas could be a surprise." Skiles opened the box and said. "I'll be damn a Myna bird! I love it; I'm going to teach it to talk so it sounds just like me."

As Madeline stepped toward the box she fell. "Madeline, are you okay," Skiles asked? "I, I don't know," she said, "I must have fainted." Frank said," Have you ever fainted before?" "No," she said, "I don't know what happened." "Do you hurt anywhere," asked Skiles? "My head hurts where I hit the floor but I don't feel any blood. "

"We should get you to a doctor," said Skiles. "I have a friend

———

who is a doctor, let me call him and see if he can come over," said Frank. "Do you think he will come on Christmas," Skiles asked? "Sure," Frank said, "He's a great guy."

Dr. Dan Langford was just about to leave his apartment when the phone rang. "Sure," Dan said, "I know about where you are but give me some final directions and I need to make a call then I'll be there."

"Hi Mom, I'm going to be late for Christmas," Dan said. "I have an emergency patient." "That's fine Dan," she said. "We will not be eating until around one in the afternoon so try to make it by then."

Dan was a young doctor and had been practicing about six months. He worked with a small group of doctors in an office nearby his apartment. Frank was Dan's mother's vet and he had met him during a visit when he took her dog in for an ear infection. Frank didn't charge him anything calling it professional courtesy and Dan reciprocated whenever Frank needed anything.

Dan was a little under six feet tall, darkish hair, and had a slender build. He was nice looking but he looked older than his age of twenty-eight. He was not a well-liked doctor in the community of professionals. He barely made it through med school and had some ideas about medicine, which were considered radical at the time.

He had dated off and on during college but his opinion on medical procedures, his politics, and especially his treatment of women led to termination on all his relationships.

He and Frank seemed to get along very well though. They both shared the same opinion of women. They both viewed them as sexual objects and most discussions they had always revolved around that.

In fact Frank had shared with Dan the little episode he and Madeline had. He told Dan how he fixed her drinks and made up some sob stories to get past that stone heart of hers. As a result Dan was eager to see her. He did have a genuine concern for her health but wanted to see what Frank was so excited about.

"Thank you so much Doctor for coming out on Christmas," I'm Skiles. "You are welcome, glad to be of help." "Hi Frank, how are you?" "I'm fine Dr. Langford good to see you again." "Madeline is in here on the couch," Skiles said.

As Dan approached the couch he knew what had attracted Frank to her. She was everything he had said. He was thoroughly going to enjoy taking care of her!

"How do you feel," asked Dan? "I'm so silly," she said. "I think I just lost my footing and hit my head on the floor when I fell. I think I'm okay." "Why don't you let me be the judge of that," he said. "Where did you hit when you fell?" "Right here on the very back, I think there is a slight bump there." "Yes, I can see the bump but there is no bleeding. Let me check some of your vital signs."

It only took Dan a few minutes to check her blood pressure and listen to her heart.

"Well everything seems normal but I want to check back with you in a couple of days," Dan said. "Sometimes with bumps on the head issues can show up later. I'm going to give you some pain pills and if anything irregular happens call me right away."

Dan turned to Skiles and said, "She seems okay, but I would like to see her tomorrow if that's possible. I have a couple of other patients in this area that I visit so I could drop by tomorrow around one. Would that be good for you?" "Why don't we make it a little later, say six and you can join us for dinner," Skiles said. "It's the least we can do for you. And Frank, if you don't have any plans why don't you come too," said Skiles? "Okay," said Frank "I can come," "Doc, is that good for you too," asked Skiles? "Yes, I can make it; I'll see you all then." "Hold on doc," Frank said, "I'll walk out with you."

"Well doc what do you think of Madeline?" said Frank as they walked to the car. "She is quite the classy lady as you described." "Yes she is classy and in addition she and Skiles are rich," said Frank." "I have on occasion overcharged a little for my services and they never question it. If you can get in good with them I'm sure you will be very well taken care of also." "Maybe so, said Dan. "But another benefit will be working on Madeline when she is sick." "I see," said Frank. "With you being a doctor you can paw over her in a professional way and get by with it, and you won't even have to get her drunk." "Exactly," said Dan!

Chapter 7
1945
Madeline and Dan

The next day at 6 p.m. both Dan and Frank knocked on the door. Madeline opened the door and invited them in. "Skiles will be out in a minute," she said, "please follow me to the dining room."

As they walked to the dining area Dan thought the house was nice and roomy but didn't seem extravagant for a millionaire. He did notice that Madeline was dressed a little extravagant. She was wearing a very low cut almost formal dress. Her shape complimented every inch of the dress or did it compliment her? It didn't matter she looked terrific.

"Good evening," Skiles said as he walked into the room. "I'm so glad both of you could come. We love to entertain and during the winter it slows down a bit and there are not a lot of people around. You both will have to come swimming this summer; we'll throw a couple of parties. Frank, you have been swimming here before haven't you?" asked Skiles. "Yes Skiles, I was here a couple of times, your pool is magnificent."

"Do you swim Dr. Langford," asked Madeline? "Oh please all of you call me Dan. Doctor sounds so formal and I want you both to think of me as a friend. And yes, I do swim. I think its great exercise for the body."

"So Madeline how have you been feeling since I was here," asked Dan? "Well, Dan to be truthful I am having a lot of headaches." "Are they where you hit your head or elsewhere," he asked? "Where I hit my head doesn't bother me at all, it seems to be here above my forehead, but let's wait until after dinner before you look at it." "Okay, that's fine," said Dan, "I'm hungry anyway."

"Did you cook this meal Madeline," asked Frank? "I wish I could take credit for it," said Madeline "but we have a cook named Emma and she prepared it. In fact you just missed her." "It's very delicious," said Dan.

Dan could not keep his eyes off Madeline. She was stunning. Not only was she beautiful she was an excellent host. She was the kind of woman you could fall in love with but that was one of Dan's problems. He could fall in love with any beautiful woman one after another after another.

After dinner Dan examined Madeline but could find no medical reason for her headaches.

"Let me give you something a little stronger for the pain," Dan said "and if they continue we may have to do some tests." "Okay," said Madeline, "thank you very much for coming out." "My pleasure," said Dan; "I enjoyed the dinner and the company."

As Dan and Frank were putting on their coats Skiles said. "Let me walk out with you, I'd like to show you my latest decoration." "If you are referring to the blue lights around the porch I noticed those," said Dan.

"Actually," said Skiles, as they reached the front steps. "I wanted to talk to you about Madeline. I think there is something wrong with my wife. I have noticed she seems to be fine most of the time like she was tonight. But for example this morning she forgot to put on a bra. Then we were talking and she started saying stuff that didn't make sense. We were talking about the cats and all of a sudden she started talking about her mother right in the middle of the sentence." "What did she say about her," asked Dan? "She said she needed to take her shopping, and that is the strange part. Her mom passed away when she was six."

"Hmm," said Dan. "I'd like to witness this behavior. The fall could have caused a mild concussion but I suspect something else is going on."

"I have an idea Dan," said Skiles. "I don't know what your schedule is but would it be possible for you to stay with us for a week or so. We can put you up in the guest room and you can witness for yourself her behavior. I'd pay you well for your service." "Well," said Dan. "I could work out of your home but I wouldn't want Madeline knowing I was here spying on her. It would be best if she thought things were normal."

"Why don't we do this," said Skiles? "I'll tell her they're painting your apartment and I invited you to stay while the work was being done." "That's sounds plausible," said Dan. "I'll pack a

33

few things and come over tomorrow evening." "Great, I'll tell Madeline and if you can make it by six you can have dinner with us again."

As Skiles left Frank turned to Dan and said. "Talk about luck." "Not only do you get to fondle Madeline during her exams but now you get to spend day and night with her." "Come on Frank, after all I can be professional at times and think of things other than sex. Madeline may have a serious problem." "Wait a minute," said Frank! "You are falling for her aren't you?" "What makes you think that Frank?" "Because doc, I saw the way you looked at her at dinner." "Well," said Dan, you can think what you like but I do have a real concern for her."

The next day Dan arrived around one. As he drove through the farm area he noticed something he had never seen before, people! He had always been there either on a holiday or late in the evening after all the workers had left. There were not a lot of workers around, probably just enough to take care of the animals he thought. It was still winter and there was not much farming to do. There was however more workers around the house than in the farm area. Skiles had a supervisor who ran things around the house and a couple of young boys under him to do most of the work. He knew Skiles had a cook and housekeeper although he had not met them yet.

"Hi, I'm Dr. Dan Langford." "Come on in I'm Louise Buckner, I'll show you to your room. We have been expecting you. Emma, our guest is here." "Hello doctor, I'm Emma Jones, I help Louise and do most of the cooking." "Oh, both of you, please call me Dan, it's a pleasure to meet you both and I have already enjoyed some of your cooking Emma. It was very delicious." "Thank you Dan," she said.

"So are Skiles and Madeline here," he asked? "No Dan, Skiles took Madeline to her work to get some dresses and mannequins," said Emma. "Skiles suggested she work from home for a while." "Exactly what does she do?" he asked Louise. "She works for Ayres. She helps design dresses and then models them."

"And pardon me for being ignorant but what does Skiles do other than run this farm," asked Dan? "Well, I know he owns a car dealership, a chain company, several parking garages, and beyond that I'm not sure," said Louise. "I just know he is always busy."

It was almost 4:30 p.m. when Skiles and Madeline returned. Dan went out to the car to greet them. "May I help you carry in your things," asked Dan? "Sure," said Skiles, "I was glad to see your car here when I pulled up. How long have you been waiting?" "Just a couple of hours," Dan said. "Louise and Emma have been keeping me company."

"They also told me you were moving some of Madeline's work here so she could stay at home for awhile. I think that's an excellent idea Skiles." "Well, I'm not sure," said Madeline. "He thinks my headaches might be something serious and he wants me pampered."

"I hear you are also staying awhile with us," said Madeline. "Yes," said Dan. "I'm having some apartment work done and your husband offered me a room for awhile."

"So Madeline, how have you been feeling since I was here last," asked Dan? "I'm still having some headaches and Skiles says I do and say crazy things but I don't remember if I do." "Well while I'm here we can see if I can help you get back to normal."

Madeline liked Dan. He seemed very concerned about her health not only as a doctor but as a friend. For the first couple of days, while Skiles was away at work, they would sit and talk for hours when Dan didn't have to run off to see other patients. She found him someone she could confide in about her marriage, her past, and dreams for the future.

Dan himself was afraid he was falling in love with Madeline. It was true, as Frank thought, he was attracted to her from the first but it was becoming more than that.

Dan had thought about all the women he had dated, how he misused them and wondered if maybe Madeline would change all that. But then, how could she, being married was a showstopper.

So no-matter what his feelings for Madeline were, all she would ever be to him was just another woman to use and then move on. Oh, how he hated himself at times for the way he was. He just wasn't a nice person!

It was the first Saturday since Dan moved into on of the guest rooms. So far since he had been there Madeline showed small signs of pain but Dan had seen nothing to suggest she was having spells of confusion. It was 9 a.m., Skiles had gone to the dealership and Dan was waiting for Madeline to come to breakfast. She normally was up and out by at least 7 a.m. so he was beginning to worry. Skiles said she was still sleeping when he left and that was over an hour ago.

"Madeline, are you okay in there," he said as he knocked on the bedroom door? There was no answer. "Madeline," he softly said as he quietly opened the door. There was still no answer.

As Dan entered the room he saw Madeline lying on the bed. She seemed to be asleep but had thrown the cover completely off her. She was wearing a very thin silk gown that didn't hide very much. Dan had imagined many times what she was like under those dresses she designed and now his imagination had not been disappointed. The gown flowed down across her breast and as it split in the middle both breasts was exposed just beyond the nipple. The gown was very short. It barely covered the upper part of her thighs. It clung to her body like a glove and you could make out the little mound of flesh and hair between her legs.

He stood there with wild thoughts running through his mind fighting his emotions, his desires, and his professionalism as her doctor. He thought about her marriage and that now might be the only opportunity he would ever have to be with her. He remembered what Frank had told him and thought maybe she had liked what Frank had done. After all she never mentioned it to anyone as far as he knew.

As he moved closer to her, she began to stir. "Dan, is that you?" "Yes Madeline it is." "I was having a dream that you had left me. Why are you dressed? Please come back to bed, I'm lonely."

As Dan lay down beside her, he brushed his hand gently across her breast. Madeline responded by pushing her body against his. She then unbuttoned his shirt with one hand and his pants with

———

36

the other. "Are you sure you want to do this Madeline?" "Why wouldn't I?" she said, "We are in love aren't we?" "Yes, I love you," said Dan as he entered her.

It was 9:45 a.m., when they both got dressed. Dan left the room first and a few minutes later Madeline came out. "Dan, where did you come from," said Madeline. "Did Skiles go to work?" "Yes, Skiles is at work, what's the last thing you remember Madeline?" "Uh, I'm not sure. Let's see I remember Skiles getting dressed and I think I went back to sleep. I was dreaming about something, but I can't remember what it was. Then I heard a noise out here, I got dressed and here I am."

"Are you having any pain," asked Dan? "No I feel great, why are you here? Did Skiles tell you I was sick again?" "Not really Madeline, Don't you remember I have been staying here for the last few days while my apartment is being renovated." "Oh yes I remember that, how silly of me. Would you like some coffee Dan?"

Chapter 8
1945
Madeline's Diagnosis

Dan knew Skiles had gone to the car dealership and found the
phone number Skiles had given him.

"Skiles, this is Dan." "What's wrong Dan, is Madeline okay?"
"Well yes and no. She is showing some signs of things I haven't seen
before and I wanted to prepare you. It's not an emergency I was
just wondering when you will be home?" "I was getting ready to
leave when you called." Where is Madeline now and what's she
doing?" "She is in the kitchen drinking coffee; I didn't want her to
hear me calling you." "Okay, I'm on my way," said Skiles.

Skiles was worried about his wife. He loved her so much and
she was so young. God forbid anything happen to her. He just didn't
know how he would cope with a loss like that. She was such the
perfect mate. They shared so much and were so alike in everything
he just couldn't lose her. He just couldn't!

Dan was waiting for Skiles in the living room when he
arrived. Madeline had developed a headache and Dan had given her
a sedative. "So, tell me Dan what's going on," said Skiles.
"Madeline's memory issue is getting worse. I have a couple of ideas
Skiles but I want your permission to have a colleague of mine take a
look at her." "Fine," said Skiles "another opinion will not hurt."
"Another thing Skiles, if I may, I'd like to stay here awhile longer. I
don't think Madeline knows whether I live here or not and I think I
need to be near her." "Great," said Skiles "I love having a doctor
around.

Dr. Timothy Franklin was indeed a colleague of Dr. Dan
Langford. He did not occupy the same office, in fact he didn't work
in Indiana but they were med school buddies. All during school they
shared some of the same ideas about how to treat patients. Dr.
Franklin worked with the mentally insane at the state hospital in
Columbus, Ohio.

It took Dr. Franklin a couple of days to clear his schedule but

———

he soon arrived at the farm. Skiles insisted he stay at the farm and he put him in the room next to Dan.

He and Dan spent the next few days observing and talking to Madeline. She seemed to be getting worse mentally but physically there was not much change. She still had headaches but they controlled them with pain medication.

"Skiles, I think we are ready to discuss a plan of treatment for Madeline," said Dan. "Let's all four go into the piano room where we can be a little more comfortable," said Skiles.

"Both Dr. Franklin and I agree that we are not 100% sure what is wrong with Madeline," Dan said. "We think she either has a brain tumor or she has some mental disabilities. There is no way to tell at this time. We thought about x-rays but brain x-rays are not all that reliable yet. There have been some success but the risks are not worth what we might get. If we were to find something the treatment we want to propose would be the same anyway, so I don't see a need to try x-rays."

"The treatment we are proposing for Madeline has many names," said Dan. "It has been called BioResonance Tumor Therapy, Cell Comm System, Rife machine, Zapper, Super Zapper Deluxe, zapping machine, electromagnetism, bioelectricity, magnetic field therapy, bioelectromagnetics, bioenergy therapy, and others. I know that's a long list but I want you to be comfortable with it in case you hear or read about one of them you will know they are all the same."

"The thought going into using this therapy," said Dan "is that for some reason the body develops imbalances within its electrical frequencies and those in turn disrupt its chemical makeup. These imbalances can cause ulcers, headaches, burns, chronic pain, nerve disorders, spinal cord injuries, diabetes, gum infections, asthma, bronchitis, arthritis, heart disease, and cancer. In general, practitioners of electromagnetic therapy claim that if we can correct these frequencies we can trick the body into healing itself."

"So how does it work Dan," asked Madeline? "What we will be doing is sending a measured amount of an electromagnetic

---

charge around your body," said Dan.

"Keep in mind we are not sending any current through you we are only creating a magnetic force field. We think if we submerse your body in water it will conduct just enough energy from this force field to realign your internal frequencies. By doing that we are letting the body return to its normal rhythms thinking that will make it heal itself."

"Is this a proven treatment," asked Skiles "and is it dangerous?" "It's not dangerous," Dr. Franklin said. "I have used it before. As far as effective, there are pros and cons on that. I have some case studies I will be glad to share with you if you'd like." "That won't be necessary," said Skiles. "I can accept success or failure as long as there is no danger to her."

"I have another question," said Skiles "How long do you expect this to take Dan?"

"What we want to do is try this once or twice a week for two or three months, said Dan." "We don't want to do too many at once. We are looking for a gradual frequency change in the body over time. If after that time there is no improvement we feel she probably does not have a tumor and is suffering from some mental disability. At that point we might want to talk about performing a Lobotomy." "I think I've heard of that," said Skiles "but exactly what is it?"

"It's a small surgical procedure that was first used in 1939," said Dan. "What we do is sever the nerve fibers connecting the frontal lobes to the thalamus."

"I'm a little concerned," said Skiles, "The first procedure doesn't sound too bad but I'm not sure about the Lobotomy." "Hopefully," Dan said, "we won't have to do that. I'm confident the resonance therapy will work."

"Madeline what do you think," asked Skiles? "Well, gentlemen right now other than a headache I seem to be myself. You know I don't remember doing all these other things you say I do. So, I am willing to try the electric thing since its safe but I'll have to think about the other one. Now, if I get worse and can't make that decision I will leave it up to Skiles."

"Okay," Skiles said, "when can we get started? "First," Dr. Franklin said, "We will need some equipment. We need a glass tank that will hold water for Madeline to lie in. Once we have that we will need some wiring, a small generator, gauges, and some way to control the current." "I'll get to work on that," Skiles said. "I'll have my electrician get the generator and wiring. One of you will need to explain to him exactly what kind of controls you will need. As far as the tank, I'll have my foreman find one, make one, or whatever."

"One more thing," said Madeline. "I want to call my mother to tell her before we start."

Chapter 9
1945
Madeline's Treatment

Spring was in the air at the Test farm. Trees and flowers were blooming. The farm hands were once again planting crops, and getting the equipment ready for a long summer. Everything was just perfect except for one. Madeline wasn't doing very well.

Dr. Franklin had helped Dan during the first couple of treatments with the electric current but other commitments had now called him away. That was fine with Dan, by now he didn't need the help. He remembered back to the first treatment. They had to dress Madeline in a swimsuit and heat enough water to submerse her in the tank.

The electrician had done a great job with the generator and all the wiring. The tank looked like a big fish aquarium without the wires of course. There were a total of ten terminals they welded using lead on the tank. Non-insulated wire wrapped around the end terminal, then was twisted and connected to the next terminal and so forth. This was done several times so as to have enough wire to create a magnetic force around her almost like a giant magnet. They controlled the current through a lever with gauges showing how much she was getting.

There didn't seem to be any side effects from the treatment but then there didn't seem to be any results either.

Dan was still living at the farm and managing his other patients as he always had. The treatments didn't take too long and the remainder of the time he spent with Madeline.

When Skiles was home the two of them would play chess and became quite good friends. Skiles had put his trust in Dan and even though Madeline wasn't getting any better he knew Dan was doing everything he could for her.

Skiles also realized that Dan had fallen in love with her. Skiles never knew about the rumors among the farm workers and he never said anything to make Dan think he knew but Skiles knew. He also knew Madeline was fond of Dan. He didn't know how fond because Madeline didn't even know. Her mind just didn't work very well anymore.

Dan had long decided that the Lobotomy they had planned would not be done. Whatever was going on with her was not mental illness.

He suspected it was and had always been a brain tumor as early as one month into the Bio Resonance procedure.

He had changed his mind about other things to. It didn't matter anymore about the sexual side of a woman. Madeline had taught him something, she had taught him what real love was.

As he looked back on his life, he was sorry for the way he had treated the ones that cared about him. He was sorry for all the hurt he had caused. Yes, Madeline had taught him that.

Even as she slipped in an out of her episodes she shared her feelings with him. Yes, it was possible to love two men at once she said. She still loved Skiles but she had a love for Dan too. She couldn't understand it and she didn't try. She accepted it and took every moment she could get whether it was with Skiles or Dan.

Madeline was slipping fast but she had to accept that too and be strong. Her disease, whatever it was had began to take a toll on her body. She had become so frail and weak that most of the time she just stayed in bed.

It was the first Friday in May. It was a beautiful warm day and she wanted to go outside. She had only been out a couple of times over the last month and she was determined to go.

"Skiles please get the wheelchair for me" said Madeline." "I'd like to go see the pool and the flowers out in the garden." "Of course Madeline, I'll be glad to take you out," he said.

"Well look at you," said Emma, "you going outside huh?" "Yes, I am," said Madeline. "I'm going to enjoy this day."

Skiles rolled her out of the front door and down the east side of the house past the kitchen.

"Look Skiles," she said. "There's a cat in the window eating the pie Emma has cooling." "Hey Emma," yelled Skiles, "you better check your pie." "What are you doing you crazy cat," yelled Emma, as she approached the open window. The cat just looked at her and

43

kept eating.

"Skiles dear, please go get me the cat, I want to hold it," said Madeline, "and bring the pie with you."

"Nice kitty," said Madeline as she stroked its fur. "So you like

lemon pie she said?" "Then so be it. I dub thee Sir Lemon Pie." Skiles just laughed and said. "That is kind of a silly name for a cat but then I guess it's just as good as any."

On the way to the pool Madeline wanted to stop at the sundial. It was situated about a foot from the walk that ran between the house and the pool. "I remember the day we bought it," said Skiles as he stopped the chair and walked around to kneel beside her. On the dial was an inscription of words from a poem. The poem was "Rabbi Ben Ezra" by Robert Browning. The words said "Grow old along with me, the best is yet to be."

Madeline said, "I'm so sorry Skiles that I will not be around to live out those words." "Now don't try to humor me," she said. "I know I'm getting weaker and my time is short. I don't need to hear those things like I'll get better or I'll be around a long time yet."

Skiles saw a tear drop from her face and he quickly moved back behind the wheelchair. He didn't want her to see him cry. It would do her no good. "I'm ready," she said. "Lets go on up to the pool now."

"Can I get you anything," asked Skiles? "Yes, I want some fresh lemonade." "That sounds great," he said; "I'll have Emma make us some."

"Well hello there beautiful" Dan said as he approached the pool. "Oh how you do go on Dan, you know I'm not beautiful. Those days are long gone." "You are always beautiful to me," he said. "So where have you been today she asked?" "Oh, I had a couple of patients to look in on. One had a cold and the other is recovering from a broken foot."

"Hello Dan," said Skiles, as he returned with the lemonade. "Do you have time to join us for refreshments?" "Sure," he said.

"Hey Dan, did Madeline tell you about the black cat's name?" "I haven't told him yet Skiles, I---

"You what," asked Skiles? "Madeline, Madeline."

Chapter 10
1948
Time Slowly Heals

It had been three years since Skiles lost the love of his life. He still hosted parties for his family and friends but he never got too involved with them. His personal secretary Lucy Gordon handled most of that.

Lucy was hired not long after Madeline's death at the suggestion of Dan. Lucy was quite a looker. She was 22, and very attractive, however she was not hired for her looks but rather her business degree. In fact Skiles never paid too much attention to her other than to talk about business. At the time his businesses and the farm were flourishing but he wasn't that interested in them thus Lucy did most everything that was needed. As a result Skiles had a lot of free time which he spent mourning his loss.

Skiles also hired Keith Wiley whom he called his timekeeper. With Keith and Lucy taking charge of things Skiles was able to distance himself from most of the farm operations and his key businesses.

Skiles had moved the glass tank they used for the treatments into the sunroom where all Madeline's mannequins were stored soon after her death. He would look in the room as he walked past but rarely would he go in. Dan still came by to see him and he enjoyed his company. Dan was married now and seemed to have found happiness. They didn't talk much about Madeline when they were together because Dan knew Skiles was still in mourning and it was best to keep quiet.

They never talked about the Bio Resonance procedures. That subject was always kept very quiet. Only a handful of people knew and it was suggested to them that it was a private matter and should stay that way. In fact Dan signed the death certificate as pneumonia.

Everyday Skiles would have fresh flowers brought in from the garden and placed on the kitchen table. He always remembered she wanted to see the flowers on the day she died. In the wintertime he would have them delivered from the florist.

Yes, it was taking Skiles a long time to come to grips with his new life. As for Dan he missed Madeline to. But unlike Skiles he had moved on because of what she had taught him about love and life. He was a different man now and even though he would always miss her he knew she would be happy for him the way he was now.

Chapter 11
1950
Bonnie

It was now January 1950. Skiles had returned to the business world and with Lucy's help had expanded into a couple other areas of commerce. Lucy had done a good job running everything for him. America had been and was still in a building boom after the war. Most of his employees that had been with him for years were still there. Only a couple had left and they had been replaced.

One replacement was Jim Tyler. He was the son of his foreman Ned. It didn't seem that long ago that Ned's wife gave birth to Jim but here he was not only grown but had a son of his own named Tom.

Another one was a young twelve-year-old boy name Doug Raines. Doug's family did not work for Skiles but lived nearby. One day Doug's father came to the farm and talked to Skiles about Doug. He told him Doug's mother had some issues at birth. He didn't go into a lot of detail, as they were a very private family. He only told Skiles Doug was oxygen starved during birth. As a result of this they noticed a slight "slowness" in Doug as a toddler and later some learning disabilities when he entered grade school.

Skiles assigned Doug near the house to take care of the cats and dogs. He and Skiles would walk the dogs daily and Skiles became very fond of him. Skiles did notice that he was a little unlike most kids but it didn't seem to interfere with his work. He asked Dan to spend some time with him to see what he thought about his retardation. Dan told Skiles he didn't think he was any danger to himself or anyone and would be okay.

Skiles Test heart was on the mend. One day he even had the glass tank and all the mannequins removed from the sunroom and placed in the storage barn. He started shopping again and enjoyed getting out. He even thought about dating but never quite knew how to go about it until one Saturday while grocery shopping.

He was in Broad Ripple one afternoon. Broad Ripple is a

---

suburb of Indianapolis. It is about ten minutes west of the farm.

There was a small grocery store there named Kuhn's Market. It was a little mom and pop store owned by John and Martha Kuhn. The store was originally owned by John's father and was located near downtown Indianapolis. John had always liked the Broad Ripple area and when his father passed away they moved the store there.

They were a nice couple in their early fifties. They had tried for years when they were younger to have children but were unsuccessful. Then all of a sudden a "change of life baby" came along. They named him Aaron Oscar. He was now eight years old and was quite the little gentlemen. He would help carry out the groceries for you, put them in the car and then stick out his hand for a tip. He was a funny little guy and very serious about his money.

As Skiles entered the store he walked past one of the two cash registers. Normally Martha would be on one register and John would man the other one if they got behind but today there was someone new there.

"Hi Martha, I see you hired some help," said Skiles. "Yes," she said, "we are just getting so busy; John couldn't keep up any longer. Her name is Bonnie."

Skiles picked up some vegetables, fruit, bread and a candy bar. Skiles had a little sweet tooth and always liked something sweet during the day. He preferred chocolate with raisins and nuts.

Skiles was the second person in line behind this young man who looked to be in his early twenties. Skiles noticed the man was in no hurry to get checked out. Apparently he was more interested in Bonnie than his groceries. Bonnie however didn't seem to be paying him too much attention and he finally finished and left.

"Hello sir," said Bonnie, "how are you today?" "I'm good thank you," said Skiles. "Do you come in here a lot," Bonnie asked? "Oh, I get in about once or twice a week," he said. "Shopping for the little lady at home huh?" "Oh no," he replied. I am a widower."

"Oh, I'm sorry," she said. "I figured a handsome man like you would be married." "Handsome," said Skiles. "I think I'm far from

---

49

handsome at my age." "I don't know," she said. "I have always found older men very attractive and you don't look that old." "Well, thank you for the compliment, my name is Skiles," he said. "That's an unusual name," said Bonnie, "unusual but nice. If you didn't know my name is Bonnie and it's very nice to meet you."

Skiles wasn't sure what to think. He didn't know if Bonnie was just being kind or was flirting with him.

"May I help you out with the groceries sir," asked Aaron? "Sure," said Skiles, knowing that this would cost him what pocket change he had but he wasn't thinking about money just now. He was thinking and wondering about Bonnie.

Chapter 12
The FBI

Being it was Saturday, most of the help had gone home by now. Skiles had to unlock and open the North gate leading to his house. All the gates were locked now everyday around 4 p.m. Not only were they locked but he had to reinforce them all and make them taller. For some unknown reason a couple of years ago someone had started a rumor. Apparently Skiles had become so distraught over the loss of his wife he had placed her in a glass casket and guarded her all the time. It was rumored he had a dog beside him and a shotgun. Every night he would turn on all those hundreds of blue lights and sit there crying for hours.

Skiles figured that someone had seen the glass tank and all the mannequins in the sunroom and along with a wild imagination made up one hell of a story. The story had spread and by now his property had become the spot for all the local teenagers to go. They would tear down his fences, climb over gates and do whatever it took to get up close to the house. The place was becoming quite an urban legend.

As Skiles got out of his car to unlock the gate another car pulled up behind him. "Mr. Test I presume," one of the men said. "Yes, can I help you," asked Skiles. "Let us introduce ourselves," one said. "I'm J. Edgar Hoover of the FBI and this is Jeff Needham, from our Indianapolis office."

"Well," Skiles said "I never knew I was important enough for the big guy to come all the way from DC." "Believe me Mr. Test you are," said Jeff. "Well if I really am," said Skiles, "then drive on in and let me lock the gate behind you and you can follow me up to the house."

Mr. Hoover was impressed with the property as they drove toward the house. There was a beautiful wooded area near the road and as you got closer to the house there were pastures on both sides of the lane. They passed a hay barn, a herd of cows, a pig barn, another hay barn, and then some other out buildings. What Mr. Hoover wasn't impressed with was the house. It just didn't seem to fit. Oh, it looked like a house that you would see on a farm but knowing what he did about Skiles he would have thought the house would have been more luxurious. It was sort of simple looking compared to other homes occupied by millionaires.

"May we help you with the groceries," asked Jeff? "No thanks," said Skiles, "I don't have any more change." Jeff looked puzzled and Skiles said, "It was just a joke about tipping. It's a long story."

"Have a seat gentlemen, can I fix you a drink?" "I'll take a beer if you have it," said Edgar. Jeff said, "Make that two." "Would you like a glass for the beers," asked Skiles? "That would be great," Jeff said. "Okay," Skiles said, "then why don't you just come on into the dining room and we can talk at the table. I think I'll just have a coke and some candy. Would you guys like a snack with your beers?" "None for me," said Edgar. "I'll have some nuts if you have them," said Jeff. "Sure," said Skiles.

"Okay," said Skiles "what is this about? I hope it is not about the rumor of my dead wife in a glass casket." "No, I assure you," said Edgar "it's a little more than that."

"Are you familiar with Senator McCarthy and the term McCarthyism," asked Edgar? "Yes," said Skiles, "I follow politics, but I don't see what it has to do with me." "It has come to our attention that you have a cousin named Jack Test," said Edgar. "Yes, I do, he is my Uncle's son on my Dad's side of the family." "Do you see him much," Jeff asked? "Not really, I haven't talked to him or seen him for several months. I think the last time I saw him was at a swimming party I held here."

"Well we have reason to believe he has become active in the local communist party here in Indianapolis," said Jeff. "That does not surprise me," said Skiles "but again, what does that have to do with me?" "We were hoping you could help us by passing any information about him that could help our cause" said Jeff. "And what is your cause," asked Skiles? "What we are trying to do Skiles," said Jeff "is stop this unpatriotic activity. As you know there are groups of people out there who want to take this government down using political means and we intend to stop them."

"We have to balance what we do with the rights of the citizens," said Edgar. "However, having said that sometimes we may stretch things a little if we know or can prove any kind of subversion."

"We know you are a very patriotic citizen Mr. Test." "We know about your support of our soldiers and your war effort in providing tank parts." "Well, yes I am," said Skiles. "This country has been good to me and I love it and I'll be glad to help you. If that little SOB is trying to do anything in the way of subversion we have to stop him."

"Great," said Edgar, "then Jeff here will be your contact but this whole thing has to stay between us. I'd like to install a phone with a direct line to Jeff if that's okay?" "That's fine with me and I'll even pay for it", said Skiles! "I'll also go you one better. I'll throw a swimming party and invite Jack. Maybe he will loosen up with me about what he is doing. Also I know someone who can do a little research on Jack if you'd like. That might help since I don't have a lot of contact with him," said Skiles. "That would be great as long as it's kept quiet," said Jeff. "Not to worry Gentlemen," said Skiles. "My friend knows how to keep quiet and when I get useful information I'll give Jeff a call."

"Hello, Larry Thomas's office, may I help you?" "Yes, this is Skiles Test calling; I'd like to speak to Larry if he is in." "Just a moment Mr. Test, I'll get him for you."

"Skiles old friend, how are you?" "I was just thinking about calling you. It has been so long since I have seen you. I think it was when Madeline died. So what can I do for you?"

Larry Thomas had met Skiles while working at his dealership as a salesman. At the time he was going through the police academy and worked on weekends to make a little extra money. He eventually dropped out of the academy. He said it was way too structured, so he thought he would use that experience as a private detective. It seemed to work for him, as he had become very successful with two other agents working for him.

Larry was a short but rather large man. He was

---

thirty-nine but sitting around a lot at the office and in a car had begun to take a toll on his body. His weight kept piling on and he had to resort to walking five miles a day to slim down. So far after one year he had lost fifteen pounds.

"I am in need of your services," Skiles said. "Could you come out to the farm this afternoon around three?" "Sure," Larry said, "I'll be there."

Skiles was out by the garage when Larry pulled up. Larry was driving a Nash he had purchased from Skiles's dealership. It was similar to the big boat type that Skiles drove.

"How many cars have you bought from me over the years," asked Skiles? "Oh quite a few Skiles, you know we put a lot of miles on a car following all those shady characters!" "Come on in I'll fix you a drink and tell you what I need," said Skiles.

"Larry what I am about to tell you is in strict confidence. I'd like for you to handle this yourself as not to involve anyone else. I'd also prefer you did not write down anything but try to do it all from memory. I don't want any information in any form that can be traced."

"You have got my attention," said Larry. "As I think you know, I can keep my mouth shut when needed." "That's good," said Skiles.

"Here is the deal," said Skiles. "The FBI thinks my cousin Jack Test is involved in the local communist party here in town. They are investigating him and I have agreed to help. I want to find out if it's true and just how far he has gone with it. If he is doing anything at all in the way of subversion I need to know."

"I have his address and a picture of him in this envelope. Also there is the name and number of my FBI contact in here. As soon as you memorize it all, burn it. I do not want you to call my contact I'll do that. I just needed you to know who he was in case you run across him in your investigation. I'm sure they are following Jack and I'm sorry I don't have a picture but I'm sure you will know him if you see him. He dresses like a cop!"

"It sounds pretty serious Skiles," said Larry. "I have known a couple of folks who have been sent to prison for this type of thing. I'd hate to think one of your own is plotting against his own country. I'll get started on this right away and I should be able to get back to you in one to two weeks with any findings."

"Thanks Larry, you will be doing me and the country a great favor. Here is some cash to get you started. When you need more just let me know."

Chapter 13
1950
Bonnie and Skiles

Skiles was running out of coffee or so he thought. It didn't matter he just needed to get back to the store in Broad Ripple. He had thought a lot about Bonnie since his first meeting and wondered if perhaps anything at all could ever happen between them. It had been so long since he had even thought about another woman, he wasn't sure he knew what to do or even how to act. He also just didn't quite know what to think about Bonnie. Maybe he was wrong but she had to feel something or she would not have acted as she did. As for him, she was young but he had a strong attraction to her.

As he pulled up to the store he saw Bonnie coming out. He hurried and parked, jumped out of the car and walked toward her. Hopefully he thought to himself that she had not seen him. He was acting like a sixteen year old.

"Well Hi Bonnie, are you leaving," asked Skiles? "Yes, I just got off work," she said. "I looked for you all day and I didn't think you were coming in." "You were looking for me," he asked? "Well, sort of," she said. "I had been thinking about you since the last time you were in and thought maybe you would come in today."

"Say, I don't want to be too forward but are you hungry," asked Skiles. "Yes, I could eat," she said. "Good, why don't you hop in the car and we'll go to this little restaurant up the street." "Sounds good to me," she said.

Bonnie was not like most young girls. Oh, she was pretty. She had dark hair, slender build and a cute face. You couldn't say she was beautiful, just cute. You know there are four types of women. Cute, Attractive, Pretty, and Beautiful. Unless you are a man it's hard to explain that but that is just the way it is. You can be cute or attractive and sexy. Or you can be beautiful or pretty. If you're beautiful or pretty you aren't normally sexy or don't have as much sex appeal as a cute or attractive woman. So Bonnie was cute but her maturity level seemed to be much higher that the eighteen years old that she was.

"Where do you live Bonnie," asked Skiles? "I have a little flat up the road here," she said. "I moved into it about a month ago. It's not much, just a temporary place. I just moved here from Ohio. I was living with my folks but got bored with things around there so I left."

"Did you get mad at your parents," he asked. "Oh, no it was nothing like that, we have a great relationship. I was just hanging around after high school dating guys. I just got tired of their kid games. I think that is why I'm attracted to older men. I just can't take the silliness."

Just then Skiles was thinking how silly he must have looked by hurrying to meet her in the parking lot. He needed to act more his age going forward.

After eating Bonnie said it was too early to go home, maybe they could take a drive if Skiles didn't mind.

"I know," he said. "Would you like to see where I live?" "You move pretty fast don't you Skiles?" "Oh, I didn't mean anything like that he said." "I'm just teasing," she said, "I'd love to see your place."

As they neared the north gate Bonnie got a strange look on her face. "Skiles, are we going in there?" "Yes," he said, "this is where I live." "You have got to be kidding," she said. "I have been on one date since I moved here. This neighbor guy brought me out here one evening and tried to get me to jump the fence and go in. He told me all about the glass casket, the wife, the dogs, and the blue lights."

"Well, did you jump the fence," he asked? "No, I'm a big chicken." "I assure you Bonnie that none of those rumors are true. This is just my home. It's a farm, nothing more. Now I admit there are some things here you will not find on most farms. I have a large number of cats. People dump them in this area all the time and I haven't the heart to turn them away. But you will see there is nothing here to be afraid of."

As they pulled up to the garage, she couldn't believe it. How in the world did she ever get a connection like this? Skiles must be loaded she thought. Not only did she find an older man, but a rich old man. That is the thing some women dream of, not particularly her, but some women.

As the day slipped away, night fell on the property. Skiles had given her the grand tour of the place. They had walked out to the cow barn, visited the cat lot, and the pool.

At the pool Skiles turned on the lights. "Gee," she said. "This is beautiful. All those lights make the place. I wish it was warmer; I'd love to go swimming." "It won't be long now," said Skiles. "As soon as it's warm enough you can swim all you like." "I'd love that," she said "but I'd better go now. I have to get up early for work."

On the way back Skiles told her all about himself and his family, or lack of a family. He told her about Madeline and his years of mourning, his businesses, and even how he had been thinking about coming back to the store to see her again. That was unusual for Skiles. He was not the type to talk about himself or his feelings. And he wasn't the type to be so forward with someone.

"Skiles," she said. "I'm attracted to you but I'm a little scared. I think I want to date an older man but I need to go slow. It may or may not be the thing for me, I just don't know. I know I came on pretty strong to you and I don't want to hurt you but I am scared."

"You shouldn't be scared," he said. "I don't know how I feel about a younger woman. I just think you go with it and see what happens. Hopefully no one gets hurt and since we don't want to create any hurt I think we will be fine," he said. "Besides I'm not saying I'm ready to marry again, and you may not want marriage. I do know already that I like the pleasure of your company at times and if it turns into something more, then that's okay."

"Okay," she said. "Let's do it. I'm free all weekend if you want to see me." "Why don't you drive over to the farm Saturday morning," he said. "I need to go shopping for some clothes and maybe you would enjoy going with me." Okay, I'll be there around nine," she said. "Great," said Skiles. "Some of the farm hands will be working that day so the gate will be open."

Shopping was turning into an all day affair. It had taken Skiles one hour to find what he needed. When he told Bonnie to pick out something for herself, she dragged him from here to there. Skiles bought two dresses, one pair of shoes, two nightgowns and lunch!

Later that evening when they were back at the house Bonnie said to Skiles. "I think I'd like to stay the night Skiles. I don't know how you feel about that. You have talked to me about a lot of things but not religion and sex before marriage."

"As for me, I first had sex when I was sixteen," she said. "I believe in God but beyond that I have never been involved in the church." Skiles kind of stuttered at first then said. "I too believe in God but I have never been a religious person.

You also need to know I haven't been with a woman since Madeline died. If fact it may take me awhile to get back into knowing what to do."

"As far as marriage, I just don't know," said Skiles. "I always thought one time was all I would ever want but now I just don't know."

"I guess we can take it as it comes," said Bonnie. "I know what society thinks but I have an aunt who swears she may live with a man but she said she would never marry again. In fact she thinks that one day marriage will be obsolete. That may be stretching it a bit but who I am to know, maybe she can forecast the future!"

Skiles was very nervous. He kept thinking about the last time he made love to Madeline. Could he perform? Would he feel right? He didn't know but he was about to find out. Bonnie had gone into the bathroom to get ready for bed.

The nightgown Skiles had bought for Bonnie was white with lots of lace. As she came toward him he became very aroused. He was sure at that moment he would be able to perform. Bonnie was a cute girl and the nightgown was just the thing Skiles needed. It showed just enough but left some to his imagination. Imagination was what it was all about for Skiles. Seeing a woman naked didn't do as much for him as seeing one half naked. It just seemed more exciting if he didn't know it all at the beginning.

Making love to Bonnie was different than Madeline. For one thing Skiles was not in love with Bonnie or at least not yet. He was

---

59

very infatuated however and perhaps that made him able to perform but it was more sex than anything. His animal instinct was alive and well but his emotions were just not there yet. He liked Bonnie, she made him laugh, he loved being with her, and he loved that first sexual encounter. Maybe in time he would love her, right now he just wanted to enjoy her.

Bonnie wasn't sure what she felt about Skiles. He was the third guy she had been with and obviously the oldest. The other two were younger and didn't last as long as Skiles. With them it was come and go. With Skiles it was come and stay. And then there was this other thing that Skiles didn't know. He didn't know about her restlessness and how after awhile she might move on. She liked Skiles but would he be enough to make her settle down?

For the couple of weeks Bonnie stayed with Skiles more than she did in her flat. She had grown fond of him and him of her. They had fun, but did a little more shopping than Skiles was used to. He didn't mind spending the money it was just Bonnie took so much of his time. He was so busy with her that he missed the walking of the dogs with Doug. Doug missed him to. Skiles had become a father figure to him. His own father was always around but Skiles was different. Doug didn't understand the difference he just felt it.

As far as how Skiles felt about Doug it was as if Doug was the child Skiles never had. He and Madeline had tried to have children in the first couple years of their marriage but nothing ever happened. Skiles thought perhaps he couldn't make babies, but that thought was about to change.

Skiles and Bonnie had been dating now for two months. Since Skiles didn't think he could have kids he never used any protection during sex. However, one Thursday afternoon Skiles got quite a surprise.

"You are pregnant," said Skiles! "Yes, I wasn't sure but I went to the doctor yesterday and he said I was."

"Oh, Bonnie, I am so happy. I didn't think I could have kids. Madeline and I tried but it never happened."

60

"I wonder what it will be," said Skiles. "Oh well it doesn't matter. I always wanted a boy but then I always wanted a girl."

"So, Bonnie what do you think now about marriage?" "I don't know Skiles; I want to think about that for awhile. I think we can take care of the baby even if we don't get married."

"Well then at least you need to move here to the farm so I can take care of you," he said. "I'm okay with that;" she said "I'll start packing tomorrow."

Chapter 14
1951
Kelly

"Mr. Skiles, the phone, it's for you," said Louise. "Hello," said Skiles. "This is Larry; I need to talk to you." "Why don't we meet somewhere," Skiles said? "This isn't' a good time to come to the farm." "Okay, let's meet up in Castleton," said Larry. "There is a Methodist church across the street from the Castleton School. Let's meet there in the parking lot."

It took Skiles ten minutes to get to the school. He wondered what Larry had found out about Jack but he had an idea it wasn't going to be good. He had invited Jack over to swim but so far he had not come.

"Skiles I'm sorry but I have some bad news for you. Jack is in pretty deep into this communist party. I am hearing that he is trying to buy votes for the elections next year. And it's not just him. He has other 'comrades' that he is trying to get elected. Now, I don't have any proof yet, but I think I'm getting close."

"I hate to hear that Larry but I suspected it. I'll give Jeff a call and update him. In the meantime I want you to keep me posted at least once a week."

"Also, and I hate to do this but I want you to write down our progress and mail it to me," said Skiles. "I'll open a mail box up here at the post office and you can send the information there. I know I didn't want anything written but I think it will be safer than meeting like this. I'm afraid someone will see us. Call me tomorrow and I'll give you the mail box address."

Kelly Test was born on April 28, 1951. She was twenty one inches long and weighed seven pounds and two ounces. Bonnie spent three days in the hospital but all was fine with both mother and child. On the day she was coming home, Skiles told her that he had a surprise for her.

"What is it," she asked? "Your mother and father are here." "Oh, they came," she said. "The last time I talked to mom she said

---

she wasn't sure but I'm so glad they made it. I can't wait to see them and show them our baby."

"How you think they feel about us not being married," Skiles asked? "I'm not sure but I think they would prefer that we were," she said. "Even though they are not religious they feel a child belongs in a home with two married parents." "Then do you think we should get married," asked Skiles? "I'm still thinking about that," she said.

Charles and Gladys Hanover were elated to see their granddaughter and of course Bonnie. Skiles had given them the guest room upstairs and invited them to stay as long as they wanted.

Everyday all day long it was almost a fight to see who got to hold Kelly. However Bonnie won most of the time since she was doing the breast-feeding.

After a couple of days had gone by and nothing had been said yet about marriage Skiles took Charles on a tour of the farm and approached him about the subject.

"Charles, I want to talk to you about Bonnie and me not being married." "I appreciate that Skiles, but it isn't necessary," said Charles. "You see Gladys and I both know that Bonnie will never get married."

"I was not aware of that," said Skiles. "All she ever told me was she would think about it." "That's right," said Charles. "She will be telling you she will think about it forever."

"You see there is something you may not know about Bonnie. She likes to play around. Now, I know you may be thinking that she is too young to continue feeling that way forever. And don't get me wrong when I say she likes to play around. Sure, she likes to play the field but she does wait at least a few months between men. It's just that she does not like to be tied down."

"She had a boyfriend her junior year in high school," Charles said. "He treated her like gold. He was the sweetest, kindest kid you could want. She broke his heart and never looked back. She dated two different guys within six months her senior year. Both guys were great and thought the world of her but she didn't care."

63

"When we first heard about you and her we thought maybe since she had gone for an older man she might be changing. And as long as she has been with you and now with a baby we were even more hopeful."

"So what makes you think she hasn't changed," said Skiles? "Gladys told me," he said. "Bonnie and she had a long phone conversation about two months ago. Bonnie told her that after the baby was old enough she would be leaving. Gladys asked her what old enough meant. Bonnie said she didn't know and it didn't matter. It could be two years or ten. Bonnie told her that having a baby didn't mean she couldn't do the things she wanted and it didn't mean she would be tied down. She also said that she cared for you and didn't want to hurt you if that's any consolation."

"Now, I know you love Kelly, she is your daughter, but if you haven't already, don't fall in love with Bonnie. She may stay with you since you have money and can keep her in a style she enjoys, but love you enough to marry you? I don't think so."

Skiles got quiet. He was hurt; there was no doubt about that. He had already fallen in love with Bonnie. It wasn't the deep love he had for Madeline but it was enough to satisfy him. He had a lot of plans for the three of them and this news sort of shattered his dreams.

"Well," said Skiles. "I appreciate what you're saying and I knew she kept putting me off on the marriage, I just didn't know why. And I guess it doesn't matter, I'm very fond of her but I have to be honest, I don't love her. I would marry her for Kelly's sake but then if what you say were true she would still leave. So let's hope she stays with me until Kelly is old enough to understand."

Charles could tell Skiles was lying about not loving her. Maybe Skiles didn't want to show that side of him to Charles or maybe Skiles didn't want him to know he was that vulnerable. Whatever the reason Charles respected him and accepted what he said whatever the reason.

"Hey Skiles, there is a boy coming this way," said Charles. "Does he work for you?" "Yes, that's Doug; he is one of my favorite employees."

"Hi Doug, are you looking for me," asked Skiles? "Yes, please excuse me but I wanted to tell you I was getting ready to take the dogs out for a walk and something is wrong with Fuzzy. I didn't

know what to do about it."

"Would you excuse us Charles, I need to check this out," said Skiles. "Sure, I'll talk to you later. By the way, I think we will be leaving tomorrow afternoon, it's time we got back home." "Okay," said Skiles, "you know you are welcome anytime. Just come on back when you can. No matter what Bonnie does, I think it's important for a child to have grandparents."

"Fuzzy is acting a little funny," said Skiles. "Why don't we put her in the car and run her up to Franks. I need to go to the post office anyway." "You want me to go with you," asked Doug? "Sure why not, it will be fun," said Skiles. "Maybe we will stop at the store for some ice cream."

"I don't think it's anything serious," said Frank, "I think she has eaten some wild grass or something. It happens." "Thanks," said Skiles "and when you get a chance come see my daughter." "I will," said Frank, "I'll be down later in the week and I'll come up to the house." "Good, I'll see you then Frank."

After ice cream and a trip to the post office they headed home. It was fun being with Doug again and Skiles told himself that he had to make it a point to make time for him. Doug was just too good of a kid and he wanted to be sure he knew that he was well liked and appreciated.

The trip to the post office did not yield good news. Larry now had all the proof they needed against Jack.

The next day Skiles met with Jeff Needham. It wasn't a

---

pleasant talk for Skiles. Even though Jack had and was doing wrong, he was still his cousin but Skiles couldn't let that bother him.

Jeff didn't tell Skiles what they would do with Jack, just that they would take care of it and it was better if he didn't know.

The next day the phone line was removed and Skiles never heard from the FBI again. Several days later Skiles received a phone call from Jack's father. He told Skiles Jack was missing and wanted to know if he had seen him. Skiles told him he was sorry he was missing but hadn't seen him in months.

Chapter 15
1955
The First Affair

Kelly was four years old today. Winter had come and gone and spring flowers were popping up everywhere. There were Daffodils from one end of the south lane to the other and all around the pool.

It was fun times again at the farm. Winter had been rough. They had lost a few cattle during a blizzard, one of the hay barns had caught fire, and one of the dogs had died. Skiles had two different types of dogs but both were huge. He had five Saint Bernard dogs and a couple of Great Danes. Fuzzy, the one they had lost was a Saint Bernard.

Bonnie was still with Skiles. They had been getting along well or so Skiles thought. He had been away a lot over the last couple of years taking care of his businesses but when he was home things seemed okay.

During the summers Bonnie had spent a lot of time at the pool. She looked forward to her daily swims and especially when Jim Tyler was cleaning the pool house. She knew Jim was married and had a son, but she didn't care. She was going to make a play for him.

She had thought many times about leaving Skiles, but she wasn't ready just yet. She thought Kelly was too young and she wasn't that unhappy so leaving could wait. She did love her daughter and besides she would have to give up the lifestyle she had become accustomed to.

So instead she was finding some temporary happiness in Jim. He wasn't a great looking man. Not ugly at all, just an average looking guy. The one thing he did have going for him was his body. Jim was in his mid 30's and did a lot of work at the farm, which kept him in shape.

Bonnie didn't do much work but she didn't need to. After Kelly was born she returned to her slender build. Her dark hair was cut short now and sometimes it was blond. She liked it short it was

---

much easier to take care of and fix after it got messed up.

It was the beginning of summer when she first began to notice Jim. That summer was rough for her. Her restlessness was about to get the better of her. She had gone to the pool one Thursday afternoon. She had just gotten back from shopping for a new bathing suit. Skiles was gone to one of his businesses and Emma and Louise were watching Kelly.

Bonnie normally did her changing upstairs in the bedroom. Today however as she entered the pool house she noticed Jim coming from behind the diving platform. There was a small building back there where they kept the pool chemicals. He was carrying some chemicals so she assumed he would be walking around the pool for several minutes while he put them in the water.

As she reached the elevator her mind began to wonder just what Jim would do if he were to look at the pool house and see her inside changing. After all she could change there on the ground level and not have to go upstairs. If he looked in she could just pretend she didn't know he was there.

She had never thought that much about exposing herself to him or anyone else. She also never tried to hide her body from anyone who would look. She and Skiles had lots of pool parties with a lot of drinking and dancing. During those parties she would watch the men look at her when she bent over or wore something tight. So, yes she would change there, just inside the door with her back to the pool and if he looked in, he looked in!

Jim saw Bonnie as he came from behind the platform but he wasn't sure whether she saw him or not. He had seen her there swimming and lying around the pool several times and would go out of his way to move a chair or clean the pool house just to get a closer look at her. He thought she was very sexy looking and all her clothes seem to fit her just right.

Bonnie was naked now. Her back was turned toward the pool and she was bent over putting on her new bathing suit. Jim walked by at that moment and glanced through the window. It was just a normal glance like he had done a hundred times but this time there was something to look at. At that very moment, Jim Tyler had a

---

thousand thoughts run through his mind. Should he turn away and just walk on? Should he stop and take it all in? Should he turn and walk in on her as if he didn't see her there?

Just as he was about to turn and walk on, Bonnie pulled her suit up to just below her breasts as she turned around. Jim was frozen in time. Bonnie just stood there for a second, and then slowly pulled her suit up all the way. She smiled at Jim and walked to the back of the room.

Jim moved to the poolside and began to put the chemicals into the water. Bonnie came out of the pool house and lay down on a lounge chair. As he came near her, she asked, "Hi Jim, how are you today?" "I'm fine," he said. "I'm sorry about a few minutes ago. I didn't know you were in there changing." "I'm fine with what you saw Jim. No harm done, don't worry about it," she said.

It had been a week since she had exposed herself to Jim. That little incident aroused her and all she thought about was how to do it again without Jim thinking it was on purpose.

It was a hot June morning. It was only 10 a.m. but with the heat and humidity it was a perfect time to take a swim. As she came out the back door on her way to the pool Jim was coming up the walk from the garage basement.

"Good Morning Bonnie," said Jim. "Hi, Jim, I haven't seen you in a couple of days, have you been off?" "Oh no," he said. "We have been baling hay so I haven't been up near the house as much."

"Has the pool been cleaned," she asked. "I think its okay," he said, "but I can go out with you and check."

When they got to the pool Jim looked at the water and said, "I think I need to put just a little chemical in that end over there." "Okay," Bonnie said. "I'll just go change."

Bonnie went inside and stood by the window watching Jim. She liked the way he walked. She liked to watch his hips move, she liked everything about him.

Bonnie was in the center of the room with her back turned toward the pool. She had just taken off her clothes and had thrown her bathing suit over her shoulder. She figured she had just enough

---

time to make it to the window before Jim came back. But then she heard the door behind her open. She turned around and Jim was standing there looking at her.

Bonnie was not shy, she did not attempt to cover herself. She just stood there and said. "Looks like you caught me again."

Jim didn't say a word. He had walked in on purpose. He had gotten half way to the platform before he realized that Bonnie might just be playing him. After all, she smiled the first time he saw her changing and this time she told him she was going to change. Was that a hint to him? He had to find out for he too had been aroused by what had happened last week.

Jim didn't think he was a bad husband and he had always been faithful to his wife. He appreciated his job and liked Skiles but he was still a man and any man can be tempted given the right time and place.

Jim moved toward Bonnie. His eyes moved from her face down over her breasts. Her bathing suit covered one of them but the other was exposed. He was a foot away from her when he stopped. Bonnie reached out her hand for his. She then moved it between her legs. As Jim began to caress her, she reached for the bulge that was now protruding from his pants.

Bonnie had needed a man for a long time. She and Skiles slept together but their lovemaking didn't satisfy her. She liked change and this was just what she needed for now.

1955 came in with a roar with the arrival of *Rock 'n Roll*. Bonnie was in love with the music. Skiles bought a huge jukebox and filled it with every hit record that was released. He hooked up speakers all around the pool. You could hear music all the way out to the farm area.

She loved all the songs but over the course of a few years she had picked out five favorites "The Fool" by Sanford Clark, "I Was the One" by Elvis Presley, "The Joker" by the Hilltoppers, "Tragedy" by Thomas Wayne, and "The World Is Getting Smaller" by Mark Dinning. She had a routine she followed at every party. She would play her five favorite songs, and then she would play fast songs.

70

The fast songs put her in a dancing mood where she could show off her moves and body. It was just what she needed to add more spice to her little affairs.

Bonnie loved to dance and she even bought a poodle skirt to wear at parties. The skirt was a perfect fit for her now. She had learned with Jim that men are always looking and if you danced just right and wore the right kind of panties you could turn a lot of heads.

Yes, Bonnie had become quite the exhibitionist. Bonnie even went further than just showing what she had. There were many elevator rides up to the bedroom with men. Some got a look, some a feel and some got to go all the way.

One party was especially a good night for Bonnie to show off her dancing talent. In was summertime 1959 and it was her 27th birthday.

"Skiles, remember the other day you asked me what I'd like for my birthday?" Yes, Bonnie, I remember but you haven't told me yet." Well, I'd like a live band to come play at a pool party," she said. "I was talking to Lucy and she told me about this band called

the 'Dawnbeats' that plays great rock n roll. She saw them play at the Fountain Square tavern last Saturday. They also play at sock hops with 'Bouncing Bill Baker of the radio station WIBC and were on Channel four last Saturday afternoon. Do you think you could hire them and give me a huge party?" "I'll see what I can do," said Skiles. "I'll ask Lucy about them."

It was a Saturday in mid August. The day was extremely hot and humid and Bonnie was all excited about her party. She was trying to figure out what to wear to keep cool. She settled on her poodle skirt with white socks and black and white oxford shoes. She figured a plain white blouse and of course white panties would match everything just fine.

She also had to pick out a bathing suit to wear when the swimming started. Maybe she would buy a new one for the party and she knew just what to buy. The bikini was the newest thing and she wanted one.

The party was set to start at 7 p.m. The band arrived at six and Bonnie was there to greet them. She wanted to be sure they knew where she wanted them to set up and what to play.

"Hi, I'm Bonnie. "Nice to meet you Bonnie, I'm Bob Carrie, this is Dick Donahue, Don Herald, Phil Ramey, and Morgan Schumacher. We also brought this new guy along that is going to play bass for us. His name is Johnny Bennett. He is trying to get a band started called the 'Blue Angels' and wanted to see how we operate."

"We were surprised when we were contacted to play here," said Bob. This lady, I think her name is Lucy, came and asked if we would play at the 'House of blue lights' and we about fell off the stage. We had heard the rumors for years about the place and we didn't hesitate at all to accept." "Yes, this is quite the place," said Bonnie

"Bob, here is a list for you of songs I want you to play," said Bonnie. "I also understand you just released a record called Midnight Express. Please feel free to play that also. I want to hear it. Then whenever you take your breaks, feel free to go inside the pool house and help yourself to the refreshments. Then when you wrap up, you are welcome to go swimming." "Thanks," said Bob, "but I don't think we brought any swimming trunks." "I think we have extras downstairs in the dressing rooms or if not, just wear your underwear," she said with a big grin.

The first song began at seven. Bonnie thought the band was excellent and wasted no time doing her dance in front them. She was twirling around and flipping her skirt up and down being sure every member of the band saw her white panties.

The band had played for about two hours and Bonnie was getting hot. She had danced with every guy there and now it was time for a swim. She retired to the upstairs bedroom, took a quick shower, and put on her bikini. She admired herself in the mirror and practiced her entrance walk. She wanted to strut herself around the pool to the diving board. She was a little nervous since all the other girls had regular bathing suits on but she was determined to make a splash!

The sun was beginning to set as Bonnie walked out the door wearing a bright red towel that covered her waist down to her knees. All the lights had been turned on around the pool and that gave a nice contrast to her solid white bikini top that just barely covered her bouncing breasts. As she moved toward the high dive she took off the towel showing the remainder of the all white bikini and heard a couple of "wolf whistles" from the guys. She reached the diving board, made her way to the end and dove in. As she hit the water the top of her suit came off and as she came up from the dive she played the shy act by staying under the water. Of course there were several guys willing to help her find the top.

After getting her top back on she came out of the water and sat on the edge where the blue lights were. She positioned herself facing the pool house with her feet in the water. The blue light cast a soft hue on her white bikini and if you looked close you could tell there wasn't much of her body left to the imagination.

It was getting late, the crowd had thinned out, Skiles had retired for the evening, and Bonnie was getting horny. She had been watching the band members to see who, if any, were paying attention to her. She noticed they all were so she thought she would plan a little surprise for them after all the guests were gone.

"Bob, I'd like for you guys to hang around until everyone is gone," said Bonnie. "I'd like for you to play one more song for me but inside the pool house." "We can do that, said Bob, "what song would you like?" "I'll tell you later," she said "and you don't have to set up the whole band, just one guitar and maybe a drum will do."

Bonnie had changed back into her dancing outfit, the band had moved inside, and Bonnie said, "I want you to play 'The Stripper' for me. I've always wanted to dance that and this may be the only chance I'll ever have.

As the music started she began with her blouse. Her moves were good enough that she could have been a professional. The smoothness of her movements and the agility of her body made the dance flow as if it were a small waterfall flowing over tiny rocks into a pool of water.

Bonnie did not leave anything to the imagination by the time she had finished. The last piece of clothing to come off was the panties.

As the song ended all the guys clapped and Johnny said, "Beautiful, just beautiful." Bonnie turned her back to the band and said. "I'm going upstairs to bed if any or all of you want to join me."

Skiles was spending more and more time with work and Bonnie was spending more and more time playing. Skiles decided to hire a nanny for Kelly. At first Bonnie became very angry and told Skiles she was not neglecting their child! No matter what she said Skiles was determined to hire one anyway. He knew Kelly was not being ignored. Even when Bonnie was not with her there was always Louise and Emma. However, it just seemed the thing to do. Later on even Bonnie began to think it was a good idea. It would give her more free time.

Skiles ran an ad in the Indianapolis newspaper. He asked for a live in nanny with references. There were four responses to his ad. He interviewed all of them at the farm and said he would make his decision within a week. Immediately after the interviews he called Larry.

"Larry, I have another investigation job for you," said Skiles. "Do I need to come over Skiles or can we do this one over the phone," he asked? "The phone will be fine," said Skiles; "there is nothing secret about this. I'm going to give you the names of four persons. These are the applicants I have for Kelly's nanny. I'd like you to find out anything you can for me to help me make my decision."

Mrs. Kathryn Kistner stood 5'6" slender build with short dark hair. She was on the back side of thirty but not far back. She had been a nanny for eight years with a family on the west side of Indianapolis. Being a nanny was all she had ever done since college. The last family had provided a small two-bedroom home behind their house for her. She cared for their two small twin boys until they reached their early teens. The family had ran into financial troubles and had to let her go.

She had been married but her husband had been killed in the Korean War and she was thankful for the job Skiles had offered her.

Skiles had fixed up one of the upstairs bedrooms for her. Her job was Kelly and nothing else but Skiles soon found out she was much more than he had hoped for.

Kathryn grew very fond of Kelly. She treated her as if she was her own. She was also fond of animals. She, Kelly, and Doug would spend hours playing with the cats and walking the dogs.

On weekends she would cook meals for the family. She even got along with Bonnie. Yes, once again, Skiles was lucky and as time would show his life was about to change again.

Chapter 16
The Sixties
Bonnie Leaves

Bonnie was tired and bored. Kathryn had basically taken over her daughter. Jim had become boring, and she could hardly stand to look at Skiles. She still liked the parties, it was the only time she felt alive. She now drank all the time, spent too much time in bed trying to sleep away her problems. She was very moody and there were days she would just sit and cry. She had to talk to Skiles!

Skiles was sitting in the piano room playing with the Myna bird Madeline had gotten him. Bonnie wondered how long that silly thing would live. It was getting close to its normal life span of twenty years. All it did was cuss at you when you walked in the room.

"Skiles, can I talk to you a minute," Bonnie asked? "Sure, have a seat, what's on your mind?"

"It's my life Skiles, I'm so unhappy. I was thinking about taking a long vacation, maybe a year or two. I just need to get away." "What about Kelly," he asked? "I know she will miss me but not that much," said Bonnie. "I don't spend much time with her anyway. Kathryn is always with her and at times I think Kelly feels more like Kathryn is her mother instead of me."

"I always wondered when this day would come," said Skiles. "I have seen you go down over the years. I know you haven't been happy with me for a long time and I won't try to keep you here. I'll set you up a bank account that should last you awhile. If you need more money, just let me know."

"Thank you Skiles. I hope this does not hurt you, it was not my intent to do that." "I know," he said "and just remember you have a home here if and when you decide to come back. All I ask in return is that you stay in contact with Kelly. I don't want her growing up not knowing where her mother is." "I will Skiles and thank you for understanding."

"Need to get away, need to get away, the sob needs to get away," said the bird as Bonnie walked out. Skiles was upset but he

---

had to laugh at the silly bird.

Bonnie was gone for six months. She had traveled the world and was now running out of money. She had kept in contact with Kelly as Skiles requested and was now on her way back. She did not plan to stay but a couple of days, just long enough to replenish her bank account, and spend a little time with her daughter.

Nothing much had changed since she had left. Kelly was happy to see her. Skiles offered her more money without her asking. Her world was okay now. She had her freedom, she had money, and she loved to travel. She had everything except she was lonely. The loneliness was horrible at times and she knew she could always stay at the farm but that wouldn't get rid of the loneliness. She had to find something or someone else to play with to survive. She was just that way.

Kathryn was happy at the farm. The life she had there was like a dream. She loved Kelly, she loved the animals, and she had fallen in love with Skiles. He was so gentle, loving, and kind. She had never known anyone like him.

She knew Skiles and Bonnie lived a strained relationship. She also knew it was Bonnie who kept that distance for Skiles would have married her in an instant for Kelly. She knew Skiles was unhappy and disappointed with Bonnie even though he never spoke badly of her. He would always make excuses for her and Kathryn respected that.

She had been silent as she watched Bonnie come and go in and out of their lives. Bonnie was gone again, maybe for good this time, and she wanted more than to be just a nanny. She wasn't sure if Skiles had any feelings for her beyond friendship. What she did know is that Skiles would never marry her as long as Bonnie was alive. He didn't want Kelly to have a stepmother and he always wanted to keep a place for Bonnie to come home to. She knew all this but if they could have just a few moments of pleasure together, then maybe that would be enough.

It was Monday afternoon, Skiles had come in from outside

and was going into the piano room. As he walked through the doorway a chill run up his spine. There was no sound coming from the birdcage. His bird had passed.

That bird had meant the world to Skiles. It was 1944 when Madeline gave it to him for Christmas. He remembered the day so well because it was the beginning of her illness.

Skiles took the bird and placed it in newspaper. He then took it outside and found Doug. Doug was heartbroken also. Doug was fond of all the animals but the bird was one of a kind. He told Skiles he would build a casket for the bird and asked what name he should put on the headstone. Skiles said, "You know Doug I never named the bird." I just referred to it as the bird. I'll tell you what to do though. Why don't you put 'The Loud Mouth Bird' on the headstone? I think Madeline would like that. No wait," Skiles said. "Make that 'The Foul Mouthed Bird,' not only was he a fowl but he did have a foul mouth. Sometimes I wonder where he got all those words from," said Skiles with a little smile on his face.

Later that day they buried him in the pet cemetery. Kelly, Doug, Kathryn and Skiles were in attendance. They all four had tears in their eyes as they walked away.

Skiles was very upset about the bird. He and the bird had been through a lot together. As he sat there looking at the empty room a smile came to his face. He remembered one night a couple of years ago.

He was in the kitchen when he heard the dogs barking. He thought to himself, not again. He knew there were kids out there. It had been a week since he had encountered a couple that had sneaked in and were swimming in his pool. He was going to scare them and run them off but Skiles wasn't like that. Instead he invited them to continue swimming and even provided them soft drinks. All he asked in return was to tell folks that this wasn't a place with dead people but his home.

This time however, Skiles thought he would pull a little trick on them if they came around the house. He turned off all the lights except for a small blue lamp in the piano room where the bird was. He opened the door that led to the outside so they could see and hear through the screen. He knew if they came into view of the bird he would talk. Skiles then hid in the other room where they couldn't see him.

It wasn't long before Skiles saw them. There were four of them. They looked to be around sixteen years old. There were two girls and two boys. As they approached the door the bird yelled out. "SOB, you're an SOB." One of the boys said. "Look it's a bird talking to us!" Skiles then yelled out. "No, you are the SOB you silly bird. I'm going to take this gun and shoot you." The bird said. "Shoot the SOB, Shoot the SOB." The kids took off running and Skiles had his little laugh.

Yes, Skiles missed the bird. He had been dealt a lot of tragedy in his life but that didn't get him down. He always said life was what you make it and he was blessed in a lot of ways despite the tragedies.

Chapter 17
Present Day
Laura

It was late afternoon when Brian returned to his office. As soon as
Jack saw him, he wanted a full report. Brian told him what he knew
so far but until he knew what or who was in the casket, it was too
early to make any conclusions.

"I understand Brian," said Jack "but I want a story to run on the
front page of tomorrow's paper. While you're waiting on the press
conference take a look at these pictures and articles from our
archives. I had the research department put a package together for
you. This thing is going to go national and I want this paper to be
where people go to for the whole story. I want to use the whole
front page starting with the history of the legend up to finding the
glass casket buried," said Jack. "Oh, by the way," said Brian. "Do you
know anything about the house of blue lights web site that has
been taken off the web?" "I didn't know it was gone," said Jack. "I
looked at it a long time ago but it lacked a lot of information. I guess
that could be part of your investigation, and get going on that
interview with what's her names dad!" "Her name is Laura," Brian
shouted as he left the room.

The press conference was called at 7 p.m. It was going to be
run by Troy Bennett, the current coroner. They were holding it in
the old auditorium near the police station. Brian knew Troy. They
had talked several times but they were not the best of friends. Troy
didn't care much for reporters but he made an effort to help them if
it benefited his career.

The auditorium was within walking distance for Brian but
Amanda had to drive. She parked in a lot near the building and ran
into Brian just as he walked by the entrance of the lot.
"So we meet again," she said. "Yes," said Brian, is this called good
karma." "Not sure if it's good or bad," she said laughingly.

"Ladies and Gentlemen, I'm Troy Bennett, the coroner for the
city. Let me make a statement and then I'll take a few questions. As

you know we found a casket on the property that had previously been a nature park and before that was the home of a Skiles Test. Now I know you all know about the urban legend but I'm not getting into anything involving that. My job is to present the facts.

The facts are we found two bodies in one casket. I say casket but it was more like a big glass tank. The woman appeared to have been in her early twenties. The man's age is going to take a little more time. His decomposition suggests he was not prepared for burial like the woman and just placed into the casket soon after death. Of course we haven't identified either of them yet, the time frame for that is unknown. I'll now take a few questions."

"Amanda," said Brian, "why don't we cut out of here? Bennett doesn't know anything other than what he told us. If he does, I'll pump it out of him later. I want to make you a proposition and I don't want to do it here." "Okay," said Amanda.

"Let's take a drive," said Brian. "I'll bring you back to get your car later." "Where are we going Brian," she asked as they drove away? "We are going to visit a friend of mine, Bill Johnson," he said. "Bill is a computer geek. He is my go to guy when I have computer issues and I want to see if he can find out who hosted the house of blue lights web site that went missing."

"Okay, so what's this proposition you have for me," Amanda asked? "Well," Brian said. "I know that you have contacts and information regarding the House of Blue Lights. I know the coroner Bennett. I have a lot of newspaper articles to research and I thought since you are TV and I am newspaper." "I accept," she said! "I haven't finished yet," Brian said. "You don't have to," said Amanda. "I know what you are going to say. You want to partner in this investigation and share information. I will agree to do that as long as you and I work out an arrangement on when each of us releases information. I don't want to be scooped by the paper." "I think that's fair," Brian said. "But," Amanda said, "I think I have one up on you. All you have is articles, and a coroner contact. I have more contacts including one you don't know about. I know detective Reynolds who has been assigned the case. So you can pump Bennett all you want but I think I can provide an inside avenue

———

81

that would be more help." "So you are saying this is sort of one sided," Brian said? "Does that mean you want something extra from me?" "Maybe, I'm not sure," she said. "I will have to let you know when the time comes."

"Come on Bill answer the door," Brian said. "I know you're home, I hear your clock ticking!" "I'm coming, I'm coming," yelled Bill as he tried to get to the door before the bell rang again.

"Well, Howdy Brian, I haven't seen you in four days. How's the laptop doing?" "Just great Bill," he said. "Come on in and bring your friend with you," Bill said.

"Bill, this is Amanda, Amanda this is Bill." "Nice to meet you," said Amanda. "Same to you and next time don't bring him with you," said Bill as he chuckled.

"So what's up guy," asked Bill? "We need a favor," said Brian. "Have you ever heard of the House of Blue Lights?" "Of course," said Bill. "Anyone who lives around here has heard of it and I do watch the news." "I hope you watch Channel seven," said Amanda! "Channel seven huh, is that where you work," asked Bill? "Yes, she is a reporter for them;" said Brian, "now let's get back to the blue light thing. It is my understanding that there used to be a web site about it. Then all of a sudden it went down and." Bill stopped him, "and you were hoping I could tell you why," said Bill? "What is this," asked Brian? "First Amanda knows what I'm going to say and now you. You guys must have the same personality trait." "Didn't mean to be rude," said Bill. "I'm just an impatient person. I'm always finishing other people's sentences before they do."

"Okay, let me see if I can find out anything here," said Bill. "It looks like the site was purchased in 2000 and was taken down in 2009. The first Internet was in 91 and the first dot com was in 97. So it looks like they purchased it after the boom started but didn't keep it long." "Does it say who owns or owned it," asked Amanda? "Well yes and no," said Bill. "The problem is I can't tell you who because that information is sealed. That is strange too because only the government does that kind of crap." "Why would the government own a web site like that and try to seal the fact they

---

own it," asked Amanda? "It doesn't make sense," Bill said. "Anyone who looks at this can tell it's the government but I'm sure if I dig deep enough I can find out who in the government it is."

"Okay," said Brian. "If you don't mind do some more digging and give me a call when you find something. And one more thing, let's all agree here and now to refer to the House of Blue Lights as the 'farm' going forward. After all it was a farm and I'm tired of saying those four words. Everybody knows, especially you two, what I'm going to say as soon as the word house comes off my lips." "Agreed," Bill and Amanda said together.

"It's getting late," said Brian. "I want to run through a drive thru and get a sandwich and then I'll take you to your car. Would you like something?" Yes, there is a Rally's hamburger place just up the road; I'd like one of those and a small fry. I love their fries," she said.

As they neared the lot where Amanda had left her car Brian commented how much the traffic had died out. "It was almost 10 p.m. and he was rarely downtown at that time of night. No traffic was nice but there was another benefit. There were all kinds of parking spots along the street.

"I'll park here on the street and walk you up to get your car," Brian said. "That's nice but you don't have to. I think the garage is pretty safe." "No, I want to," he said. "I want to see what kind of car you drive." "All you had to do was ask silly. I drive a little gray Toyota. It's just an old car that gets me there and back. It's not my dream car, I can tell you that." "What is your dream car," asked Brian? "I want a Lexus," she said. "When you see me drive one of those you will know I have made it to the top of my career."

"How far up are you," he asked. "My car is on the third floor," she said. "Do you mind if we take the stairs," asked Brian? "I don't care much for elevators.

The stairs of the parking garage were not much different than Brian's newspaper building except there were no windows. As they neared the top Brian said, "Amanda, do you think you could introduce me to Laura tomorrow evening. If you guys don't have

83

any plans, I'll buy dinner. I'd like to question her about her granddad." "Let me give her a call," said Amanda.

"Laura, this is Amanda, do you have plans for tomorrow evening?" Well," said Laura," I had a dinner date with this movie star but I could cancel." "You are so dramatic," said Amanda. "How would you like to be treated to a real free dinner instead of a pretend one?" "Sounds okay," said Laura. "Good," said Amanda, "Let's plan on around seven. Brian is that good for you?" "Sure," he said. "Who is Brian," asked Laura? "I'll tell you when I get home if you are still up." "What should I wear," said Laura? "Are we going someplace fancy?" "Just casual," said Amanda. "I am going to ask Brian to take us to Logan's. I am craving peanuts and one of their baked sweet potatoes with cinnamon."

Laura's condo was just off Allisonville road as you entered the town of Fishers. Fishers had recently been awarded the best and safest city to live in the USA. Fishers was situated north, northeast of Indianapolis. It was a suburb of Indy and was bordered by Carmel, Lawrence, and McCordsville. It wasn't long ago the town consisted of a few buildings and a little pig path through downtown. But as Indy spread out it was the natural progression of things. Now Fishers was bustling with shopping, dining, and the usual traffic jams.

Brian saw Amanda's car in the drive and parked behind it. The garage door was closed so he assumed Laura's car was inside. He was wondering what she drove. He always wondered what everyone drove. He couldn't help himself, he just loved cars.

There were flowers on the front porch hanging from a beam that ran across the top of the porch. The porch was small but had room for the two chairs that were sitting there.

He didn't trust doorbells to always ring and there was a knocker on the door so he used it.

"Come on in," said Amanda. "Let me take your jacket; is it a little cool out?" "Yes, it's a nice spring but still a little cool, I'm waiting for summer temperatures myself."

It was a typical two-bedroom one-floor condo with a two-car garage. It had a small deck out back with a small fenced in yard. The living room was large with all tile floors and a huge area rug. The kitchen was just off to the right side of the living room as you walked toward the back door. There was a large counter type bar separating the two and standing behind it was Laura.

If Brian was infatuated with Amanda, he was smitten with Laura. Her red hair flowed down on her shoulders in these little curls that bounced when she walked.

"Laura, this is Brian. Why don't you two get acquainted I'll be ready in a minute?"

"So, where do you live and work Brian," asked Laura? "I live in Zionsville," he said. "In fact, I have a condo similar to yours. I work for Indianapolis newspapers as a reporter." "That's nice," she said. "I guess Amanda told you already that I'm between jobs." "That's not a bad place to be if you can afford it," he said. "Sometimes, I wish I was between jobs, but only on Mondays. The rest of the week is okay." "It's kind of like that Manic Monday song by the Bangles huh," said Laura. "Yes," said Brian, "you could say that."

"So, Laura, what kind of car do you drive?" "Car," she said. "I don't drive a car; I drive a truck, why do you ask?" I'm a car buff," he said, "and a truck, that's great! I love trucks, what kind is it?" "It's a bright red 2002 Chevy S-10 extended cab four wheel drive with twenty two thousand miles on it. My dad bought it new and gave it to me after I kept begging him for it. I've had it a couple of years. Before that I had an old mustang." "Define old," said Brian. "It's wasn't a classic so don't get all excited," she said.

"Ready to go," asked Amanda? "Whoa, you look terrific," said Brian. "Oh, this little ole thing," Amanda said. "It's just something I threw on." "Here is your jacket Brian," said Laura. "Amanda do you want a sweater or jacket?" "Just grab the tan jacket for me," Amanda said.

As they drove to the restaurant, Brian thought, just something she threw on, huh? Amanda had come out of the bedroom wearing a silk blouse with more cleavage showing than a cat had fur. Her skirt was about six inches above the knees and to his amazement he wondered how she could move as tight as it was. As far as Laura, she was dressed casual but even with that she was a knockout. She was wearing very tight jeans and a loose pullover. Both women were a 10 on looks, but it was yet to be seen what the total score was after he knew them a little better.

Logan's was a nice little restaurant about fifteen minutes from the condo. They had decent food at a good price and he also liked the bucket of peanuts they place on all the tables. The thing was you couldn't stop eating them and if you weren't careful you would fill up on them and not be hungry when your dinner arrived.

As dinner progressed the conversation fixated on the farm. Laura said her grandfather was still alive but not in good health. He was around eighty-five and his memory was fading fast. She said that however her dad might be able to help and she would ask if he would meet with them.

After dinner, Brian took them both back home. Before Amanda got out of the car she reached over and gave Brian a kiss on the cheek and handed him a piece of paper. The paper had her home and cell phone number on it. The nice thing about that he thought was the home number was also a way to get in touch with Laura.

Brian, what are you thinking, he said to himself? One woman at a time, and don't pit friends against friends! He went home and went to bed.

Chapter 18
Present Day
Detective Chip

It had been an exhausting week for Brian. Bill had not called back yet, he and Amanda had been doing research but they were at a stand still. He had talked to Bennett. Bennett was not that helpful at first until Brian promised him exclusive quotes in the stories he wrote. Then after that Bennett still didn't have much to say, he was waiting on forensics. Amanda had talked to detective Reynolds but he was waiting on Bennett. Laura's dad had been out of town and he wasn't expected back until Monday and today was Saturday. So Saturday was sleep in day or at least until 9 a.m. when the phone rang?

"Brian, get up, get dressed and get going," Jack said. "But it's my day off," yelled Brian! "The news doesn't take days off Brian; they just found another body at the House of Blue Lights!"

"Hello," said Laura, "Hi, this is Brian, is Amanda up?" "Hold on Brian, I think she just got up. Amanda, Brian's on the phone." "Hello Brian, what's up?" "They just found another body at the farm," he said. "I'll pick you up in thirty minutes."

Amanda and Laura both were waiting in the driveway when Brian arrived at their condo. "I just have to go with you," Laura said. "Amanda has an extra press pass and I need the excitement! If you let me tag along Brian, I'll give you a Yankee dime." "What's a Yankee dime," he asked? "Google it silly," said Laura.

The scene at the farm was worse than before. There were all these crazies carrying signs from everything from respect the dead to save Mother Nature. They had to park even further away than Brian had the last time. Just as they had gotten out of the car an unmarked police car pulled up next to them.

"Amanda, would you guys like a lift," came a voice from the car? "Hi Chip," Amanda said, "we sure would, it's a little chilly out

---

today." "Just hop in the back," he said. "Chip, this is Laura Needham, and Brian Fallon." "I presume you are all press", Chip said. "Yes," said Amanda. "Laura works with me and Brian works for the paper." "Oh, yes," Chip said, "I have heard the name. I was talking to the coroner yesterday and he mentioned your name Brian." "I hope it was nothing bad," Brian said. "Oh no," said Chip. "He was just talking about how you were going to get him some publicity. He is such a political hound, but he would be a good contact as long as you stay on the good side of him."

Chip Reynolds was a good cop. He had started as a street patrolman 10 years ago and worked his way up to detective. Some guys have to wait longer for that position but Chip had taken it upon himself to further his education during his patrolman time. He had taken every forensic and criminal investigation course the force offered as well as the local colleges. He stood 6', weighed 190 pounds, and was considered by most women to be, as they used to say in the 50's, Tall, Dark, and Handsome! He was married with one small boy. He had known Amanda a short time but he considered her his friend. He liked to have friends in the media. They always came in handy when you needed help with charity functions. They also could be helpful when you needed a favor that involved media coverage for crime related things. He also liked looking at her. After all Amanda was a knockout.

"Stick close to me and I'll get you as close as I can," said Chip. "Do you know anything about this body yet," asked Laura? "What I know so far is that there is not much left except bones. The body was not buried in a casket or any type of container, or bag." "Was it found near the glass casket from last week," Brian asked? "No," said Chip, "they told me it was several yards away.

I see you guys have a couple of cameras. Please don't take any pictures until I clear you," said Chip as they neared the scene. "What's that," asked Amanda as Brian pulled a paper from his pocket? "It's a map I grabbed before I left home. It's an aerial view of the property from the 1950's that we had in our archives. I wanted to see where this body is in relationship to the other two."

None other than Joe Bowling had uncovered the body of

—

bones. It was the first dig site he had been allowed to dig after finding the first casket. Of course Tony was still very nervous over this whole thing. His site had been down for a week now and he had instructed everyone to work Saturday. He was afraid with this find they would shut him down for a month and dig up the whole area looking for bodies. If they did that, he hoped the state would give them an extension on the contract. As far as Joe was concerned, he was done. He told Tony he wanted to be reassigned. He said he couldn't take this strange and peculiar stuff any longer. Of course Tony ignored his request and told him to just stay calm.

Joe had separated some of the bones as his backhoe dug them up. He stopped as soon as he saw them but by then some damage had been done. The forensics guys were in the hole trying to remove the remainder by hand. The hole was about 4 feet deep.

"Stay here guys, I'll be back in a minute," Chip said as he went over to the forensics guys.

"Can you tell anything yet," asked Chip? "All we know is it's a grown male. There is no ID anywhere around here, so it's going to take a while before we know who he is."

As he returned to Amanda, Brian, and Laura Chip said, "Okay you guys can take a few pictures from here. We want to keep the scene closed off. All they can tell me right now is that it's a grown male."

"I just noticed something Chip from looking at this map," Brian said. "The first casket was found where the house used to be. This grave was where the pet cemetery was." "I don't know if there is any relevance to that or not," said Chip. "What I do know is we are going to do some more digging to see if we come up with more graves."

"That's all I can do for you guys," said Chip." I've got to get some more equipment and people here or I'd take you back to your car." "Oh, we're fine," said Laura. "Thank you so much for your help."

"This is exciting," said Laura as they walked back down the hill to the road. "I'm not morbid but I've been so bored lately, I'd do almost anything for a thrill. Do you guys mind if I help you in your

---

investigation? I can do research." "I don't mind," said Amanda. "I don't either," said Brian. "In fact, maybe you can spend some time with your grandfather. You never know what the mind can remember even at eighty five."

"I was wondering about something," said Amanda. "When they demolished this place why didn't they find any of these graves?" "Maybe they were buried after the demolition," said Laura. "Well I'm not sure how they demolished the place," said Brian. "If they just tore down the buildings and hauled them away they would not have done much digging."

"Brian, I think your phone is ringing," said Amanda. "Yes it is," he said. "I can just barely hear the ringer. Hello. Yes Bill, do you have something for me?"

Several minutes went by and Brian walked away from them while he talked to Bill. When he returned, Amanda asked him if anything was wrong. "Nothing is wrong," said Brian. "It's just this case gets stranger by the minute. It's as if it's some great conspiracy. I don't mind telling you it is getting under my skin. I want to solve this so bad but we keep running into obstacles. It's like I want to be a Sherlock Holmes but sometimes I feel more like one of the three stooges. Bill told me the missing web site was owned by the FBI and the agent's name it was in was Jeffery Needham!"

"You've got to be kidding me," said Laura. "Why in the world would my granddad own a web site about the House of Blue Lights?" "That is one of the mysteries you need to find out for us," Amanda said.

Brian, Laura, and Amanda spent the rest of the weekend doing research. They had found some information on Skiles' family but not much more than that. Monday came and Laura had set up an appointment for them to meet her father. Detective Reynolds had dug up half the farm by now looking for more bodies but none were found. Bennett still had nothing to tell them. Laura had spent some time with her grandfather but had only gotten small bits of information. They met Jeff Needham Jr. at his home late that evening.

"You folks have got quite a mystery on your hands," said Jeff. "I've been talking to Laura and it looks like you have more questions than answers." "Yes we do and we are hoping you can help us," said Amanda. "Well," Jeff said. "I don't know a whole lot about anything. Dad never talked about the place that much. He would mention things from time to time but I don't think there was anything of importance in what he said."

"I do remember he and I were at a little store in Castleton one day. The store was called Mathews Grocery. It sat there on 82nd street where the Rally's hamburger joint is now located. Castleton was just a little dot on the map back then. There was a barbershop, an old high school turned into a grade school, a grain elevator and a few houses. This was early 60's I think. Oh, and that building that is there by the railroad tracks, Odin Corp. That building was there, I find it strange that it never got torn down or changed. It looks empty but there may be someone in it. And one more thing, the grain elevator was owned by Test."

"Anyway while we were there some of Test's farm hands came in. Dad said they bought their cat and dog food there. I remember it because they bought these big hunks of frozen chicken. Dad said they cooked it fresh every day to feed the cats."

"The guy driving the truck was Jim I think. I don't know his last name. I do remember one of the guys was called Ledbetter and there was this other guy I remember quite well. Dad said he was slightly retarded. I was just a kid and I kept staring at him but I couldn't tell he was retarded. His name was Doug Raines. Now, I believe Doug could still be alive. I ran into him a couple of years ago. I was in the Wal-Mart off 96th street. I saw him but wasn't sure at first who he was. After a couple of minutes it came to me and I approached him. I told him my name and asked him if he was Doug. He told me yes but he didn't remember me from the store. I have no idea where he lives and of course he may be dead by now for all I know."

"What disturbs me is this thing with Dad and the web site. If you are telling me it went down in 2009 that was after he retired. To my knowledge at that time Dad had no computer and had already started to have some dementia. That has to be a mistake."

"Does granddad have any old papers from his job," asked Laura? "I think he does have some folders from work but I don't know what is in them. He keeps them in that metal filing cabinet of his." "Would it be possible to see them," asked Brian. "Sure," said Jeff. "I'll go over and get them tomorrow."

"You know I feel like an idiot," said Brian. "I never asked where he lived. He is not living alone is he?" "Oh, no he is in this assisted living center at 96th and Mollenkoff road," said Jeff. "It won't be long before we will have to move him to a nursing home."

"Oh, one more thing I remember, the storeowner said Skiles daughter had a nanny. He couldn't keep from talking about how good-looking she was. I'm sorry I don't remember her name; maybe Doug can help you if it's important."

Brian's cell phone had been ringing all morning Tuesday but as usual he didn't hear it. Brian had been busy locating Doug. He was still alive and lived in a small house not too far from the farm. He took his phone out of his pocket to call Amanda when he noticed he had a call from Amanda's home phone.

"Hi Laura," this is Brian; "Sorry I missed your call." "Brian, get over here right away. You won't believe what's in this folder of granddads." "Is Amanda there," Brian asked? "No," she said, "she had to go to the station but she knows what's in here. She and I went over it this morning when dad dropped it off."

When Brian arrived at Laura's condo she yelled at him to come on in. Laura was standing in the living room with a paper in one hand and a cup of coffee in the other. Laura had on a very thin silk nightgown. It was so thin it left hardly anything to the imagination.

"Oh, I'm not dressed am I?" as she looked down in embarrassment? "I have been so excited I forgot what I *wasn't* wearing! I'll be right back." "Hey before you do," said Brian. "I'll take that Yankee dime you owe me now. I looked it up on Google." "Okay," she said, as she reached up and gave him a kiss on the check.

There were mostly handwritten notes in the folder. There was a list of farm worker names but the paper was curled on all edges and most of the names were blurred and not readable. You could make out five of the names, Ledbetter, Springfield, Lockhart, Brinkman, and Oakley. There was some reference to McCarthyism and an arrow drawn to one name and that was Jack Test. There was also a typed memo stating the House of Blue Lights web site was no longer relevant and could be closed down.

"You want something to drink Brian; I need another cup of coffee." "No, I'm fine," he said. "When do you think Amanda will be back?" "In a minute," she said, "I see her car pulling up now and she has someone with her."

Amanda and detective Reynolds came through the door. "I had to tell Chip about the information Laura and I found in her granddads file," said Amanda. "Remember the little article we found over the weekend saying Jack Test went missing back in the 50's. Chip thinks one of the bodies they found could be him." "He could be right," said Brian. "I didn't put two and two together until now but it makes sense."

"How about the web site thing," asked Laura? "I'm not sure but I think it must be connected someway," said Chip. "I have a friend at the FBI. I'll give it to him and see what he can come up with." "So how are you going to prove whether or not one of the bodies is Jack," asked Laura? "Not sure yet," said Chip. "We may have to exhume a family member to check DNA."

"Listen guys," said Brian. "I have found Doug. Chip you may not know who that is but he used to work for Skiles Test. He doesn't have a phone so I was going to drive over there to see if he can shed any light on these bodies. We should take this list of farm worker names we found and ask if Doug knows any of them. Are you interested in going with me?" "Sure I'll even drive," Chip said. "Oh, by the way Laura can I assume you were not being truthful when you said you worked with Amanda as press? That is what you told me when we met but I think I figured out you really don't." "Sorry Chip, I didn't know if you would let me go along if I wasn't press." "It's okay," he said. "You are forgiven."

93

Chapter 19
Present day
Doug Raines

It was early afternoon; the cool weather had turned cooler. There was a dark cloud moving in from the west and rain was forecast for that evening and night. Laura and Amanda had dressed for the cooler weather but Brian left the house this morning without his jacket. At least he had long sleeves on and Chip seemed to be warm and comfortable in his uniform.

Doug's house was a small Cape Cod type dwelling. It was located in Lawrence which was a couple of miles from the farm. In fact the farm was in Lawrence Township but it had an Indianapolis address.

Doug's house was shrouded in bushes and trees. The driveway was gravel and very narrow. Chip pulled the car in as far as he could. The house looked run down with the gutters and soffits hanging down. The siding was wood and looked like it had not been painted in years. There was no garage and there was a car sitting beside the house. It was a late 60's Chevy sedan. It didn't look too bad for an old car other than a little rust from sitting out in the weather.

Amanda and Laura wanted to wait in the car. They didn't like the look of the place or the Beware of Dog sign hanging next to the door. Chip knocked on the door and heard a dog barking. After a couple more knocks and frail looking man came to the door. "Are you Doug Raines," asked Chip? "Yes," he said. "I'm detective Reynolds and this is Brian Fallon. We would like to ask you a few questions about the House of Blue Lights." "I am not sure what I can tell you about the place," Doug said. "It's been so long ago." "If we could just come in for a minute," Chip said. "Okay, let me put the dog up, he doesn't like strangers."

The inside of the house actually looked good. It was dated but very clean and orderly. "Please sit down," said Doug. "I would offer you something to drink but I'm out of everything but water. My house keeper is coming by later today with some supplies for me."

"Thanks, but I think we are okay," said Brian.

"So Mr. Raines, I understand you worked for Skiles Test," said Chip. "Yes, I did. I started working for him when I was very young. I stayed there until he died and then I was the caretaker of the property until they tore it down. I saw the news about the bodies, but if that is what you are here for I don't know anything about those." "So in all your years out there you never saw anyone bury a body or saw anything suspicious," asked Chip. "No nothing. If I had seen anything like that I would have said something to somebody."

"Where did you live when you worked for Test," asked Brian? "I lived at home until I lost my family, then I moved into one of Mr. Test's tenant houses. After his daughter died I moved into the house and took care of the property until they tore it down. I then moved here and have been here ever since."

"I have a list of names here Mr. Raines," said Brian. "I'll show you the list and see if you know any of them." "Are any of these names someone you think might be the bodies," asked Doug? "These are just a list of names of people we think might have worked for Test," said Brian. "At this time we don't have any reason to believe they are the bodies."

"The names are familiar," said Doug. "I knew this Ledbetter guy but I never worked with him or the others. They worked out in the farm area and I worked up at the house."

"Do you know if any of them are still living," asked Chip? "I wouldn't know anything about that," he said.

"What happened to your family," asked Brian? "Mom and Dad were both killed in a car wreck, and my brother was killed in the Vietnam War." "Did you know a Jack Test," asked Chip? "You know there were a lot of people coming and going all the time out there. I don't remember anyone by that name but my mind is not as sharp as it used to be."

"How well did you know his daughter," asked Brian? "I didn't know her very well; I was just the help and didn't get too involved with the family."

"Did you know the nanny," asked Brian? Doug stuttered for a moment then said. "I barely knew her and don't remember her

---

95

name." "Well thanks for your time," said Chip. "Oh, one more thing," Chip said. "Did you work anywhere after you left there?" "I just worked at a few odd jobs. I had quite a bit of money saved when mom and dad died, so I didn't need much to live on."

"Okay so tell us how creepy it was in there," said Amanda. "It was nice inside, you wouldn't think it would be after looking at the outside but it was," said Brian. "As far as his knowledge, he didn't impress me any."

"There was one thing that bothered me," said Brian. "Remember we found out that Skiles daughter left everything to Doug in her will? He told us he didn't know her very well." "So why would she leave everything to him," asked Chip? "Not only that," said Brian, "he didn't remember the nanny's name and he said he only worked odd jobs. I don't see how he could buy that house and live on odd jobs. Even if he had saved a lot of money, it was quite a few years after Skiles died before he would have gotten Social Security." "Maybe his parents left him a lot of money," said Chip. "I don't know," said Brian. "He just didn't seem like he was telling us all he knew." "Maybe," said Chip. "I'll run his finances and see what turns up."

Chapter 20
Present Day
One Identified

Today was Tuesday May the eighth. It had rained the night before but the morning sun was drying up all the moisture. The high was expected to be around seventy today with plenty of sunshine.

"Good morning Amanda," Laura said. "Did you have another late night," with Brian? "No, I was with Chip." "So are you and Chip becoming an item?" "Well, not an item," said Amanda. "I do like him but you know he is married and I am not the type to break up a home. On the other hand he has alluded to her not being very happy with his job because of all the hours he works. Therefore, she may not be quite as happy as he is."

"So what are your feelings for Brian," asked Laura? "Well you know when we first met I was attracted to him. I do think a lot of him but it's almost like a brother sister relationship. I'm not sure there is any romance there. Why do you ask Laura, are you interested in Brian?" "I do like the way he walks," she said laughingly, "but I always figured he liked you." "I'm not sure how he feels," said Amanda. "I know he likes me but so far it's been all business. We have not slept together but then we both have been so busy with this Test thing there hasn't been much time for romance."

"Speaking of the devil," said Laura; "I believe Chip is pulling up in our driveway. I'd better get dressed. I don't need a repeat of what happened the other day." "What was that," asked Amanda? "Oh, nothing really, I was still in my nightgown when Brian came in and it was a little embarrassing." "You are such the slut Laura! I wish I could be more like you."

Chip had found out that Jack Test's parents had both been cremated and the next closest relative was Skiles. He had asked the judge for an order to exhume Skiles based on what evidence he had so far. He had also found out that Doug didn't have any money. The only transactions were his monthly government checks and their immediate withdrawal. Apparently Doug used cash for everything and whatever he did receive from the will he must have spent it or buried it.

Brian had been busy since the last time he had seen the 3 sleuths (Chip, Amanda, and Laura). He had not bought any of Doug's stories. He was either too senile or he was hiding something and Brian figured it was the latter. Brian figured out he needed that special person who could fill in the blanks. He had some options here. One was finding someone from the list of farm workers. One was the nanny who he didn't have a name for, and one was Bonnie, the mother of Skiles daughter Kelly. Bonnie not being an actual member of the Test family had been left out of most of the documents he and Amanda had researched. Her name had been mentioned only a few times. Brian's research had turned up an Ohio family with the name of Bonnie Hanover in their family tree. However, he might need Chip's help. Chip's badge could always get into places he couldn't just being a meager reporter.

All four sleuths had a dinner engagement to go over their notes. They met at the Applebee's restaurant in Fishers and took a back booth. Amanda and Laura drove together. Amanda was wearing slacks and a pullover top. Laura was wearing a tight black leather skirt with a matching blouse. Both women still looked like movie stars to Brian and at some point he had to start thinking about a little romance. Too much work was getting him down.

The four of them had chosen Laura to be the coordinator since she was between jobs and had more free time. She was happy to take all the information, sort it out, and make some kind of sense out of it. To her it was exciting. Until this Test thing came along her life had been very boring.

"Here is where we are," said Laura. "First this is what we know. The female body had been embalmed. There was no apparent damage to any part of her body. The cause of death has still not been determined. Her age appears to be early twenties." The male body with her had not been embalmed. They think he died from a broken cervical fracture or in other words someone

---

cracked his neck really good. His age appears to be mid to late twenties give or take a couple of years."

"The male body found near the pet cemetery that was all bones was not embalmed nor was he buried in any container. His decomposition happened very quickly. They estimate his age at death was around thirty give or take. His cause of death is unknown at this time."

"We don't know any of the three names of the bodies. We thought the bag of bones guy might be Jack Test. He went missing back in the fifties. The only thing is Jack would have been a little older than thirty and the time line for burial would have to be 1950 not in the seventies. So now we are thinking that it may not be Jack."

"We are waiting on the DNA information from Skiles and also waiting on some word from the FBI on the mysterious web site thing. We don't know if there is any connection to Jack and the web site but we are curious since the web site and McCarthyism is both tied to the FBI."

"We have talked to Doug, a former worker at the farm but he is either too senile or is hiding something. We think he may be hiding something since he has funny banking habits and doesn't seem to have any history of making money."

"We have started an investigation to the whereabouts of a Bonnie Hanover. We think she might still be alive and may help us fill in some of the blanks about Jack Test and or these bodies. We also know there may be a nanny out there somewhere and hopefully Bonnie can give us some information on her."

"I'm working that list of farm workers and I think there may be others out there connected to the farm that is still living, but I want to exhaust the ones we have before I continue. I think since researching takes a lot of time hopefully we won't need to look any further than this small list we have to solve this mystery."

"So," said Brian. "We four sleuths don't know Jack and I don't mean Jack Test." "That's true," said Chip "but we are further along than we were on day one and it's only been a few weeks. Sometimes these things take a long time. And keep this in mind. We

---

99

have one positive thing going here. We all have become good friends." "I'll drink to that," said Laura!

"Excuse me," said Amanda as her phone rang. "Okay," she said, "I'll stop by. Sorry guys, my boss needs to talk to me. Could I get one of you to run Laura home for me she said?" "I can do it," said Brian.

Brian opened the car door for Laura. He couldn't help but look at her legs as she got in. She just simply had scorching hot beautiful legs.

On the way to her home they talked about the case and she told him she was thankful for the opportunity to get involved. She was having fun and she had not had much fun lately. She had not dated in months and most of the time going out just involved being with Amanda.

"I don't understand," said Brian. "You are a beautiful woman, why aren't you involved with someone?" "It's hard to explain," she said. "I had a job and plenty of guys hitting on me but it was always just about sex. It's not that I was looking for marriage, but I wanted more than just a one-night stand. A woman still likes to think a man should like her for her mind too."

"I understand," said Brian; "I'd feel the same way if I were a woman. Men are basically pigs he said. We all eventually come around to appreciating a woman for her mind, if we stay with her long enough, but at first its sex. I'm not trying to make excuses but God made us the aggressor and if you can keep a guy long enough you might find he has the capacity to love you and not just your body."

"So what you are saying Brian is if I give a guy enough time he will get tired of the sex and then he will like my mind." "No silly, I'm just saying, there are good guys out there that would find you very smart as well as attractive. Of course they are going to want sex, but if you can just relax and enjoy the sex then I think you will find they will learn to appreciate you in other ways."

"Another thing you might think about is marriage. Don't give the guy any sex until he marries you." "There are two things wrong with that Brian. One is I may not like the guy sexually if I don't try him first," she said with a laugh. "Second, is how can I be sure of him and our compatibility a year later. We may find each other boring." "That can happen whether you have sex or not," said Brian. "There are no guarantees in life."

"Want to come in for a minute," she said as he pulled into the drive? "Sure, I'd love to; maybe I can talk you into trying the dating scene again and get you out of your rut."

Brian must have stayed for over an hour. Laura liked that. It had been a long time since the conversation was just about her. She couldn't understand why Amanda hadn't moved forward with Brian. He seemed like a great guy. He was smart, good looking, and grounded. He didn't seem like the fly by night or the one night stand guy. And maybe he was right. Maybe she had been too hard on guys and needed to get back out there again.

As Brian got up to leave Laura walked him to the door. "Thanks for the talk," she said as she reached up to kiss his cheek. "You're welcome," he said, "and thanks for the Yankee Dime!"

The DNA from Skiles came back. It was no match for either of the two guys. It did however match the girl. There was no other conclusion other than the girl had to be Skiles's daughter Kelly. But if that was Kelly, who was buried in her grave at Crown Hill Cemetery? It was time to talk to the funeral director.

Chip, Brian, and Amanda walked into the Crown Hill Cemeteries office. Preston Hammond got up from his desk to shake hands. "Thanks for calling me in advance," he said. "I am not quite sure what I can do for you. You said it was something about Kelly Test. Did you want to exhume her also?" "We hope we don't have to," said Chip.

"You were here when Kelly was buried, is that correct," asked Brian? "Yes, I embalmed the body and buried her." "Then could you tell us why her body showed up in the glass tank out at the former House of Blue Lights?" Preston's face turned pale, he sat back in his seat and after a long pause said. "Do I need a lawyer?"

"Look Mr. Hammond," Chip said. "I'm not looking to arrest

someone. I'm not even sure if a crime has been committed. All we want here is the truth as to what and why this happened." "Okay," Hammond said "but I want immunity." "I can't guarantee you that," said Chip. "What I will guarantee you is that if you cooperate I'll talk to the D.A. If you haven't committed some horrible crime and have only played around moving bodes, I think you'll be okay."

"Okay," Preston said. "You may have read the death certificate. It lists her cause of death as a broken heart. I know that sounds strange but it has happened a lot in history. I think the mind just shuts down because it can't cope with the grief. She was grieving over her lost love, her mother and I have to assume her father also."

"Anyway this guy named Doug who worked for Mr. Test came to me before the funeral. He said her last wishes were to be buried on the property not in the cemetery. He wanted me to give him the body so he could bury it. I told him maybe we could just bury her there if we could get the state to okay it. He said it had to be done in secret but he wouldn't tell me why. He was just very adamant about it. I told him it was just something I couldn't do it was unethical."

"Then he offered me a large sum of money. I admit I shouldn't have done it but I had been having some financial trouble. I had some investments go bad and all that money was just too tempting."

"So I took the body out to him one night. When I got there he said he didn't want the casket. He said he had this glass container that was used in some Medical treatment of Skiles's wife. We went to some storage barn, got the glass container, carried it down into the basement of the house and put it in a hole he had dug. We then took Kelly down and put her in it."

"Doug had a lid there next to the hole and I asked him if I could help him with it and he said no, he would do it later. We then went back out to the car, found some rocks and put them in the casket I had brought Kelly in. We put just enough in to make the casket weigh what Kelly did. I brought the casket full of rocks back here for the service. I had told Doug we would have to fake a paper stating her last wishes were for a closed casket. Kelly's mother didn't question it and so everyone thought Kelly was in there. Everything just fell into place until now."

"There was no other body there in the basement where you put Kelly," asked Chip? "No, and that surprised me when I saw on the news that there was two bodies in that container. I have no idea where the other one came from."

"Okay, Mr. Hammond, I don't know what the prosecutor will do but I'll keep my promise on helping you if needed," said Chip. "How about the press," Preston asked. "Will this be plastered everywhere?" "This is big news," said Amanda. "We can smooth it out a little but we can't keep the lid on this. I'll do what I can."

As they walked to the car Brian said, "That was quite a story, I guess that means a trip back out to see Doug Raines." "Yes, it does," said Chip. "Mr. Raines has a lot of explaining to do."

As they pulled out of the cemetery Chip's phone rang. It was the FBI. They were waiting at his office. They had some information about his request.

"I need to drop you guys off," Chip said. "I'll run you back to your offices and I'll call you later with what I find out."

The FBI told Chip that Jack had not been killed. He had been deported to a foreign country and put in a prison. The states had treaties and agreements with some countries to make exchanges like than when it was in the national interest. Jack had died about 5 years ago from an infection.

As far as the web site, they thought it would be better to create and control one possibly to keep any family from posting things about Jack. It was a silly thought they said in retrospect but sometimes they do silly things. It was supposed to expire after notice that all of Jack's family had passed. The agent J. Needham retired and it did get pulled off the web but in the process the information was not unsealed. That now had been corrected. All the information on Jack and the web site was now public.

Chapter 21
Present Day
Bonnie and Kathryn

Two squad cars pulled up in Doug Raines driveway. Chip noticed as he pulled in that the car was gone. After searching the property they discovered Doug had fled. All his clothes, personal belongings, and the dog were gone. They interviewed a few neighbors but no one saw him leave. In fact most of the neighbors had never talked to him. They said he always stayed in the house. All Chip could do now is put out an APB out on him.

When Chip returned to the office his boss was waiting for him. "Chip, we got a break on this Bonnie woman," he said. "We owe those guys in Columbus a nice fresh batch of donuts. It's all here in the file." Chip took the file, read it, and headed for Amanda's home.

"We found Bonnie," said Chip as he walked into Amanda and Laura's home. "Anyone want to take a day trip with me tomorrow? She is in Columbus, Ohio in a nursing home." "I'll go," said Amanda.

Laura started to say that she would go also but she didn't want to intrude. Amanda had been with Chip a lot and she suspected things were getting serious between them.

"I don't think I'll go," she said. "You might want to call Brian to see if he does."

Brian had a previous engagement but wanted them to call him as soon as they found out anything. He did not want to wait until they returned. Everything was moving fast now and time was of the essence. Jack had been pressuring Brian for days trying to get him to commit to a full story for the paper. Brian kept stalling him saying it was too early. Of course Jack disagreed and said he could always follow up with the rest as it came to him.

It was 5 p.m. on Thursday when Laura received a call from Amanda. She told her they were bringing Bonnie back with them but couldn't get the arrangements made until tomorrow. Bonnie said if they would bring her back to see Kelly one last time she would help fill in the rest of the blanks as best she could. She said they would be staying overnight and told her to call Brian and give him the name "Mrs. Kathryn Kistner." That was the name of Kelly's nanny. Laura immediately called Brian and told him what Amanda had said.

"Okay," said Brian, "why don't we get together later and go over what we have? If you can start the online search maybe we can find her tonight and if she is close by we can go see her tomorrow." "I can do that," she said. "What time will you be here?" "About 8 and I can bring dinner if you'd like." "Okay," she said, "surprise me!"

At promptly 8 p.m. Brian knocked on Laura's door. Laura was already in her pajamas. She was not dressed provocatively just in pajamas.

"I hope its okay that I'm in my pajamas," she said. "I just wanted to be comfortable." "Its fine with me," he said, "I'd like to get comfortable to." "Then come here," she said.

He moved toward her. She took the food from him, put it on the table, and then removed his sport coat. She jerked his shirt out of his pants and asked, "how's that?" "Great," he said, "I'll just take off my shoes and make myself at home!"

"Did you have any luck with the name Kistner," he asked? "Yes," she said. "I have three names but I haven't called them yet."

"What criteria did you use," he asked. "Well I figured she had to be at least eighty years old. If I reveal any more than that I'd have to kill you. You know I can't let all my secrets out. What I can tell you is that she made it easy for me because even though she remarried she always kept the Kistner name. I can also tell you I used some friends on Facebook to help me."

"I didn't think you had that many friends," he said. "You don't need but one when you are on Facebook," she said. "That is true," he said. "I am a member but I haven't been on it in a long time. I just find I have better things to do." "How about twitter," she said. "Nope, not yet, I'm not into that one either."

Dinner was quick; they wanted to get to the calling. The first call was a disconnected number. The second call hit pay dirt.

"Hello," said Laura. "I'm looking for a Mrs. Kathryn Kistner that used to work for a Skiles Test. Is that you?" "I think you want my mother," she said. "May I ask what this is about?" Laura explained why they wanted to see her. The girl said her mother had already retired for the evening but they could call back tomorrow.

"That was too easy," said Laura. "Sometimes it's that way," said Brian. "So let's make a plan of attack," he said. "Attack," said Laura. "We don't even know if she remembers anything and you want to attack the old lady." "You know I wouldn't do that. I will be gentle and treat her with the utmost respect," said Brian.

It was getting late and Brian knew he should leave but he was enjoying Laura's company.

"I'd better go;" he said, "it's probably past your bedtime." "Oh, don't go yet, just another thirty minutes or so. I'll put on a little music for us." "What music are you going to put on," he asked? "I have this old record album by the Mystic Moods Orchestra called 'One Stormy Night', she said. "Have you ever heard it?" "I don't think so, what is it about?" "It is an actual recording of rain and a thunderstorm. It is very relaxing," she said. "So you like records," he asked? "Oh, yes," she said. "I have a huge collection of old records. I got them from my grandparents, and parents. I have records from the thirties, on up. Most of them are rock and roll mixed in with country." "You are my best new friend Laura; I love the sound of records. I have a few myself but not as many as you."

"Would you like a glass of wine or something," she asked? "Wine would be nice," he said. "It will feel good to relax for awhile; I have been so tensed up lately."

"Sit down on the floor right here," she said "and let me work the tension out of your shoulders. I want you to listen to the rain on the record, take a drink of wine, close your eyes and relax."

Laura's hands were soothing on his shoulders. He was tensed up but even if he hadn't been it was still nice to feel her hands on him. They had touched each other before and there was those Yankee Dimes but this was different. This was not a casual touch you do in conversation.

"That feels so good," he said. "I know what you can do if you ever decide to go to work." "Is that right," she said. "Well, you haven't felt anything yet." Laura reached around unbuttoned his shirt, jerked it off him. Pulled his t-shirt off and said, "Don't move." When she came back she had a bottle of alcohol and a bottle of lotion.

Laura spent the next fifteen minutes giving Brian the next best thing to sex, a soothing massage. He was like putty in her hands and she enjoyed it just as much as he did. She loved his broad shoulders, and his bulging muscles. It felt good to touch a man and she couldn't understand why Amanda was throwing this away for a married man.

"I am so relaxed I can't move," he said. "Good," she said, "I have you right where I want you. Now move over you swine away from the table and make a little room for me." Brian moved toward some open space, Laura threw a couple of pillows at him, sat on his stomach and said, "Now just try to get up." He looked up at Laura and said. "I don't want to go anywhere."

She then leaned down toward his face. Her long red hair was touching his chest and soon her lips were on his. An hour later they stopped. They had worked their way from one end of the living room floor to the other with one passionate session after another. Laura had never loved like that before. Brian was so strong yet gentle. He knew just how, where, and when to touch her. As for Brian it was just what he needed. It wasn't just the sex it was something that had been building in him from the first time he saw her. He didn't recognize it at first but he knew now what it was. He had fallen in love with Laura.

The bed was more comfortable once they made it there. "One Stormy Night" was still playing "I can't believe that song is still playing," said Brian "or is it raining outside?" "I have an automatic record player," she said. "It will play forever." "Speaking of playing can you make me an mp3 Cd?" "A Cd, come on how about moving up into the world of new technology? Everyone now is using a flash drive for their music?" "Unfortunately my car doesn't have a usb port, so I'll have to settle for a Cd for now." "Okay, give me a list of what you want on it and I'll make you one." "Okay, I'll text you the list tomorrow, right now I need sleep."

The night went quickly and Brian woke to the smell of coffee and breakfast cooking. Laura was standing over the stove wearing nothing but his shirt. "Hey you swine how do you like your eggs," she asked? "Scrambled," he said "with lots of bacon" as his went over and kissed her neck. "Don't think just because I slept with you last night and I'm making you breakfast that you can take advantage of me again this morning," she said. "I wouldn't dream of it," he said.

Laura had to keep the teasing coming. At this time she didn't know how to be serious. She didn't know how Brian really felt and if he didn't share the same feelings that she did then last night could have been a mistake.

"You look cute in your underwear Brain, is that what you usually wear around the house?" "Well, sometimes I wear a shirt but mine seems to be missing," he said. "I like your shirt," she said. "I think it fits your personality but I'm curious. What do you normally wear to bed? "I wear a T-shirt and my jockey underwear, how about you?" "Just a nightgown or maybe just panties or sometimes nude, it depends on the day."

"Hey after breakfast, I need to go home and change. Would you like to go with me," he said? "Sure," said Laura, "just let me shower first." "One more thing," Brian said as they got up from the table. "I know you took a giant step last night and I know you are a little scared but don't be. I'm in love with you Laura, I think I have been from the first time I ever saw you. I don't know what took me so long to realize it. Maybe I was waiting on you or maybe I was afraid like you." "It doesn't matter," she whispered "I'm in love with you too."

While Laura was in the shower Brian figured he might as well work on his song list while it was fresh in his mind. When he had told Laura that he loved records he was being more than honest. He actually lived them at times. Growing up music was always a big part of his family. Whether working on cars with his dad and grandfather or sitting on the porch relaxing with his mom music was always playing. Brian found that music affected his mood. A happy song filled him with energy and excitement. A sad song could bring a tear to his eye and a sad instrumental like Mantovani's Greensleeves would simply wipe him out. He loved to listen to John Barry's movie songs. The music in Somewhere in Time and Hanover Street were his favorites.

"You look fantastic and adorable Laura; I hope I can look as good as you after my shower." I'm sure you will you little preppy thing. What do you have there in those manly hands of yours?" "I made my song list while I was waiting for you, see what you think," he said.

You Can Have Her by Roy Hamilton
But For Love by Jerry Naylor
Lovin Her Was Easier by Kris Kristofferson
It's Time to Cry by Paul Anka
Just Ask Your Heart by Frankie Avalon
Five Hundred Miles by Heaven Bound
And the Grass Won't Pay No Mind by Mark Lindsay
Triangle by Janie Grant
Happy Days and Move Two Mountains by Marv Johnson
Another Fool Like Me by Ned Miller
Tragic Romance by Cowboy Copas
Ballad of a Teenage Queen by Johnny Cash
City Lights by Ray Price
Come and Stay With Me by Marianne Faithful
My Back Pages by the Byrds
Mission Bell by Donnie Brooks
A Satisfied Mind by Porter Wagoner
The Old Home by Hank Williams
I've Lived A Lot in My Time by Jim Reeves
Time by Nancy Sinatra
Trouble in The Amen Corner by Archie Campbell
Love Is Blue by Paul Muriat

"I'm impressed," said Laura, "These are sort of rare oldies the kind they never play on the oldies stations. And you even have the artists." I know," he said. "That is why I want them; I never get to hear them on the radio." "If you like records," she said. "I have something else you might like. You remember music guides?" "I'm not sure," he said. "They were those little sheets of paper the radio stations used to put out in the days of rock n roll. It listed the top forty or top one hundred songs and they changed every week. You have heard of billboards hot one hundred haven't you?" "Yes, I have heard of that." "Well, that was a music guide." "Great, I'd love to see those sometime."

By the time they arrived at Brian's house and he showered it was close to 11 a.m. When he called Kathryn's number she answered. Her voice was sort of crackled but understandable. She invited them to come out and see her and would they mind bringing her some White Castles. Brian thought that anybody who liked those onion-laced hamburgers he called Belly Bombers couldn't be too old or senile to remember. He now had high hopes.

Kathryn lived at 96th and Olio road in an upscale condo community. That told him another thing about her. If she could live there, she was still able to take care of herself and must be still be in good shape.

A middle aged looking woman answered the door. She introduced herself as Katie, Kathryn's daughter. "I'll take the sandwiches," she said, "please come on in. Mother is in the dining room so if you will follow me. There is one thing you should know about my mother before we go in. Mother considers herself to be very proper. Please refer to her as Mrs. Kistner. She is big on last names. I think all her years being a Nanny and training young girls to be proper has rubbed off on her. Although I'm not sure how proper one could be if they love White Castles," she said with a chuckle.

Kathryn was already sitting at the table waiting on her White Castles. She had a big smile on her face as she greeted us. "I'm so sorry I missed your call last night but I'm afraid I retire rather early these days. Thank you so much for the sandwiches, Katie will pay you for them." "Oh, that's not necessary," said Laura. "We were happy to do that for you."

"Does Katie live her with you," Laura asked? "No, but she does live in the condo next door." "I assume Katie told you why we wanted to talk," said Brian. "Yes," she said. "Would you like to join me or like something to drink?" "I'm fine," they both said.

"So according to the news you know Kelly was in the glass tank but you don't know anything else do you," said Mrs. Kistner? "No we don't, do you know who the other two bodies are," said Brian? "I'm not positive," she said "but I think I have an idea of who one of them is."

"Why haven't you come forward with that information," asked Laura? "There is one good reason," she said. "I wanted to protect the people I loved. If you had never discovered the woman was Kelly I figured you would drop the case and all the secrets would be kept." "What do you mean by secrets," asked Brian?

Kathryn dropped her head and didn't speak for a minute. When she raised her head Laura and Brian saw a tear streaming down her face. "Have we upset you Mrs. Kistner," asked Laura? "I'm sorry," Kathryn said. "It has been so many years and as you age there is sadness about life and things that have happened to you. And yes, there are secrets. There are always secrets and some of them aren't pleasant. I'm alright now, so where were we?"

"So who do you think one of the other bodies is," asked Brian? "Before I tell you," she said "I need to give you a little history. If I just give you the name you will not understand why and that is a very important part of the story. I want history to remember not just who but why."

"I came to work for Skiles Test in 1957. I had been a nanny before and I loved children. It was the one thing I could do well and enjoy every minute of."

"I had been married but my husband had been killed in Korea."

"Skiles fixed a room for me upstairs. I lived there the entire time I worked for him."

"Kelly's mother, Bonnie left soon after I came. She was gone for a while, and then she would come back. Finally she left and never came back. She didn't go far though. She called Kelly at least once a month as a promise to Skiles. She was afraid if she didn't keep in contact with her Skiles would cut off her allowance."

"Now, keep in mind this is just my thoughts. I don't know how she felt about her daughter. I did know how she felt about Skiles but that's another story in itself."

"Bonnie lived somewhere in Broad Ripple. In fact I believe she lived in the same place, when she wasn't on the road, until Skiles died. That was unusual for her based on how we knew she was. She never stayed anyplace very long."

"If you ask me how Kelly felt about her mother. I think she loved her but she always had a lot of resentment towards her for leaving. From time to time I would hear them arguing when Bonnie called. In fact there were times that Kelly wouldn't talk to her at all. Other than fighting with her mother, Kelly was a sweet girl and easy to care for. She was also a loving child. She would kiss on Skiles all the time. In fact, she always kissed him every time he would leave her. She did that until the day he died."

"She also became very fond of Mr. Raines or maybe we should call him Doug. I do like to be on a first name basis with my closest friends. Doug worked for Skiles around the house. He took care of the animals and helped me entertain Kelly. I believe he was somewhere around eighteen or so when I came there. Doug was a little slow as we called it then. He had some mild retardation. The slowness didn't seem to affect his duties or his passion for the animals or even Kelly. He may have been retarded but he had a deep capacity for love."

"He and I became great friends and as Kelly grew Doug's fondness of her as a child turned into love as she became an adult. Now I don't know how a slow person loves but I suspect they are just like us if not even more passionate about it. Doug was also very protective of Kelly. He watched over her as if she was a baby chick."

"Then there was this thing that changed Kelly forever. I remember one day after her sixteen birthday things got crazy. She met a boy. The boy she met was Tom the son of Mr. Jim Tyler. Mr. Tyler had worked for Skiles for years. It was thought that Bonnie and he were having an affair but no one ever saw them. As far as Tom, he was Kelly's first love. She loved that boy like no other. Tom, on the other hand turned out to be not as passionate about his feelings for Kelly. There was a song by Rick Fortune that came out in 1962 called 'Sand in My Hair.' It was about this guy who wanted a perfect girl. I think Kelly could have been that girl. But this guy was restless, he jumped from one girl to another and he knew he was like that and hated himself for it. Well, that song was Tom all over. And if you are interested and want to understand Bonnie I have a song for her also. Listen to the Waylon Jennings song 'The Hunger'. It's about a woman that goes from bars to bedrooms."

"Now, I can't tell you all the particulars of the romance between Tom and Kelly. I know while he was away in the Army she stayed true to him the entire time. I doubt that he did the same. I know from experience he was not what she thought. I'll go into that later but right now I want to tell you about Skiles and me."

"After Bonnie left, I became very close to Skiles. I had already fallen in love with him but I didn't know what his feelings for me were."

"I hate to be impatient," said Brian "but we need to know about the bodies. You said you might know who one of the two is."

"Now, Now, not to worry, all will come in good time," she said. "It's very important to me on how I present this. You need to understand the why or what I tell you will seem awful. The memory and dignity of all those people must be preserved. So, just a few more minutes and you will have your answer but right now you need to excuse me. I must go to the bathroom. I'll be right back."

Kelly had turned 16 two months ago. Her dad had bought her a

1967 Chevelle SS convertible. It was Marina Blue with a white top. It reminded her of the car her mom had. Skiles had bought Bonnie a 55 Ford Thunderbird convertible

when they first came out. Bonnie had been driving Nash Ramblers and anything else Skiles had at the dealership until then. Of course the Ford didn't look anything like Kelly's Chevy but it was blue and that was enough resemblance for her. She couldn't tell one car from another anyway. She just liked blue convertibles.

Tom Tyler was looking for his dad. He had just gotten off work. Work for Tom was AIT school at nearby Ft. Harrison. Tom had been drafted soon after high school. He had taken his basic training at Ft. Knox, Kentucky and by some stroke of luck ended up near home for final training before going to Vietnam. He wasn't sure he would go there but everyone else did and why would he be any different.

"Nice uniform" was what he heard as he came up from the garage basement. Kelly Test was standing there next to her car. She was dressed in shorts with a button up blouse hanging outside them. She was a slender girl and very cute with her short haircut. Tom was six foot, slender built and sporting an almost no hair haircut due to his military life. He was a good-looking man that most women found attractive.

"Nice car," he said back to her. "Thanks," she said, "Are you lost, Ft. Harrison is over that way," pointing to the southeast? "Actually, I'm looking for my father, Jim Tyler. I'm Tom." "I'm Kelly," she said. "Yes," he said, "my father told me about you." "What did he say," she asked? "Oh, just that Skiles had a beautiful daughter with a fast car or was it a fast daughter with a beautiful car. You know, I'm just not sure," he said. "You are a funny guy," she said. "I think your father is out by the pool, that way, pointing toward the west." "How about a ride in that fast car," he said as he walked away. "I'll think about it," she said.

Jim Tyler was coming out of the pool house when he saw Tom. "Hi, son what's up?" "Mom wanted me to tell you she was going over to her sister's house and wouldn't be home so dinner is on you." "Are you going to be home," Jim asked? "Depends," said Tom, "I just invited myself for a ride with Kelly in her convertible." "Oh, you met her huh?" "Yes, she is really cute." "You might want to be careful with that one Tom. You know she is only sixteen." "I know," said Tom, "I'll be careful."

"So how about that ride," he asked Kelly as he came back by the garage? "Okay," she said, "hop in. Let me run in and tell Kathryn where I'm going."

Kelly drove out the west lane onto Johnson road. She took it to Fall Creek and turned right. "Why haven't I seen you before," she asked? "Didn't you go to Lawrence?" "Yes and No," Tom said. "I went to the junior high there but then I started going to the Catholic school up on Shadeland just past fifty six street." "Why would you do that," she asked? "Didn't you like Lawrence?" "To make a long story short," he said, "my mom and dad were having some martial problems. They started going to church and one thing led to another and I ended up there."

115

"What about college," she asked? "My plan is to get my military obligation out of the way, get a job, and then go to college part time. How about you Kelly, what are your plans?" "I'm going to college, I just don't know where yet."

Tom was driving when they returned. He loved the car. He was driving an old clunker himself and he saw no need to buy a new car until he returned from Vietnam.

"Thanks for the ride and drive," Tom said. "You're welcome," Kelly said, "anytime." "I may take you up on that," he said. "In fact, maybe you would like to go to a movie sometime." "I'd love that," she said. "Do you have our phone number?" "I'm sure Dad does and if not, I know where you live," he said.

Tom and Kelly was a couple all summer. Tom would spend his off days at the pool with her and in the evenings they would go out with friends. Kelly had grown very fond of him and him of her. There was however a problem. Tom was used to having sex and Kelly refused him. Tom didn't push it because she was under age. He was satisfied with a little petting for a while but that didn't last long.

There was a bar just outside Ft. Harrison called the Snafu where a lot of soldiers went. Tom didn't frequent the place but one of his soldier friends did. His friend was always "fixing" Tom up with someone. On those days he always found an excuse to cut short the evening date with Kelly or sometime cancel it all together. He told Kelly he had some kind of duty and of course being in the Army it sounded reasonable to her. However, it didn't sound that way to Skiles. Skiles didn't like Tom that well. He never said anything to Kelly but he was Jim's son. Skiles didn't mean to hold it against Tom that perhaps his father had slept with Bonnie. Skiles had no proof of that but he had always suspected. However, it was more than that. There was just an air about him. You could call it intuition or whatever; Skiles just knew he was no good for Kelly and it was time to call his old friend Larry Thomas again.

Larry followed Tom and reported back to Skiles about his night time flings with other women. Skiles knew he couldn't tell

Kelly, she would get mad and he never wanted her to know he was interfering in her life even if he did know what was best for her. He could however confide it Kathryn and perhaps she could talk to her.

"You had him followed", Kathryn said to Skiles? "I know it sounds bad but Kelly is my life and I don't want to see her get hurt." "It might be too late for that," she said. "Kelly is already in love with him." "Love," said Skiles, "puppy love maybe. Kelly is just too young. Her whole life is ahead of her, I just can't let her waste it on a cheating man. Will you talk to her? You don't have to tell her he is cheating; just approach it from a different point of view." "You mean like what life is about and there is a big world out there you need to discover," said Kathryn? "Yes, that's good," said Skiles. "If you do that for me I'll be forever grateful." "I'll try," she said.

Kathryn knew it would do no good. She had been there before and Kelly would have to learn just like all the others had for centuries.

"Kelly, may I talk to you," asked Kathryn? "Sure, what's up," she asked? "It's about Tom. I know how you feel about him, but do you think it's a good idea to stick with only one boy. You know he will be leaving soon for Vietnam. A year is a long time to wait on someone. You are so young and you have so much of your life ahead of you. There is college and."

"Stop," she said. "Did my father put you up to this; I know he doesn't think much of Tom?" "This has nothing to do with your father; I just see you and think you are making a mistake." "I appreciate what you are saying, but we're in love."

"When I go to college he can go with me. He wants to go to college after the Army anyway." "Just be careful," Kathryn said. "Your heart is vulnerable when you're young and always remember love is blind." "I'm not sure what that means," Kelly said. "It means what it says. You are blind to every fault the other person has when you fall in love with them. Your eyes open up after it's too late and the faults take a toll on you."

Of course Kathryn was right in everything she told Kelly and Skiles was right about Tom also.

Tom grew up in an abusive home. His mother and father fought all the time and when he was younger his dad beat him for what seemed like no reason at all. His dad also introduced him to pictures of naked women and talked about how they were sex objects.

Tom grew up early and had his first sexual encounter at the age of fourteen with a neighbor girl. Tom and she had ridden their bikes to the farm one Saturday. Tom said he wanted to show her all the animals. They ended up in the hay barn and after some heavy petting the girl gave in. After that Tom lived and breathed sex. He chased every girl at school and in the neighborhood that he thought might put out. Sending him to a private school didn't seem to matter either. Whatever he was taught in school was not practiced at home. Tom was destined to be the way he was and nothing would ever change that.

Tom left for Vietnam in the fall and Kelly went back to school. Kelly wrote him everyday. She missed him so much but Tom only wrote once a month if that. He was assigned as a company clerk and was stationed at Vung Tau. The base was near the ocean and was an in country R&R center. This center gave him excellent opportunities to have all the women he wanted. There were a lot of local women who sold themselves for entire weekends. You could screw yourself to death for about two dollars a night.

Vung Tau was one of the safest places in Vietnam to be. It was a port of entry for most of the equipment that came in country. There were thousands of soldiers and civilian employees stationed there. Therefore he was never in much danger and had plenty of free time for drinking with his buddies and sleeping around with all the whores around the camp. As time permitted and if he was having a slow day he would write Kelly a letter.

Chapter 23
The Farm

Doug Raines was in love with Kelly. In all his 29 years other than his family he never loved anyone. And even the love for his family was unlike what he was feeling for Kelly. Doug didn't understand love. He knew the term but didn't understand why Kelly was different. He didn't want to be with his family all the time and he didn't miss them like he did Kelly when he was away from them. Although he loved Kelly, he never told her and he never asked her out on a date. Doug was just retarded enough that he didn't understand what to do with the feelings he had. In his mind taking care of her was what love was about. He looked after her and took every precaution to keep her safe around the farm.

And he didn't like Tom Tyler. I'm sure a lot of the anger he had toward Tom was jealousy but there were other things. Tom was not a nice guy. He liked to pick on Doug and call him names. He would never do it in front of Kelly though. Tom knew Kelly liked Doug and they were very close. Skiles, Kelly, and Doug were always together on the farm, and when Skiles was gone it was Kelly and Doug.

Kelly knew Doug had some type of feelings for her. It was his gentle way of talking to her and the way he was always trying to do or get things for her. She was very kind to him and careful not to hurt his feelings whatever they were. She also trusted Doug. She knew he was an honest and honorable man. She was always comfortable around him and he was easy to talk to.

They would spend hours together with the animals and Skiles had plenty of animals to spend time with. There were sheep, goats, pigs, dog, cats, and cattle. They took the dogs out for runs down the north lane everyday during the summer. They would play like children in the hay barns and follow the cows into the milk barn to watch the milking.

They named some of the cows, as well as a couple of the sheep. One lamb was named Princess, and the other Rosealina. They named one cow Virginia and there was one they really liked.

Her name was  Hoedown. She was a Holstein with an all black face except for one small patch of white near her horns. She was very gentle and Doug would put Kelly on her back and lead her around the pasture until one of the bulls got after them.

But of all the animals their favorites were always the cats. Just before lunch Kelly would have Emma fix them sandwiches so they could go to the cat lot and have lunch with the cats.

The cat lot consisted of a huge fenced in area just east of the house across the driveway that went down the south lane. Inside the lot there was a small cement pond where the cats could drink as they roamed around the area.

There was a large building to the north of the pond that was heated and kept open for the cats. There were small individual cathouses along the east end of the lot. All of these houses had a small heated compartment in the rear. This was a perfect place to have kittens or just go to keep warm in the wintertime.

The heaters might have been a good idea but one night it was suspected one of them caught fire. This resulted in the loss of several of the houses and cats. Of course Skiles rebuilt the damaged pens and replaced all the heaters.

At the north end of the lot there was a huge sand pile used for the litter boxes that were also in the houses.
The number of cats in each house varied. Sometimes a couple was in there and sometimes up to seven or eight could be found. Not all the cats stayed in the houses. Most of them either ran around the farm or inside the cat lot. The small houses were for either the sick, hurt, or mothers of kittens.

There were also several dogs on the farm and their pens were north of the cat lot. They were next to the drive that went from the house area to the farm area. There were two pens, one for the females and one for the males. Both pens had a couple of doghouses although they were not heated like the cathouses were.

Doug would feed the animals twice a day, once in late morning for brunch and once in late afternoon. The dog's diet consisted of Hill's brand horsemeat. The cat's diet consisted of cooked chicken, cottage cheese, and fish. They would eat out of metal pie pans that would be washed daily.

The food and the pan washing occurred in the basement of the garage. There was a ramp on the northeast side of the garage that led down to the basement.

It was not your typically basement. It was an area about fifteen feet wide and opened on both the east and west ends. Inside the area was a stove for cooking and just outside the west door was a freezer and refrigerator where they kept all the different pet foods. Just inside the west end as you walked through the door from the outside was another exit out of the basement. This exit would take you to two different places.

When you walked into the exit you would see this huge wood and coal fired boiler with a huge water tank on it. This was used for heating the house. As you walked around the boiler you would then have two choices. You could take the stairs up to the garage where the cars were parked or if you turned right just before the stairs you would enter a tunnel.

There were several underground tunnels on the property. These were used for rainy days and in the wintertime. The tunnel behind the boiler ran from the garage into the basement of the house. There was another tunnel just before you entered the house basement that forked off to the right and ran to the pool house. Once inside the house basement you could also find another tunnel running underneath the front lawn to the cat lot.

The garage also had two more areas of interest. On the southwest end was a small room. This is where all the washing and ironing for the household was done. Skiles liked starched and ironed white dress shirts. He even wore a fresh white shirt in the summertime when he dressed in casual shorts. He had a full time lady, Zena Matthews, that did all the household laundry and you could walk by there most anytime during the day and she would be ironing a white shirt.

Upstairs over the garage was a restroom and the office of Keith Wiley, the time keeper. Keith had an accounting background from the military and was in his early forties when he first started with Skiles.

Keith's responsibility was tracking all the farm workers time and paying them. However Keith let his responsibility go a little too far at times. He was a good employee and worked hard for Skiles but he was so hard on everyone. This was especially true of anyone he could see from his office window and all the farm workers. If he saw you sitting down just to take a break he would time you. He would then dock your pay for that amount of time. He would sneak out into the farm area and watch the farm hands at lunchtime. If you did not go to work immediately after you clocked in he would dock your pay. He pinched every penny as if it were his and his last.

Keith shared his office with Lucy Gordon. Lucy, who had once done an excellent job for Skiles in the forties and early fifties, had by the late sixties put Skiles in a business downturn. In all fairness, some of the problems were not Lucy's fault. Since the early fifties Skiles once again had given Lucy the freedom to make a lot of decisions for him. Some of these decisions were not well thought out and as a result his auto dealership and one of his parking garages in downtown Indianapolis had to be sold.

Skiles was also having some cash flow problems since the only real profitable business left was the chain business. The IRS had started one audit on him and the farm was barely breaking even. He was down to a half dozen full time farm hands and a few part time. The part time hands only worked during the harvest season or during the summer when they would bale and put up the hay.

He sold a couple of farm trucks and one tractor but it wasn't for the money. They were getting old and needed repair and he didn't want to spend the money.

There was one farm hand Skiles had to fire. He didn't enjoy doing that but the guy was drinking on the job. The worker had modified one of the farm trucks to hide his alcohol. He had taken the speaker grill apart from the dash and modified it with a spring. It looked like a regular speaker grill but you could pull it open and find a little compartment just large enough to hold a bottle. Skiles would not have fired him except he was giving alcohol to the part time kids that were under age.

Even though Skiles was having a lot of business issues he still had plenty of money he kept in a safe that no one except himself knew about. This money was to be Kelly's and he had to protect it at all cost.

Chapter 24
1968
Tom Returns

In May of 1968 the Vietnam War for Tom was over and Kelly
wanted to throw him a welcome home party. Skiles wasn't too keen
on the idea but he didn't interfere. He told Kelly that he was
planning a graduation party for her next month and they could
combine the two if she liked. Kelly asked Lucy and Kathryn if they
would help her and they agreed. Tom said he didn't need a party
but Kelly insisted he be part of the plans.

On his return from Vietnam Tom ended his career with the
military and took a job at an auto manufacturing plant in
Indianapolis. During his first month home he spent time with Kelly
but continued his carousing. Their relationship became one of
arguments over the phone and more bad times spent together than
good. But none of that mattered to Kelly. She knew she could make
him happy. She knew once she was out of High School and they
both went to college everything would be fine. She loved him more
than life itself and she just had to make it work.

It was June and the party was set for the first Saturday after
Kelly's graduation. Kelly had invited lots of friends from school and
Skiles invited all his workers, friends, family, and past
acquaintances. Kelly instructed Tom to invite whomever he wanted;
after all it was supposed to be his party to.

The blue lights were turned on all over the area. Skiles had
decorated the pool house inside and out. After dark it was really
going to be something to see. He wanted this to be a special night
for Kelly and it was.

Kelly wanted to start the party with a song for Tom. She
found a song called "Welcome Home Baby" by Shelly Fabare. Just
prior to playing the song she made a little speech.

"I want to thank all of you for coming to the party and I want
this to be a special night but not for me. Don't misunderstand, I am
grateful to have graduated and I'm very thankful for this party but

---

you know this is a dual party. I'd like for all of you to join me in welcoming home Tom. We need to thank him for his service to our country and tell him we appreciate the sacrifice he and others have made. So Tom, if you will come over here and join me, I'll start the music."

Tom walked towards her with the roar of clapping and whistles from the crowd as they yelled "speech, speech." Tom reached Kelly, turned to the crowd and said. "I'm a man of few words but I want to thank all of you and yelled Let's Party!"

Bonnie came to the party and that meant a lot to Skiles and the world to Kelly. Her mother and her still were not the best of friends but Kelly has happy to see her. Kelly had spoken to her several times over the last year but had not seen her.

Bonnie still looked good; she came with her latest beau. He was an older man similar to Skiles. Kelly introduced her to Tom and he liked what he saw. He began giving her the normal compliments that she didn't look old enough to have an eighteen-year-old daughter.

He and Bonnie talked quite a bit that night. Bonnie knew he was interested in her but she also knew he only wanted sex. She was also interested in him for the same reason. She knew they could slip out behind the pool or make a later date but instead she just brushed him off. She had done enough to Kelly without sleeping with her boyfriend.

Bonnie could have had Tom or Jim Tyler again who was there. It had been a long time since her and Jim had rolled in the hay but she left that night with whom she came with.

Tom, on the other hand was horny as usual. Kelly would not sleep with him and even though she was 18 and no longer jailbait he had not pushed the issue. She was close he thought. After all they had done everything but go that final step.

Lucy had been in the pool when Tom arrived. In fact she never went home after work. She kept a bathing suit there. Sometimes when she and Skiles would talk business they would use the pool house and sometimes they would take a swim.

She had met Tom when he first starting dating Kelly. He had come up to her office and made small talk. Lucy knew he was like all the other guys and just wanted to screw all the women he could while he could. She didn't mind that, she liked sex herself. In fact there were a couple of girls she ran with that called her Loosey Lucy. She just laughed at them even though the name sort of fit her. She had never married but instead preferred to remain single. She liked her freedom and didn't need a man to take care of her. Skiles paid her well and her freedom left her plenty of time to party and play around.

"Are you going to stay in the pool all night," Tom said to Lucy? "The water is great," she said. "You should come in." "Maybe I will," he said "but I'm not sure what I did with my swimming trunks." "Who says you need any," Lucy said? As soon as she said that she thought she had probably made a mistake. Flirting with Tom wasn't a good idea. No only could she get fired, she liked Kelly and didn't want to hurt her.

"Well, maybe I'll just do that," Tom said. "I never liked clothes that much anyway." "I'll be back, I need another drink, and can I bring you one?" "No, I'm fine," she said.

Kathryn was sitting near by and heard the conversation between Lucy and Tom. To her it was just more proof of what Tom was. She had talked many times and even recently to Kelly about him but it did no good. Kelly had told her they had almost gone all the way and Kathryn knew that once she gave into Tom he would just use her. As far as Lucy, Kathryn knew she had been drinking a little too much or she would have not said that. She and Lucy were not only co-workers but also good friends.

It was getting dark and the blue lights were casting an eerie glow on the pool and all the surrounding area. Tom and Kelly were both in the pool now. Tom had gone down the slide and the high dive several times. He was an excellent swimmer and was just about to climb the ladder again when he heard a noise behind him. He turned and saw Lucy coming down the path that led to the pet cemetery.

"Well Hi there Lucy," he said. "What are you doing back

126

here?" "I'm sort of stumbling around," she said. "I saw this cat that looked new to me and I was trying to catch it. I realized after a minute that I was too drunk to out run a cat so I gave up." "Do you need some help," he said as she started toward the pool house. "I think I can make it," she said.

Tom figured differently and grabbed her by the arm and pulled her against him. "What are you doing," she asked? "You know what I'm doing," he said as he forced his lips against hers. Lucy wasn't sure what she was going to do. Tom's hand was already inside her suit between her legs. Could she do this? Could she face Kelly or Kathryn if she let this happen? Would this moment of passion be worth that?

A loud scream came from behind the pool. Luckily for Lucy the noise and music had quieted down. Several people came running and one of them was Kelly. She saw Lucy trying to pull away from Tom. Doug, who had been near Kelly all night, ran toward them, grabbed Tom and knocked him to the ground.

"Get away from me you stupid creep," said Tom. "If you weren't retarded, I'd knock your face off!" "Tom, that's enough," said Kelly. "Oh, what do you know," Tom said? "I'm not sure what I know," said Kelly "but what it looks like is that you were trying to rape Lucy. I can't believe you would do something like this. I thought you loved me. It looks like everyone was right Tom you are no good. You treat women like dirt. I can't believe I waited all this time and saved myself for you."

Lucy was okay and knew she had made the right choice. She was sorry she had to scream but Tom was stronger and she would have never been able to stop him. If only she could have spared Kelly the hurt and humiliation it would have been better.

Skiles was upset. It took all his strength to hold back his anger at Tom. He wanted to throw him off the farm and tell him to never come back. Luckily for Tom Skiles turned his attention to Lucy instead to be sure she was taken care of.

Tom didn't want to lose Kelly. He had a lot of time invested in her, she had money, and he wanted to sleep with her. He figured once she left for college his time would come and if he played his cards right everything would eventually come to him. He pleaded with her to forgive him and blamed it on the alcohol. She was slow to respond at first but after a few days things returned to normal. Kelly forgave him and Tom continued just where he had left off.

Chapter 25
1969
College and Doug's Loss

Kelly wanted to go to college at Butler. She looked at Indiana University, Ohio State, and Purdue. She chose Butler for several reasons. She wanted to stay near the farm, her dad, friends, and Doug. She loved the farm so much she didn't think she would be happy far away. However the main reason was Tom. Tom didn't want to move away and give up his job. He said since Butler was in Indianapolis he could go to school part time and not have to give up his job. Kelly could either live on campus or stay at home and drive to school. It was the best of all worlds for Kelly. She chose to stay at home and drive.

Tom never got around to college. He had plans for Kelly. Why should he spend his time in school when he didn't have to? He figured he might as well marry Kelly. He knew Skiles didn't like him but he loved his daughter. Skiles would never interfere to keep her from him so why not. He could marry into money and have anything he wanted. As far as giving up his freedom, he probably could still play around as long as he was careful.

Doug didn't come to work on Tuesday. It was very unusual for him. He had never missed a day of work in his life. He had always been there even when he was sick. Kelly was worried. She was afraid something had happened to Doug. Skiles tried calling but there was no answer, so they both went to check on him.

When they pulled into the drive Doug was sitting on the porch just staring into space. As they approached him they noticed he had been crying. "What's wrong Doug," Kelly asked?

"He won't answer you," said a neighbor that had come over to talk to them. "His parents were killed in a car accident last night." "Oh my God," said Kelly. "How about his brother," asked Skiles? "I know Doug never talked much about him, I think he said he was in the Army. Is he here or still gone?"

"That's really the bad news," said the neighbor. "He joined

129

the Army years ago and was making a career there. Yesterday afternoon they were notified he was missing in action somewhere in Vietnam. His mother took it pretty hard so his father was taking her to the doctor to see if he could get a sedative. Anyway on the way back home they had the accident."

"The police were here when Doug came home. I think all the bad news at once was just overload. I'm glad you guys came; I think he may be in shock." "We'll take care of him," said Skiles. "Help me get him in the car and we'll take him to the hospital."

It had been 3 weeks since the Doug had suffered his loss. They had kept him in the hospital overnight and released him to Skiles the next day. Skiles brought him home and put him in one of the upstairs bedrooms.

The first week he wouldn't talk at all but then with the help of Kelly he slowly started to speak. His words didn't make sense at first but by the end of the second week he had made a dramatic turn around. He said he wanted to go back to work and he resumed his duties.

By the end of the third week it was as if nothing had ever happened. It's like he just wrote everything off and didn't remember anymore. The only thing Kelly saw different now was occasionally he got quiet and cried. The crying lasted a few seconds then he was okay again. He never talked during those few seconds and if you spoke to him he ignored you. Doug did this everyday at the same time for two months then stopped. After that he was fine.

Doug returned home for a short time while his parent's estate was being settled. He was forced to sell the house but Skiles let him move into one of his tenant houses. Even though Doug lost the house he did get a car. His parent's had just purchased a new 1969 Chevy sedan. It had been purchased for Doug with cash they had been saving for several years. The cash had been Doug's salary. He never went anywhere or spent any of his money so they just saved it for him. Luckily they had put the car in Doug's name so it was not part of the estate. Doug wasn't sure he needed a car. He had a license that his dad helped him get but he never drove that much. He parents took him most everywhere he went or he walked or sometimes he rode a bicycle. What driving he did he used his parent's car.

College was fun for Kelly. She loved the idea of living at home and driving to school. She and Tom were getting along great. Maybe it was the sex. Once she gave in she enjoyed it. She would drive over to his place after school, fix dinner and be waiting for him to come home from work. At times she would be waiting in the nude. They would make love, eat dinner, and then she would go home.

Kelly had also met a real neat friend at college. Her name was Diane Cummings. Kelly had many friends in High School but not one best friend. Diane would become her best friend. She was funny and very witty. She kept Kelly laughing when she was down. Skiles also liked Diane. She had heard about the house of blue lights legend and when she would come over she would always tease Skiles about it. Every time she came she would walk in, see Skiles and have a pun or a witty saying of some kind.

One day she came over and Skiles was sitting by the piano and she said, "Hey Pops why don't you wire up those piano keys to the blue lights. That way when you play a tune they would blink. Then you could wire up the foot pedals to raise the cat headstones up and down as you play." Skiles just shook his head and laughed. Things like that made home fun for Kelly and she was glad she stayed in Indy for college.

Doug and Kelly still did the same things but her mother rarely called anymore. She missed her and she missed Kathryn. Once Kelly started college, Kathryn's job was over. Skiles gave her a nice severance package and they left on good terms. She would come back every so often to visit. She and Skiles became very good friends and Kelly was happy when she visited.

Lucy was also very happy when Kathryn came back. Kathryn and Lucy had become very close over the years and socialized away from the farm.

Kelly knew that Kathryn had deeper feelings for her father

than just friends but her father never had the same feelings. Kelly wasn't sure how friendly her father and Kathryn were during the visits. She suspected they were having sex but she didn't pry and if that made them happy then so be it. After all Kelly could understand that if you loved someone and sex was all you could get then that was better than nothing.

By the second year of college the pressure was on. Kelly was talking about marriage and Tom had to make a decision. His original plan was to marry Kelly for the money. He had figured he could have his cake and eat it to but now things were different. The sex kept him happy for a while but now it was old to him and he missed the excitement of what he called getting some "strange." He had not slept with anyone except Kelly since she had started college and there was this new girl at work!

Tom just didn't know what to do. He didn't want to let Kelly go but he didn't want to get married. He also didn't want to spend as much time with her as he had been. He needed free time to do his own thing. He told Kelly he wanted to wait until she was out of college to get married. That would give him time to go to school and perhaps get his degree. Kelly tried to get him to go to school with her but Tom insisted he wanted to continue to work and go to school at night.

The place where he worked had a degree program that was free and he could take classes there. Kelly said he didn't need the degree, she had plenty of money and after they were married she would ask her dad to set Tom up in the chain business.

Tom said he didn't want to be dependant upon his wife. He was just funny about that and wanted to be the breadwinner. Kelly didn't like it very much but she accepted it for now. This made Tom happy. It not only put the marriage off for a couple more years but it gave him the free time he needed. The whole thing about going to school at work was a lie but Kelly wouldn't know. They did have a degree program at work but he wasn't going to waste his time in school. Those school nights would be spend chasing tail!

Chapter 26
1973
Tom's Big Mistake

It was now 1973. Kelly was graduating from college and Tom was supposedly still in school. His education so far had been great! What he had learned about women could have never been learned in school. He learned that married women were easier than single women. Over the last two years he had slept with half a dozen single women and over ten married ones. The married ones just wanted a one-night fling and he had gone through about every girl at work. His pickings were beginning to get slim. Perhaps he might have to go back around and hit them all again. Maybe twice would be nice!

Skiles wanted to have another graduation party for Kelly. It would not be as large as the High School one though. Skiles only wanted a few friends. Parties were expensive and Skiles had to cut back. He still had money but he wasn't making very much. He had told Kelly that he might have to sell the chain company or at least sell half of it. There was a guy who was interested in buying part of it and he had cash.

He did assure her though that he had some money stashed so she wouldn't have to worry. She told him that she wasn't concerned and she would be just fine on her own. She did ask him if there could be any possible positions for Tom at the company. She told him Tom was working on a business degree and perhaps he could use him. Maybe he could even help the business with all the new ideas he should have coming out of school. Skiles said he wasn't sure, a lot depended on the sale and what the new partner had planned.

"Tom, I need to talk to you," said Kelly. "Okay, honey, I don't have class tonight so why don't we meet at my place around five." Okay," she said, "I'll be there."

When Kelly walked in Tom knew something was wrong. She just seemed down and out. "What's wrong," he said. "My dad is not doing very well financially," she said. "You know that job I sort of promised you, well it may not develop. Do you think after you get your degree that they will give you a promotion? That way, we won't have to depend on dad." "I'm not sure," he said. "I know a lot of guys get promotions out of school but it depends on the openings at the time and I'm still a year or so away from that degree. I was sort of counting on having my own business and not just getting a promotion." Kelly said, "I know and I'm sorry."

Tom wasn't sorry at all. This was the out he needed. Without the promise of that position with the chain company Kelly wouldn't mind holding off on the wedding a little longer. Besides there was no way he was going to marry Kelly now that she was no longer rich. He figured he had a year or two, or even maybe three to milk her for whatever he could before Skiles did go belly up.

It was Saturday, June 2nd; the graduation party began late evening. It had been a nice day so far, there was a light breeze blowing from the south which made it warmer than normal. The humidity was high and the temperature was still eighty degrees when the party started.

At the very start of the party Skiles called Kelly aside and handed her an envelope. Inside were two first class tickets to the Bahamas. She had never been out of the country before. She and Skiles had gone to California once. He was on business and she flew out with him.

This would be great! Now she had a choice to make. Should she take Diane or Tom? It might be more fun to go with Diane, but what would Tom think about her going somewhere like that without him. Her dad hadn't said whom the second ticket was for. I'm sure he would prefer she take Diane but he had left it open. She would have to think about that for a while.

The party was quiet, not a lot of booze or loud music, just a few drinks with a swimming party thrown in. Bonnie had been invited but she did not show. She had called and said she was sick. Of course Diane came and was the life of the party. Even though it was quiet she at least got a few laughs.

Skiles, Kelly, and Tom were sitting outside discussing business when a shot was fired. The bullet just missed Tom and hit the back of his chair. Everyone there began running, screaming, shouting, and just trying to get out of the way as another shot was fired. That bullet hit the doorframe of the pool house just at the edge of the glass and caught the top hinge. The glass shattered and the top part of the door was hanging loose.

Kelly was lying on the cement with Tom covering her for protection. Skiles tried to remain calm so he could focus on who was doing the shooting. He thought the shot had come from the southwest and as he looked that way he saw the person responsible.

The gun was pointed downward and this gave Skiles just enough time to reach her before she could raise and fire another shot. He wrestled with her and took the gun away. She was shaking and crying as Skiles sat her in a nearby chair and he noticed she was pregnant.

"I'm going to kill that bastard," she said. "Who," said Skiles? "Tom, that's who," she said. "The S.O.B. promised me the moon, got me pregnant and left me high and dry. He told me he loved me but I knew he had someone else. As soon as I started getting big with the baby he quit coming around. I've been following him for the last couple of months and tonight I caught up with him."

The woman's crying became more intense, her composure was changing and she looked at Skiles and pleated with him not to call the police. "I didn't mean to do any damage, I just couldn't stand it, and I was just out of my mind. I need financial help and I don't know who to turn to." Kelly and Diane were standing near her now and had heard the whole thing. "Come with us," Kelly said.

She and Diane took the woman into the house. Skiles started looking for Tom. He was near enough to have heard the story and when Skiles came toward him he said. "Hey, Skiles, that woman is lying. I did not."

Before he could say another word Skiles cut him off. "You are such a bastard. I have kept quiet all these years while you crapped on Kelly. You have cheated on her at every turn. You have used her for the last time." Skiles was mad and Tom knew he had really done it this time. He wasn't sure what Skiles would do but Skiles still had the gun and he wasn't staying around to find out.

Tom ran for his life and Skiles was on his heels. As they ran past Doug, he joined Skiles in the chase. However, neither Skiles nor Doug could keep up with him. Skiles stopped first and Doug a few yards later. The last they saw of Tom he was running past the milk house headed toward the milk barn.

As they walked back Skiles suddenly fell over. "What's wrong," asked Doug? "I don't know," said Skiles, "I'm having a lot of pain in my chest and left arm." "Let me go get Kelly," Doug said. "No," said Skiles, "Kelly has been through enough besides the pain is going away. I think I'll be all right now."

Skiles never called the police. Skiles kept the gun and Kelly took care of the woman. Her name was Elizabeth Wilson. She had met Tom in a bar over a year ago. Kelly wasn't mad at the woman she was envious in a way. She was carrying Tom's baby. A baby is something she had thought about many times. She wanted to have one as soon as Tom and her were married but it didn't look like that was going to happen now.

A couple of weeks after the shooting Elizabeth gave birth to a seven pound boy. Elizabeth didn't want to keep the child and Kelly wanted to adopt it. Skiles told her it would be difficult for a young single woman to adopt and he thought it unwise to even try. Kelly knew he was right and gave up on the idea.

Kelly had not seen or heard from Tom in three weeks. Skiles had forbid him to come around the farm. His family had come the next day after the incident to get his car and Skiles made it clear to them that in no way was he ever to step foot on his property again.

Kelly hadn't said much to anyone about Tom except Diane and Doug. She could always talk to them and Doug was really the best to talk to. If only Tom could have been like Doug this whole thing would have never happened.

Doug was a good listener but he wasn't good at giving advice.

Kelly however didn't need any advice; she knew what she must do. She had to let Tom go. It had been a rough road these last six years. She had loved him so much and so faithfully. She had to let go but could she? She didn't know. She was hurting a lot but life without Tom would hurt even more. She wondered if Tom could ever change.

Kelly wondered a lot of things and a lot of what ifs. What if Tom changed? What if they could have that child she so desperately wanted? Kelly thought a lot about having a child, and giving up Elizabeth's for adoption was hard on her.

Kelly found a song called "Days of Sand and Shovels" by Waylon Jennings. It was about this guy who couldn't have children and lost his wife over it. She played that record over and over. She began playing other records too mostly sad ones. She didn't realize it at the time but the songs she played were the beginning and possibly the cause of her depression. She became moody and cried a lot. She was slowly losing her mind over a man that had never loved her and never would.

Chapter 27
1973
The Bahamas

Kelly had postponed the Bahamas trip until after Elizabeth's baby was born. She didn't have to make the choice anymore of who was going with her.

Diane was excited and knew Kelly needed to get away. Tom had been on her mind too much and if she could get her out of town it might be just the thing. Diane didn't care much for Tom. She never said much about him but she knew what he was. What she didn't know is what Kelly saw in him. Diane knew plenty of guys who would love a girl like Kelly and she was determined to help that along.

The plane from Indianapolis landed at the Bahamas at 3 p.m. Kelly wondered if she should have waited until next year for this trip. It was already July and she thought it might be too hot and early spring might have been a better time.

Their hotel room had an ocean view with a small balcony. The balcony was a small space with room for a couple of chairs and a small table. They were on the 21st floor and could see the hotel's pool. It was between the hotel and the ocean.

"Okay Kelly," said Diane. "We are here, what do you want to do?" "Well," said Kelly "it's late in the day and I think I want to wait until tomorrow to go to the beach" "Why don't we find a nice place for dinner, get a good nights sleep and start fresh tomorrow." "That sounds like a plan," said Diane.

"Let's get cleaned up and go downstairs. We can then walk around the block and see what's here," said Diane. "What are you going to wear," asked Kelly? "Should we dress up for dinner?" "Don't be silly," said Diane. "We are in the Bahamas. Everything is casual here. Let's just wear shorts and one of these little revealing tops!" "You are such the slut Diane, why don't you just go walk around naked?" "I'll probably do that later," said Diane.

The "strip" consisted of several similar hotels, small restaurants, and a few bars. They settled for their own hotel for dinner and after eating decided to go bar hopping.

There was a little bar area next to the beach at the hotel next to theirs. The bar was divided into two sections. One was inside and looked like a typical bar you would find anywhere. The outside part was the most interesting. It was an open area built right on the beach although far enough from the water so the tide wouldn't get you. The flooring was wood decking and there was a railing that ran all the way around it except for two exits you could take to the beach. There were tables and bar stools but the most interesting area was in the farthest corner from the hotel.

That corner had a higher and wider railing than the other sections and there were big padded stools with extended footrests. These stools sat up next to the railing where you could put your drinks and even have room for snacks. The view from this corner was beautiful. You could watch the sunset down through the clouds, and enjoy a slight breeze along with your snack and drink.

The bar was about half full when they arrived. There were several couples but also several single men and women. They took a seat on the padded bar stools next to a couple of girls.

"Hi, I'm Diane and this is Kelly." "My name is Tina and this is Joan," she said. "Where are you from?" "We are both from Indianapolis," said Kelly, "how about you guys?" "We are from Columbus, Ohio," said Tina. "We came down with a group from work. This is our second time here. Last year we were here, then before that we went to Vegas, and the year before that we were in the Florida Keys."

"So," said Diane, "are there any available good looking single men in your group?" "Yes, there is a couple," said Joan. "I'll be glad to introduce you to them. They are sitting over there at that table," pointing to a large table with four men and two women. "The two single men are the ones in the sport coats. They just came from a meeting. The other two are married to the two women sitting next to them. However, I can tell you from experience you will not have any trouble finding guys."

"If you sit here for a few more minutes someone will come and ask if they can buy you a drink. And then when the band starts you will get tons of dance offers."

"I would however give you this advice. Stay with tourists. This place just gained its independence and since then a lot has changed in a hurry. Do not get mixed up with any locals. They can't always be trusted and most of them are out to scam you out of your money."

"So, what's the story on the two single guys in your group," said Diane. "Well," said Tina. "Either one would be a good catch if you are just looking for a fling. They both have been around the barn a time or two but they are not someone I'd want to settle down with." "What do you mean around the barn," said Kelly? "Have they been married?" "Oh, no, I just mean they play around a lot," said Tina. "You will have to excuse her," said Diane, "she doesn't get out much."

As the evening went by several drink and dance offers came to all four of the girls who by now had become best friends. Kelly and Diane had been introduced to the two guy co-workers and had decided they were not that interesting.

"It's getting late," said Tina. "Why don't we all meet by the pool at your hotel around 8 a.m.? We can have breakfast and we will show you the best beach spot." "Sounds good to me," said Kelly. "I think I'll stay and have one more drink," said Diane. "I see a guy over there that looks interesting and he is coming this way. I'll see you all in the morning."

"Hi, my name is Justin Taylor; may I buy you a drink?" "Yes, maybe one, I'm Diane Cummings." "Nice to meet you," he said. "Did all four of you come down here together," he asked. "No, I came with my friend Kelly. We just met the other two while we were sitting here."

"Are you here alone she asked?" "No, I'm with a business convention; there are eight of us. We are from Atlanta. Where are you from," he asked?

The small talk continued for several minutes and then Justin asked her if she would like to take a walk on the beach. "I'd like that," she said, "although I'm not too sure how well I can walk. I think I may have had one too many drinks." "Not to worry," he said. "I can hold the both of us up if we stumble."

"Let's go over there toward those rocks," said Justin. "Maybe we can find a little place to sit for a while." Sit for a while thought Diane. I just bet that is what he has in mind she thought to herself. Even though she had been drinking a little too much she still knew what was going on, but the thing she knew and Justin didn't was that she wanted to go to the rocks. Drinking made her horny and she had been in a dry spell back home and Justin would do just fine, just fine.

It was two hours later when Diane made it to the room. Kelly was sleeping and didn't even hear her come in. Her time with Justin had been great and had left her a little exhausted but very satisfied.

"What's that light shining in my eyes," said Diane. "That's the sun goofy, time to get up. What time did you come in last night?" "Last night, oh, let me tell you about Justin," she said. "I'm not sure I want to hear about him, is it good?" "Good, I almost screwed myself to death. That guy is hung like a horse and I know how to ride a horse." "You are so silly Diane, get your bathing suit on it's almost time to meet Tina and Joan."

Joan and Tina were sitting at a table near the pool when Kelly and Diane came down. "Good morning guys," Diane said. "Let me tell you about my night. Did you guys know they have horse back riding on the beach late at night?"

Kelly laughed and said, "They probably do know that but they don't know all the horses are two legged."

Tina and Joan had this very confused look on their faces until Diane explained. "So Diane," said Tina. "Does this horse have any more like him in the stable?" "Justin said there were eight of them."

"Hey, I've got an idea," said Joan. "Let's order breakfast here and have them bring it down to the beach. That way we can get to the spot I want to go to." "Will they be able to find us," asked Kelly? "Oh sure," Joan said, "I'll tell them where we will be and it's not far from here."

The beach wasn't crowded yet. There were a handful of people in chairs and a couple wading in the ocean. The spot where Tina and Joan took them was a few yards from the hotel. The beach curved into a small inlet with some good size rocks, then straightened back out for a about half a mile.

"This is it," said Tina, "you can see both directions here so you know who's coming and going. The rocks provide good scenery and the tide only comes up to here" as she pointed to a tall rock near her. "And," she said "the best part is that it's near that hotel" as she pointed to the building nearest them. "What is so special about it," asked Diane? "Well," said Tina "that is the hotel where 80% of all the business men stay. Believe me we have done our research. If there are any 'horses' anywhere around this beach, they stay there." "And they walk past here," said Joan. "In fact here comes a couple now." "I think I know one of them," said Diane.

"Diane, is that you?" "Well, Justin, good morning, nice to see you again. Oh and by the way are these the same rocks that I remember from?" Before she could finish, Justin interrupted her and said, "No, different place." The girls just sort of giggled and Justin figured Diane had told them about their little late night get together.

"By the way ladies let me introduce you to my friend. This is Curtis Tompkins; he is our leader so to speak. He watches after us crazy guys. He is one of those boring non-drinkers." "It's a pleasure to meet you folks," said Curtis "and don't pay any attention to Justin. I think you can have just as much fun by not drinking as you can if you drink. That way you can remember everything." Diane said, "This is Kelly my friend that I came with. This is Joan and Tina from Ohio."

"Breakfast is coming," yelled Tina as the waiter approached. "Would you like guys to join us," asked Joan? "We will have to pass for now," said Curtis. "We were just taking a quick walk before our first meeting. Perhaps we will see you later today."

"So what do you think of Justin," asked Diane? "Quite the hunk," said Joan. "I agree," said Tina. "What about you Kelly," asked Diane? "He seems fine to me but if I had a choice I would take

Curtis." "Why Curtis," asked Diane? "He just seems a little more grounded and he has a nice smile." "A nice smile you say," said Diane. "Girls, we have got to get this little lady laid!"

It was just after lunch, Justin and Curtis had returned with a couple other guys. Everyone had paired off and left Curtis with Kelly. Kelly thought Curtis seemed to be nice guy. He was nice looking with jet-black hair, slender build, and he did have a great smile. He might even be someone who she could like if she could just get in the mood. So far the trip had been a good getaway for her but she had not been able to relax completely. She still had a lot on her mind but maybe a drink or two would help that.

"Curtis, do you see that little waiter that was near here a while ago?" "Yes, he is over there by the blue umbrellas, do you want something?" "Yes, I think I'd like to have one of those strawberry drinks with a little kicker in it." "I'll be happy to get you one," said Curtis. "I think I could use a Coke myself. I'll be back in a jiffy."

By the end of the day, Curtis and Kelly had become good friends. She had found him easy to talk to and had confided in him about her past. As far as Curtis was concerned he enjoyed Kelly. She was unlike most other women he had run across on these business trips and he liked that very much.

"Hey you two, on your feet," said Diane to Curtis and Kelly. "Where are we going," asked Kelly? "Justin said he would pick us all up at our hotel lobby in a limo and take us to a dinner play," said Diane. "A limo, "said Curtis. "I'm going to kill him! I bet he has expensed it and I'll have to explain it to the board when we get home." "Don't know," said Diane, "he said he had it covered!"

The dinner and play were good. Kelly was feeling great. She had just enough drinks to loosen up and had gone with Curtis for a moonlit walk on the beach. She wasn't sure where all the others had gone, she had lost track of them somewhere between drink number three and four. She wasn't drunk by any means just feeling good. It had been a long time since she had enjoyed herself this much.

The beach was almost empty; there was just one other

couple up ahead of them. They were running in and out of the water. The woman had a white sundress on and it appeared in the moonlight that she had nothing else on underneath it. The man looked like he had on white swimming trunks but as they got closer it became clear it wasn't trunks it was underwear.

"Hey you two," yelled the man in underwear. "You guys should join us, the water is great!" "We don't have bathing suits," yelled Kelly. "We don't either," yelled the man, "but we don't mind, come on join us."

"What do think Curtis," asked Kelly?" "Are you serious Kelly, you want to join them?" "Why not," she said. "I don't care if these clothes get wet." "I'm game," said Curtis as he grabbed her hand and starting running toward the couple.

They hit the water running hand in hand and came alongside the other couple. "I'm Terry and this is Janet," the man said. "Curtis and Kelly," Curtis said.

"Let's play," Janet yelled!

They all four ran began running in and out of the water playing tag. Kelly would grab one of Curtis's buttocks and yell, "you're it". Before she could move away he would grab a breast and say "not now". Soon the touches spread from breasts and buttocks to more private areas and to other people. And then just before a huge wave came in Curtis saw Terry dive for Kelly. His head came up underneath her dress as the wave hit. They came floating toward him with Kelly holding Terry's head between her legs yelling, "Ride cowboy ride." Then Curtis heard Janet yell, "Wait for me" and as he turned toward the sound Janet grabbed him. She dragged Curtis under the water and when they came up his pants were gone. The next to go was Kelly and Janet's dress, then the remainder of the men's clothes.

Curtis didn't know what to think. He was the only sober one there. Normally he wouldn't be involved in anything like this but seeing the two women naked was just too much for him. He didn't care what he normally wouldn't do; all he wanted now was Kelly and Janet, either one at a time or both at once.

Kelly just simply didn't care nor did she even think about

144

what she was doing or why. All she knew was she saw two men naked and she wanted both of them inside her.

The next huge wave was coming, Janet headed for the beach yelling "If you can catch me you can have it". Kelly was next, she yelled "me too" and started running. By the time both girls had gotten clear of the water both men were close behind. Curtis was closer to Janet than Kelly so he headed for her. He caught her by the leg and brought her down. As soon as she touched the sand she flipped over on her back, spread her legs and pulled Curtis down on her.

Terry was still chasing Kelly but as soon as Kelly saw Curtis and Janet she changed directions. She headed for them and reached them at the same time that Terry grabbed her arm. They both tumbled down and landed against Curtis and Janet.

Kelly could feel the movement of Curtis with Janet and it made the passion inside her stronger. She was like an animal. She reached for Terry and thrust herself up to him.

Forty-five minutes later, they were done. They had swapped with each other over and over. Terry had finished with Janet and Curtis with Kelly.

Kelly and Curtis then gathered their clothes and said their goodbyes. When they left Terry and Janet were still there naked as before. Curtis took Kelly to her hotel, kissed her goodnight and left.

As Kelly entered her room she was cold, nervous, and sobering up very fast. Diane was there and asked if she was all right. "I'm not sure what I am," said Kelly. "I just slept with two different guys." "Two! You are one lucky girl," said Diane. "I don't feel lucky," said Kelly "and be serious for once." "Okay," said Diane. "Tell me all about it." "There's not much to tell, I was drinking more than I should. Curtis and I were walking on the beach and we saw this other couple in the water. They were half naked and invited us to join them. I don't know what happened, it's just my passion took over, my inhibitions all came out and I now I feel like a cheap tramp."

"Well maybe it's good you did it," said Diane. "I think that after all you have been through with Tom you deserve to have some fun and I don't think you should feel bad. Society looks down on us for screwing around but they accept it when a man does it. What kind of deal is that? Who got hurt tonight, huh, no one."

"I don't know that anyone did," said Kelly. "I've got to sort this out and you have to promise me that you will never tell anyone. You have to promise." "I promise," said Diane.

The next day all the friends Kelly and Diane had made left for the states. They both were staying another day. That morning at breakfast there was an article in the paper about a couple that were arrested on the beach for having sex in public. In the article was a small picture of Terry and Janet.

The following morning the plane left. They arrived in Indianapolis at 6 p.m.

Chapter 28
1973
The Beginning of the End

As soon as Kelly arrived home from the Bahamas trip she felt confused. The wild fling she had in the Bahamas was exciting at the time but now she wondered if she really did that in the Bahamas? Did it really happen or was it just a dream? Was there some great passion inside her that she was unaware of? No, that couldn't have been her; she was not that type of girl. It must have been a dream, yes that's what it was, a dream.

After all she was home now, everything looked familiar. Everything was in its place but Tom. She kept asking herself, why? Why couldn't she move forward? Maybe if she could just see him one more time. Yes, maybe she could move on if she could say good-bye to him one last time. Maybe she would tell him about the fling in the Bahamas. Maybe that would make him go away out of her life. But wait, that was a dream, it didn't happen. After all Diane never mentioned it so it must have been a dream. Maybe life was a dream, what is reality she thought? She didn't know, but she did at that moment decide she wanted to see Tom. She had to know what had happened to him. Why hadn't he called? Didn't he care? She was going crazy. She needed help.

Ralph Castle's office was in the left wing of the Community East hospital. He had been a physiatrist for several years and he thought he had heard it all until Kelly. He had seen a lot of patients for depression but she was unlike any of them. Her depression went deeper than most. It was going to take a long time to figure her out.

"How are you today Kelly," Dr. Castle asked? "I don't think I'm any better," she said. "This is my third visit and I think I'm getting worse." "Are you taking your medication?" "Yes, I take it everyday but maybe we should try something different." "I don't want to give you anything too strong," he said. "I want to calm you down and get to the root of your issues without a lot of medication."

"The last three sessions you talked a lot about Tom and a little about your dad. I think this session we should talk about your mother," he said. "Are you anything like your mother at all? "I'm not restless like she is, but I am sad a lot." "I think the two might be connected," he said. "If a person is sad they are looking for something to make them happy. Her being restless may be a part of that. How does she cope with her restlessness?" "She copes by leaving her current environment and going somewhere else or moving from one relationship to another."

"Kelly, have you ever discussed any of this with her? "You mean about my sadness or hers?" "Well I was referring to hers but either would be okay to discuss." "Well, I've never talked to her about me and I did try once to talk about her."

"She was getting ready to leave on a trip and I went to her room to try to get her to stay. When I entered the room she was playing records and crying. I asked her what was wrong and she said she didn't want to talk about it." "Were they sad records?" "Yes, and you know Dr. Castle she played sad songs a lot, does that mean anything?" "It might," he said. "Do you listen to sad songs Kelly?" "Well, I have been recently, especially ones that remind me of Tom. And by the way doctor, I need to see him, do you think that would be okay?" "I think that might be okay, go ahead and let's talk about your visit with him next week."

Tom was fine or so he thought. He had missed Kelly since the graduation party. The Kelly who was always there willing to take him back no matter what he had done. He wondered if she would take him back this time. She didn't know how he really was. She had caught him in lies and she suspected he had been having relationships all these years. But this time it was a lot different. He had gotten a woman pregnant and Skiles wouldn't let him on the property. Maybe it was over or was it? The doorbell rang.

He knew who it was. He had this feeling that on the other side of that door was Kelly. What would he say? Would he try to lie about things he had done or tell the truth?

"Hi Kelly," he said. "Hi Tom, may I come in?" Tom had not

realized how much he missed her and how good she looked. For once in his life he realized he had more feelings for her than he knew. He realized what he had lost and he was sorry but he figured it was probably too little too late?

They talked for hours. Tom opened up to Kelly and was truthful. He admitted what he had done and he was sorry. He was also glad she had come to see him. Kelly said she had missed him and had not been sure how he felt but just had to know.

"What do we do now," Tom said? "Your dad hates me and I deserve it. I don't understand why you don't hate me to." "I don't think I could ever hate you Tom and maybe dad will come around," said Kelly. "If he knows you have changed dad can be a very forgiving person. If dad will not forgive you I will not go against his wishes and marry you. I will not hurt my father like that. He is such a good man, he deserves better of me. I will just be content to just see you and not let him know. Then no matter how long it is once he is gone then we can get married."

Tom wasn't sure what his feelings were after Kelly left. He was glad he had her back but could he keep her? Could he change his restless ways? Could she convince Skiles to give him another chance? Could he forget about the son he had somewhere out there or like Kelly had said during their talk, could they get him back? Only time would tell.

Kelly left Tom with a new outlook on life. Maybe since he had been truthful with her he would change. And maybe someday in the short future Skiles would come around and finally her life would be complete. However, Skiles didn't quite see it that way.

"But dad," she said. "It should be my choice." "It is your choice Kelly. I'm not telling you how to live your life I'm saying if you choose Tom you won't be welcome on the farm. Besides, how many times are you going to forgive him? Haven't you had enough?" "I can answer that with one question dad. Would you put a limit on how many times God forgives you?"

There was silence in the room. Kelly had made her point. When you love someone you never stop forgiving. Skiles walked away without answering her. He knew she was right but he wasn't God. Skiles knew men like Tom and he had to protect her now for what she would face in the future if she married him. He would do anything for Kelly but not this. He knew it would be the end of her. Tom might change for a month or two but men like him were bad to the core.

Besides Skiles had other problems he had to worry about. He was in financial ruin. He had been forced to sell his remaining share of the chain company.

The IRS had audited him and he had to pay 100,000 dollars in back taxes and they were not finished yet. The only business he had remaining was the farm and it was not very profitable.

He began selling off some of his land to a developer. The entire section of what he used to call the lost 40's was sold. He had named this section of land that bordered along 71st street after several herd of cattle had died in a snowstorm there back in forty nine. His property had now been reduced from 700 acres to just fewer than 300. He used the money to invest in the farm figuring he could get at least three to four more years out of it. Hopefully by then it would be turning a nice profit.

Skiles was by no means out of money; he just didn't have much on paper. He wasn't any longer the millionaire he used to be but he had enough to take care of himself, Kelly, and Doug.

Skiles had been hiding money for years from the IRS and his accountant. He would skim some here and there and after all it was his money even though the IRS thought differently. Now he thought it was time to do what he had been planning for a long time.

He called Doug into the house one day when Kelly was home. He took them both to his bedroom. Skiles had built two safes, one in the wall between the bedroom and bathroom and one in the floor. In the safes Skiles had counted out one million dollars that was to go to Doug and the remainder was Kelly's.

Doug didn't know what to say. He never cared much about money. He only cared about Kelly, Skiles, and the farm. Skiles told him that he had been like a son to him and he appreciated all his loyalty and most of all he appreciated the way he had taken care of

Kelly. A tear came to Doug's eyes. No one but his parents ever cared for him like Skiles. His heart was aching to tell Skiles how much he loved him but he didn't know how. Skiles understood and he knew how Doug felt without the words being spoken.

Kelly's life was miserable. She loved her father, she loved Tom but she couldn't have both at the same time. It was like she was waiting on her dad to die so she could be free and marry Tom. What an awful thought she said to herself. Life on the farm wasn't much fun anymore.

After the Bahamas trip Diane began to move on. She found a steady guy and was planning marriage. Her visits to the farm were becoming fewer and fewer and Kelly missed her friend. Doug and the animals were still there but it wasn't enough. She was slipping further into depression. The medication and the advice from Doctor Castle didn't seem to be working at all.

Tom told her that he didn't mind waiting but Kelly wasn't sure if he was lying or even if he still wanted her. It had been like this for four years now and she couldn't take it any longer. She was at the point where she didn't care if she lived or died and on top of all that she knew something was wrong with her father. He just wasn't the same.

What Kelly had thought was true, Skiles was sick. He had not said anything to Kelly but he had gone to the doctor while she was away. His doctor had told him his heart was giving out and he could go anytime. He gave Skiles a year at the most, but probably it would be less.

He didn't know how to tell Kelly, maybe he wouldn't. The doctor said he had a chance of going quickly and if he were lucky enough to do that, there was no need to tell Kelly. He could pretend everything was fine, and then one day it would happen. It would be quick and save her months of worry.

Skiles knew Kelly was depressed and he told himself maybe after he was gone she could finally be happy. He had failed in his plan of Tom going away before he died. He was sorry he had to put Kelly through all this but it was a chance he had to take. If his plan had worked Kelly would have been much happier in the long run.

Kelly's depression was getting worse. She and Tom didn't spend a lot of time together anymore, and she thought he was cheating again. She knew now her dad had been right. Everyone had been right about Tom. If only she had listened to Kathryn so many years ago. If only she could have spend these last few years having fun with her dad instead of pining for Tom. Now it seemed too late for everything.

She was sure she had lost Tom and now she was almost sure she was losing her dad. He slept more now than before and he was always tired. He also had stopped walking the dogs with her and Doug.

Yes, Kelly knew she was going to lose her father and had lost Tom. What would be left for her, her mother wasn't around either, so as far as she was concerned her life was over. It was time to make her will. She wanted Doug to have everything.

"Hi Kelly, how have you been since our last talk?" "Dr. Castle, I don't think I 'm going to lick this thing. I think I'm going to lose dad before long, I think the relationship with Tom is over, and I never see my mother. What is left for me?"

"Are you feeling sorry for yourself Kelly?" "Maybe I am, you tell me, you are the shrink"

"Kelly, I am going to tell you something. I know you have a lot of issues and have been dealt a dirty deal with this Tom guy. I also know some of this you inherited from your mother. Sometimes a parent passes on some traits that we don't like or understand but it happens. I think both you and she spend most of your life waiting to live."

"I'm not sure I understand Dr. Castle, you think mom and I are alike?" "Are you still listening to sad songs? "When I get moody I do." "Let me suggest something to you Kelly. I don't think you listen to sad songs when you are moody. I think the sad songs make you moody. I also think the same thing happens to your mother."

"So, Dr. Castle you are saying that if I listen to happy songs I wouldn't be like I am?" "I'm not saying that, but your depression wouldn't be as bad or last as long. Sad songs bring you down."

"But, I tried to listen to up beat songs. I love all these oldies, and I go through them and try to pick out happy songs. Just yesterday I played 'Footsteps' by Steve Lawrence which was a fast up beat song."

"I'm familiar with that song but did you listen to the words of 'Footsteps.' They are about this girl that walked away from this guy, that's still sad." "Okay then Dr. Castle, I give up, what should I listen to?" "I don't think you should try to pick out particular songs, I think you should look at life as it really is and not place yourself in your music. Whether a sad song or a happy song plays you should enjoy the music but not let it influence your behavior."

"What I want you to do Kelly is stay away from playing records. I want you to concentrate on living for today. Life is passing you by because you are always waiting on something. You are waiting on your father to die so you can be with Tom. You are waiting on Tom to stop cheating. Stop waiting! If you have to wait on something before you can live you will never live."

"Don't you see you have put your life on hold because there are certain things you tell yourself that need to be in place before you can move on and enjoy life?"

"Okay, Dr. Castle, I just wish I could be happy like I was when I was a child." "I know Kelly, but we grow up and when we do we have to learn to cope with life as it is and I know that has been hard for you. Let's talk again real soon, give your self a week without the records and come back in." "Okay, Dr. Castle I'll try."

As Kelly returned from the doctor's office she noticed a red Corvette parked near the dog pens. She had never seen that car before and wondered who it belonged to. Little did she know at the time, the Corvette would only add to her problems.

It had been two months since Kelly had seen Dr. Castle. She didn't have any good news for him. Things had gotten worse but it weren't sad records this time, it was something much worse but she couldn't tell him. She figured it had to remain a secret forever.

"Hi, Kelly, how have you been since our last visit," he said? I'm not any better doctor." "You haven't been playing records again have you?" "No, I stopped doing that for now; it's just there are other things on my mind." "Are these things something you want to talk about Kelly?" "I can't tell you, it's too private but I want to ask you a question."

"If you loved someone, and I'm not talking about Tom, I'm talking about loving someone like a family member. But if you loved them and they did something terrible, really terrible wouldn't you want to protect them?"

"If you are covering up something illegal you shouldn't do that," he said. "The guilt you feel will never go away it will just get worse."

"If I told you something happened, a deep dark secret, would you have to tell the authorities," she asked? "It depends, but I can't guarantee anything," he said. "I'm not going to hurt the people I love even if it makes my depression worse doctor Castle. I guess this secret is just one more thing that I have to take to my grave."

It was a gloomy day this last day of April, 1974. The weather had been warm this spring after a cold and bitter winter. It had been so warm in fact Kelly was already in her summer shorts on this particular day. What was strange about her wearing shorts was even on hot days she was cold and most of the time wore long sleeves and pants. She didn't give much thought to how she looked, nor did she care. She only cared about one thing at this time in her life and that was ending it.

"Kelly, honey can I fix you something to eat," asked Emma? "I'm not hungry." "But child, you don't eat anything any more. I am worried about you. I think you have lost ten pounds over the last week." "I'm okay," Kelly said. "Do you know where my dad is Emma?" "Yes, he is lying down for a while. He said he needed a nap."

"Dad, are you okay," she asked? "I'm just a little tired," Skiles said, "nothing for you to worry about." "Are you okay Kelly?" "Yes, I just wanted to talk to you for a minute," she said. "Come over and sit by me on the bed and we can talk," he said. "Now what's on your mind honey?"

"I just wanted to make my peace with you father." "I'm not sure I understand," he said. "It's this whole thing about Tom," she said. "You and I have skirted the issue not really talking about it. I know all you ever wanted for me was happiness. I know now you knew better than I how Tom was."

"I have been so blind all these years." "I don't think you have been blind Kelly, I think you knew deep inside, I just think you thought he would change."

"But none of that matters now dad. I have realized what you and Kathryn tried to tell me so long ago. And even though I realize that now it still hurts. I just can't seem to get over him, I don't know what is wrong with me but I'm scared dad."

Tears were in Skiles eyes as he reached up to hold Kelly. He knew what she was feeling. Skiles had felt the same way about Bonnie. Skiles tried to tell himself over and over again that his feelings for Bonnie were not real or not as real as what he had with Madeline. But no matter what he told himself the hurt she caused him would be taken to his grave.

And now this hurt that his daughter was feeling was too much for him. He, as any father, felt his daughter's pain and wanted to take it away. He wanted to hold his little girl and wipe away her sorrow.

"All is fine between us," said Skiles. "I just want you to try to move forward. You know it's not too late for you Kelly. You're still young and you can have a happy life. Don't let Tom win by taking away your chance for happiness." "I'll try daddy, I love you." "I love you too Kelly."

It started to rain as Kelly walked out the front door. It was a light rain and she loved the smell it created in the little puddles on the walk in front of her. There were little drops of rain falling off the

155

leaves and little drops falling on her face between her tears. The tears she was crying was for the sadness she was feeling and the heartache she knew she faced. She knew it was almost time for her father to go. She knew her mother was no longer part of her life, and she knew Tom would soon be just a memory.

The rain was falling harder now as she walked toward the pool house. She stopped by the Sundial to read the poem her father loved so much. As she read the poem she wished she had known Madeline or perhaps she wished Madeline could have been her mother. She must have been a special lady for her father to love her so much. As she moved away a lightning bolt hit the Sundial splitting it in half.

The thunder and lightning didn't scare Kelly nor did the continuing hard rain bother her. She reached the pool and sat down on one of the outside benches. She sat there for over an hour deep in thought as the rain finally stopped. As she got up to walk back to the house she saw Emma running towards her. Emma didn't have to say a word the look on her face said it all.

As she and Emma walked back to the house she knew the passing of her father was going to be the hardest thing she had ever faced. She wondered if God would be kind to him, a man who loved from his heart and cared for all of God's creatures. Then for the first time in days a smile came to Kelly's face as she noticed a rainbow in the sky. How beautiful she thought. God's word so simple and pure painted in a beautiful picture.

Chapter 29
Present day
Bonnie's Story

Kathryn had been in the bathroom for quite a while. Brian and Laura begin to wonder if she was okay. Katie had gone next door to her home to get something and had not come back yet. Laura went to the bathroom door, knocked and said, "Are you okay, Mrs. Kistner?" There was no answer. "Brian, go next door and get Katie," said Laura. "I think something is wrong."

Kathryn was lying in the floor her heart had stopped. As Brian knelt down to pick her up he noticed she had a tube of toothpaste in her hand. On the floor next to her was the word "Tom." He moved her to the bed and went back to the bathroom. All he could think of was that in her dying moments she had left her clue there on the floor. She figured Tom was probably one of the bodies.

That answer left more questions that it answered. If Tom was one of the bodies which one, why, and how? Maybe Bonnie would have some answers. Chip and Amanda should be back with her soon.

As they left Kathryn's Laura said, "I need to call Amanda." "Are you calling her to fill her in on what just happened," he asked. "We can, she said but that is not why. I feel I need to tell her about us." "Why do you feel that way," he asked? "Do you think she will get upset?" "I'm not sure," she said. "Amanda and I had a long talk and I think she knows I am interested in you. Also I told her I thought she was making a play for Chip. I think we left that conversation with that understanding but I just want to get it out so there is no mistake."

"That's fine with me," said Brian. "At one time I was attracted to Amanda and I thought she liked me a lot also. But things never clicked with us."

"Amanda, this is Laura, Brian and I found the nanny." "That's great," said Amanda "is she in Indy?" "Before I tell you about her there is something else I need to tell you," said Laura. "Brian

---

157

and I slept together last night." There was a short silence, and then Amanda said, "Chip and I did the same."

After they filled Amanda in on what had transpired at Kathryn's house Chip said he would have his team check Army dental records. If Tom was in the Army and one of the bodies was his they should know something in a couple of days.

The police department put Bonnie in an apartment with a female police officer that was also a trained nurse. Bonnie was tired when they arrived in Indy so Chip decided to interview her the following day. He didn't like working on Saturday but it couldn't be helped. He invited the other 3 sleuths, as they continued to use that phrase for each other, to come along.

Amanda and Laura were alone now back at home. It had been a long day for Laura with having to witness Kathryn's death and Amanda's drive back from Ohio.

"So, what are your plans for you and Chip," asked Laura? "I'm not sure what you mean," she said. "Well, is he going to leave his wife, are you going to marry him or what?" "Why would you think any of that," Amanda asked? "I don't know," said Laura. "Maybe I'm just old fashioned and think if you are going to sleep with a guy you should marry him. I also think that even truer if the guy is married." "Well you know Laura I used to feel that way too. Now I'm not sure how I feel. I'm not a home wrecker. I just wanted a little romance but mostly I wanted sex."

"So how does Chip feel," Laura asked? "He didn't say a whole lot, but by his actions, I think it was for the sex too. He loves his family and I don't think he has any intentions of leaving them for me."

"So what are your plans for you and Brian," asked Amanda? "I believe we both love each other. I can't explain it any better than that." "Did Brian tell you he loved you," Amanda asked? "Yes he did and that was the great thing about him. He knew how nervous I was and he was so understanding and compassionate." "Don't you think it could just be infatuation instead of love?" "No," Laura said "I believe in him." "Well if that's the case I'm happy for the both of you. I was attracted to Brian myself when I first met him," said Amanda. "I'm not sure what happened there. Maybe it was just these bodies and this big investigation we became wrapped up in. We just turned out to be great friends."

Bonnie didn't look well to Brian when he saw her that morning. She had not aged well. Perhaps it was the hard life of drinking, smoking, and never settling down. She never married, never had any more children, and basically wasted her life on fun times. She was broke and lived on Medicare and Medicaid. She gave up what could have been a great life with a husband and daughter. But Brian wasn't judging her; he was only judging what she did not why.

After introductions, Chip filled Bonnie in on where they were, what they knew for sure, and what they didn't know. Bonnie said she didn't know anything about the bodies. She had always thought Kelly was in the casket at the funeral even though it was closed. What she could tell them was the last time she saw Kelly, Tom, and Doug.

"It was the day of Skiles funeral," she said. "I needed a little courage to face Kelly. You see she and I fought all the time. It was never really about anything just differences between us and maybe because I left the farm and didn't visit her much."

"To get the courage I needed to face her, I thought one little drink would be sufficient. But one led to two and you know the rest of that story. By the time I had to leave for the funeral, I couldn't drive so I called a taxi."

"Now, I don't remember everything I said or did. I just know I made a mockery out of the funeral and a fool of myself."

"And, there was Tom, handsome Tom. I had thought about him a lot since that night at Kelly's graduation party. I thought Kelly was a lucky girl. Of all the men I had ever had, none of them looked as good as he did, not even his dad."

"Anyway, Kelly and I got into an argument and she asked me to leave. So, I left but before I could get to a phone to call a taxi I ran into Tom in the hallway. He said he would take me home. Kelly got upset about that but Tom insisted and said he would only be gone thirty minutes. As for me, I really didn't care, I was looped just enough that nothing mattered."

"On the way home I must have been sitting in a provocative position. Tom kept starring at my legs, which were exposed all the way up. I didn't care and when I noticed he was looking I spread them apart so he could see more. He reached over and began rubbing them until his hand made it all the way up. By the time we had reached my home, I was so horny I couldn't stand it. I tried to get Tom to go in with me but he said he had to get back, Kelly would be wondering what happened to him. He said after the funeral he would find an excuse and come back over."

"Later that evening, perhaps a couple hours later, Tom knocked on my door. I was still looped and still horny. The minute he stepped into the door we starting kissing and taking our clothes off. We made it to the bed and you know the rest. I don't know how long we had been in bed but I heard a noise, looked up and saw Kelly and Doug."

"Kelly started screaming, Tom jumped up and went to her and started mumbling something about he could explain. I crawled out of bed and asked Doug what they were doing in my home. Doug said he had talked Kelly into coming over to make up with me. I was the only parent she had left and he thought we should make amends. After all, he said if I weren't drunk I would not have acted that way."

"Tom and Kelly were really into it by now. She was hitting on Tom, crying and yelling at the top of her lungs, and then she turned on me. She kept yelling, how could you mother, how could you? This is the man I love and planned to marry, how could you? I was beginning to sober up by now and I knew saying I'm sorry wouldn't have meant anything. I just kept quiet until she finished. There was this horrible moment of silence, she then looked at Doug and said, let's go home."

"That is the last time I saw either of them. I knew what I had done would never be forgiven. I had to get away out of Kelly's life forever. So I moved to Ohio and that's where I stayed. There were only a handful of people who knew where I was going and I told them not to ever tell Kelly. One of my friends found me when Kelly died. I was at the funeral but stayed away from everyone."

"I was so hurt after that, I found it hard to live with myself. I drowned myself in alcohol, and told myself what a fool I had been. I had spent my entire life looking for my life and it was always there in front of me all the time. I had finally realized my life was Kelly. Now, I'm near the end and I have found peace in God. I have asked for forgiveness and in my heart he knows I am truly sorry."

Tears were streaming down Bonnie's face. Her eyes showed a sadness of a life spend with too much excess of things that in the end didn't mean a damn. All she wanted now was to see Kelly one last time. Chip, Brian, Amanda, and Laura took her to the morgue. She pulled up a chair, sat down and started crying. She cried for about five minutes, mumbled some words over Kelly's body, and then she died.

It was raining the following Tuesday when Bonnie was buried next to Kelly and Skiles. The doctor said her heart had just stopped and it was probably due to the stress and the hard life she lived.

Brian and Amanda wanted to wait a few days to publish the story about Bonnie's death but Jack and Amanda's boss wouldn't let them. It was just as Brian and Amanda knew it would be. The whole thing was a media blitz. It was the biggest story to hit Indy in years and it wasn't even over. They still had one more body and a fugitive to go.

The next day after Bonnie's funeral Brian received a phone call from
Laura. "Brian sweetie, I have found the Ledbetter family. The
Ledbetter mentioned in the notes from grandfather has passed
away but his son is living." "Good work, is he here in the city?" "No,
he lives down around Nashville in Brown County" "That's not too
far," he said. "Let me call Chip and see if he wants to run down
there later today or tomorrow. Did you want to go with us," he
asked? "No, I think I'll stay home tomorrow, I have some more
things to research."

It was a little over an hours drive to the Ledbetter house.
They lived north of Nashville on five acres of pristine forest with a
huge lake behind the house. The house was a log cabin type and
had a huge pole barn off to the side. Brian fell in love with the pole
barn right away because of what he saw inside it. Sitting behind
door number one was a 1957 Chevrolet. Door number two had a
1967 Chevelle convertible, and door number three had a 1953
Chevy 5 window pickup truck. All that was missing was his 1970
Chevelle.

"Gentlemen, come on in, as you probably know I'm Garry."
"I'm Detective Reynolds, this is Amanda Steele from the TV station,
and this is Brian Fallon from the Indianapolis paper." "Can I get you
anything to drink or eat," Garry asked? "A soft drink would be fine
for me," said Chip. "Me too," said Brian. "Might as well make it
three," said Amanda.

"Here you go guys; I brought some chips to go with your
drinks. I always need something to snack on when I drink. Now,
what can I do for you?"

"Are you aware of this House of Blue Lights thing going on
up in Indy," asked Brian? "Sure, I am," said Garry. "I always pay
attention to stuff about that place. You know I grew up there?"

"I am surprised though that you contacted me and even

more surprised that you knew about my dad working there." We found his name on a list of employees," said Brian. "As you know we are trying to piece together the whole story of bodies and what transpired."

"I understand," said Garry, "but the only body that I know anything about is the burned one." "Burned one," said Chip! "What burned body are you talking about? None of the three we found had been burned as far as we know." "Oh, I wasn't referring to one of your three," said Garry. "I am talking about the body that was found on the property back in 1963." "I don't think any of us knows anything about that body," said Amanda. "Please continue," said Chip. "I hope you aren't going to tell me it's buried up there somewhere and now I have four bodies!"

"I'm sorry," said Garry. "I didn't mean to imply that, I didn't think about it but I guess you three wouldn't know about that body. It has been a long time since then." "Please fill us in," said Brian.

"One morning back in 1963 my dad was out near 71st street and Shadeland. If you aren't familiar with that area it is near the Skiles Test Elementary School. He was driving down 71st street and there was a body lying off in the ditch. The body had been burned to death. Of course the police were called and they did some investigations."

"What's really weird about it is I mentioned it to my wife a few years ago. At the time of the find she was dating a guy and the police questioned his brother about it. Now, she doesn't know why he was questioned but she said he lived on 71st street so I have to assume the police were asking people who lived around there. As far as the body, I have no idea what happened to it. I don't know if they found out what happened, if he was murdered or what. I suppose you guys could look up stuff up, it has to be in your records somewhere."

"I'll look into that," said Chip. I don't think it has anything to do with our case but it might be interesting information.

"We have a list of names, we would like for you to look at," said Brian. "Do you know any of these people?" "Let me see here, yes, I knew them all. It looks like a partial list of the farm workers

Test had." "Did you work for Test," asked Amanda? "No, my dad did. I worked for this guy who ran a gas station in Nora. I was there a lot and knew almost everyone. I even went swimming out there once or twice."

"Since you were there and went swimming did you know Mr. Test or his daughter Kelly," asked Brian? "Sure, I knew them. In fact Skiles gave me a St. Bernard puppy. Kelly invited my girl friend and I out there one day to swim. Skiles had this little speedboat we played with. He was a nice man. The entire family was nice as well as most of the hired hands."

"Here, I have a picture Skiles took for me of the puppy. Here is another picture of the farm area and my car, the 57 Chevy. Skiles took that picture to. I pulled these out before you got here thinking you might want to see them." "Is that the same car that is in your pole barn out there," asked Brian? "Yes, it is, I was very fortunate to be able to keep it all these years. It is still original."

"What about the other two vehicles," asked Brian? "I am an old car buff." "Well, its funny you ask, both the truck and 67 Chevelle came from the farm. They have both had an off frame restoration. The truck was one of the farm trucks and the Chevelle was Kelly's."

"How did you get those," asked Chip? "From my dad, Skiles left him the truck in his will and the car he bought off Doug Raines." "Would you be interested in selling any of them," asked Brian? "No, I can't," said Garry. "I promised my grandson Cody a Chevelle when he was born and the other two I will pass on to my granddaughter Jaelyn and my son."

"Okay, Mr. Ledbetter, before we go would you mind writing down some of the other employees that aren't on this list. It may help us in our investigation," said Brian. "I'd be glad to, I'm sorry I can't help you with the other bodies or information. I don't think I know anything else that would be helpful to you."

As they drove away, Brian was still drooling over the cars in the pole barn. "I'd sure love to have all three of those," he said. "I don't get it," said Amanda, "they are just cars. And what's the big deal about a Chevelle?" "If you have to ask---" said Brian. Chip just laughed and then he said. "You know, Ledbetter was the only name on that list that Doug said he knew. I figure the reason is that he sold him the car. I wonder why he never mentioned that?" "Who knows," said Amanda. "We all wonder about this guy Doug. He must still be a little retarded."

Chapter 31
Present Day
Doug's Story

It was Friday the eighteenth of May. The four sleuths were having lunch and going over all their notes. They were downtown eating outside in front of the restaurant just outside the door along the front of the building. There was only room for one row of tables on the walk between the door and street. The day was warm with a slight breeze. The wind was blowing just enough to carry all the smells of the city around especially the food. Of course there was the exhaust smell and the fragrance of flowers planted along the walk. There were also a few pigeons around waiting for some crumbs to be thrown their way.

Chip's phone rang. It was the coroner. After the phone conversation Chip said, "I have some good news. The body in the casket with Kelly was Tom Tyler. The Army dental records confirm it. How he got there and who killed him is still a mystery and we still don't know who the third body is." "Looks like things are normal for us," said Brian. "This whole thing has been and still is one big puzzle." Chip's phone rang again. It was headquarters. "More good news," he said. "They found Doug Raines."

Doug had been hiding in a motel in Kentucky. He was just leaving to head further south and had gotten involved in an accident. He was slightly injured and they were holding him for extradition. Chip would go pick him up tomorrow.

Chip was home watching the late news about Tom being the second body. It sure didn't take Amanda very long to break the news. Of course he understood, this whole blue lights thing was the talk of the town and had even gone national. Chip was about to retire for the evening when his phone rang. "Hello," he said. "Is this detective Reynolds," the voice asked? "Yes, may I ask who is calling," Chip said. "This is Bud Sawyer; I'm the son of Tom Tyler."

There was silence for a moment before Chip answered. He had not expected this and wasn't sure what to say if he started asking questions. All Chip knew at this time was who the body was but nothing more.

"How did you get my number Mr. Sawyer?" "I got it from the police station. They weren't going to give it to me but since my father was the body you found they did."

"What can I do for you Mr. Sawyer?" "Oh please just call me Bud. I just wanted to talk to you about my dad. Could we meet one day next week?" "Sure, I can meet with you middle or late next week," said Chip. "Are you in town?" "No, I live in Chicago, but I can drive down. Let's say next Thursday morning around 10 a.m. if that's okay?" "Sure, I'll expect you; I'll be in my office downtown. I'll text you the address if that's okay." "That will be fine," said Bud. "I'll see you then."

Doug was silent all the way to Indy. "Come on Doug," said Chip. "We know you were somehow involved in all those bodies. If you come clean, I can make it a lot easier on you. What about all that money they found in your car, he asked? You were carrying over 100,000 dollars. Where did you get that kind of money?" Doug remained silent.

Processing Doug took the remainder of the day. Things were slower on weekends anyway and finding an attorney was becoming quite a chore. They finger printed him, inventoried his belongings, and sent a transport to pick up his car. The car would be impounded and checked. Doug would be charged with lying to police and suspicion of murder. Doug's dog, which rode back with Chip and Doug, was taken to the Humane Society.

Laura and Brian were out looking for rings. Brian had not proposed to her yet but it was only a matter of time and finding the right place to do it. Brian wanted it to be special and was looking for just the right place or circumstance. He wasn't sure yet, but it had to be something unlike anything else and very special. "I like this one Brian," said Laura. "It looks pretty but it's sort of simple," he said. "I know Brian but you know I'm not a fancy person. I don't need large diamonds, just a nice ring." "Okay, but let's look around some more before we decide," he said. "And, if I go to all this expense to buy you a ring and if I do decide to ask you to marry me, what are you going to do for me Laura?"

"You are a dog," she said. "But I have a surprise all planned for you." "Speaking of surprises, I made that Cd of songs you wanted" "Great," he said, "I had almost forgotten about them." "Oh, and you will find a special one on there you didn't ask for. I am going to play it for you the next time we make love." "Oh, and what would that be," he asked. "It's a song called "Stay Awhile" by the Bells. It's about quivering," she said.
"I have one question," he said. "When can we play it?"

Amanda and Chip had cooled their extra relationship for now. They both were busy processing their new findings in the case. Amanda spent a lot of time at home and she enjoyed the relaxation. They were down to one body and Chip had Doug in custody. She figured it was just a matter of a few short days and they would have the whole story.

It had been three days after they brought Doug in from Kentucky. It was getting late in the month and Chip wanted to get this case wrapped up. The 500 mile race was this coming Sunday and it being 2012 it was the 100th year anniversary of the number eight car that won. That car was owned in part by the Test family and with all the publicity about this case there was a lot of interest. Chip didn't care that much about the race he just didn't want the distraction to take time away from his case.

Doug's car didn't yield any new evidence and it was looking like they were not finding much proof that Doug had done anything but lie. He still refused to talk and his attorney was working on his release when the bad news for Doug came in. It seems his fingerprints matched a soldier that had been missing since 1969. That soldiers name was Daniel Raines.

Daniel had been brought into the interrogation room. He was not aware at the time that they knew his real identity. "Doug or is it Daniel," said Chip? "I'm going to be blunt with you. You either start talking or I am going to turn you over to the military."

Daniel's face turned white as a sheet and his lawyer immediately asked for a consultation with his client.

One hour later they were back in the room. Daniel told them that he didn't have anything to say. They had no proof of any murder and all they had him on was lying to them. "You may be right to a point," said Chip. "However, proof will come and don't you forget the Army."

"I have been on the phone with Army headquarters and talked to a Colonel Sanders. They are just waiting in the wings for you. They have assured me that you are facing the rest of your life in prison." "I don't have that long to live," said Daniel. "I'm a pretty old man, so what does it matter?"

"Well, I'll tell what I can do," said Chip. "The Army's prison is not where you want to be. I've talked to the DA and he is willing to make a deal with you considering your age. He will take the death penalty off the table and guarantee that you will be placed in a minimum-security prison. That has to be a better deal than Army prison."

"What about the Army," Daniel's attorney said? "Are they going to still come after him when the civilian courts are done with him?" "No," said Daniel. "I have been assured by Colonel Sanders they will not pursue their case if we reach a deal with one caveat. The Colonel said they wanted some information on some guy you were in business with in Vietnam. Do you know what he is talking about?" "Yes, I know," Daniel said. "Tell him I agree."

"Give us a few minutes," the attorney said.

A few minutes later Daniel had agreed to the deal. He had carried the burden of what he had done too long and he owed the memory of his family more than silence. The truth needed to be told.

"It all started when I was in Vietnam," Daniel said. "I was career military but the money wasn't all that good unless you were in a war zone. I knew one day the war would be over, I'd go to another duty station with less pay so I was searching for someway to make money when I got involved in this black market scheme."

169

A buddy of mine, this is probably the guy Colonel Sanders was asking about, who slept in the same hooch next to me had gotten in on this brothel business. One day I noticed he had left this book out and so I took the liberty to look at it. Inside were pictures that I found out later were of these ten whores that worked for him. He was also dealing in drugs."

"When he came in that evening I told him I saw the book and after a long conversation he asked me to help him out. He said the business had grown so much he couldn't handle it all any more."

"We were stationed at this huge ninth infantry division base camp called Bearcat. It was a few miles Northeast of Saigon. We both worked in the headquarters building and we controlled all the incoming and outgoing personnel. We also had access to all the company records of the other support outfits that were based there. As a result we knew everything about everybody and were able to approach certain guys who we knew would be interested. On top of that word of mouth alone kept us busy."

"I had only been involved with him for three months and already I was making so much money it was becoming hard to hide. We both took our R&R in Hawaii at separate times and opened up several bank accounts there in other names. We had thousands of dollars deposited. You know you could get away with stuff like that back then. Today big brother is watching you and you can't hide anything."

"Well, it came time for my buddy to rotate back to the states. He had extended his tour once but he was ready to go spend some of that money. I couldn't handle the business by myself so I started looking for another partner. What I didn't know was that the military was already suspicious of what we were doing. They had planted a snitch in the tent where I slept. So to make a long story short, they found out about what I was doing and they were coming after me. I didn't want to do hard time in Ft. Leavenworth then no more than I do now. So I staged a kidnapping."

"I had gone to Saigon one day on what we called a 'day trip' to look around for a particular type of bar. I was looking for one with a back door and alley where I could stage the kidnapping. So to shorten the story I later paid a couple of guys $1000.00 each to go with me back there one day. I worked out the story and told them just to say we were in a bar when these two Vietnamese guys came in and took me. When you have money you can do anything."

"I had fake papers and hopped a ride on a helicopter to a Marine base up north. I knew if I got to a different base where I was unknown I could catch a military transport to Hawaii. Luck would have it that there was a group of 'donut dollies' there. Now if you don't know what those are it's the Red Cross girls. They visit base camps and bring donuts to the soldiers."

"Anyway the dollies were headed for Hawaii and I tagged along. Once there I just blended in and laid low. I knew they would not be able to track what happened to me for a long time if ever so they just reported me as missing in action."

"I stayed in Hawaii for about three months and finally made my way home. I found out that Mom and Dad had been killed. I knew where Doug was but I didn't want to see him. I couldn't trust him. His mind was not quite right. So I left and went to Florida. I hid out there until the money and women ran out. I hopped on a bus and headed for Indy."

"I got to Indy, I'm guessing about a week or so after Kelly died. I found Doug and he was Looney Toons. He was sitting in the back room of the house. He had Kelly's body in this big tank. It looked like an aquarium. He had a lamp on the floor next to one end of it. The lamp had a blue light in it and it made this tank kind of glow a light blue hue. It was eerie. He had become the urban legend of the house of blue lights. I just couldn't believe it. He was guarding her like someone was going to take her away from him."

"It took me three days before I could reason with him about what he was doing and who I was and where I had been. I didn't tell him my whole story, I just told him I was a prisoner and they finally let me go. He had no concept of time and place anyway and his mind was all focused on Kelly."

"He told me he almost buried her once in the basement but couldn't. He said he moved her body and that silly casket out of the basement and put her in that room. At the time he was taking care of the property and I assume it was the family house he was in. Personally I don't know how he got that tank upstairs by himself but apparently he did!

He said that Kelly had requested to be buried on the farm. I told him he should take her back to the basement and finish the job. He said he was waiting on this guy named Tom to die. He then proceeded to tell me the story of that guy. He seemed like a real jerk."

"He said Kelly wanted Tom to be buried next to her and he couldn't do that until he died. I told him that she meant next to her in the ground not next to her the same casket. I don't think he understood that, he just started crying and said he didn't know why she didn't want him instead of Tom next to her."

"I was out of money and asked Doug if he could loan me some. He looked at me and said I'll pay you 10,000 dollars if you will go kill Tom and bring him to me. Now that really scared me. Doug actually thought of something that a sane man would think of or that's what I thought. You see, killing someone was second nature to me. I had killed so many men in the army it seemed natural. So why not kill him, dump him in the casket with Kelly and then maybe Doug could move on whatever that would mean to him."

"Then Doug really shocked me. He wanted to kill Tom but after that he said he had one more thing for me to do. He wanted me to find Tom's son. He said he wanted to give him some money. Apparently Doug was feeling bad about killing Tom yet he wanted to pay off his son. Maybe it was his way of making it right. I'm still trying to figure that one out."

"I accepted the job. Doug said Tom had taken a transfer when his plant closed and he was in Ohio. I took Doug's car or I guess it was Kelly's. Doug said she gave it to him in her will. It was a 67 Chevelle. He had another car, the old Chevy I was driving. Later I sold Kelly's car. It was a nice sporty car but it brought too much attention to me and I don't like convertibles anyway."

"Did you sell it to a farm worker named Ledbetter," asked Chip? "Yes, how did you know?" "We just know," said Chip.

"Anyway I found Tom and followed him for a couple of days looking for a way to get him. Then one night he was in this bar. I parked next to his car and waited. I wasn't sure how I was going to kill him but I figured it would come to me in time."

"Tom came out of the bar with some woman he had picked up. I thought this was going to be a little more difficult than I thought. I had not planned on a woman. But as luck would have it some other guy approached them. They began to argue. All I heard was something about Tom sleeping with his wife."

"The woman must have gotten scared because she ran away as fast as she could go. Then the argument between Tom and this guy turned into a fight. This guy maneuvered himself behind Tom and grabbed him around his neck. The next thing I knew Tom was on the ground."

"The guy just stood there and stared at him for a while then he bent over and I guess he figured that he had killed him. He got up, jumped in his car and left. I thought, hey this could not have been easier. I got out and dragged him to the car, threw him in the back and three hours later I was at Doug's house."

"We put Tom in the glass tank and buried them both in the floor of the basement. After we finished Doug was out of his mind. If I had thought he was a Looney before, he was completely off his rocker now. I just wanted my money and to get out of there. Doug took me to this safe, opened it, and took out this big wad of money. I had never seen that much money before. There had to have been a million dollars in there. I asked him where it came from and he said Skiles and Kelly had given it to him."

"I guess the temptation was just too much for me. I was broke; I had no life, and no future. I couldn't be myself, I was sure the Army was still looking for me so I did it. I figured killing one more person wouldn't make any difference. And killing Doug would put him out of his misery. He was so far gone I would have had to take him to a mental hospital."

"I killed him with rat poison. It took a few days but he finally went quietly. I buried him behind the pool somewhere, took his identity and here I am. So Doug is your third body. You happy now, I solved your crime for you?"

"So, how did you take his identity so easily," asked Chip? "Did you look a lot alike?" "You don't know," said Daniel? "We were twins. I was born first, but when Doug came out, the cord was wrapped around his neck and he suffered from a lack of oxygen. My parents were ashamed of the retardation. You know back then stuff like that was kept quiet. Not many people knew about him. They rarely took him anywhere; he stayed inside most of the time. I'm not even sure all the neighbors knew. I think we moved soon after we were born and didn't have any close neighbors anyway."

"What about this son of Tom's," asked Chip? "I never looked for him," he said. "Doug said he was adopted, that's all I know. Did you think I was going to kill my brother for money then split it with some kid? I never gave him another thought."

"One more thing, I don't suppose you know anything about Kelly's death," asked Chip? "No, I don't know anything about that, why do you ask?" "It's just we don't have any details about it. There doesn't seem to be much information from the time her father died until she died." "You would have to find someone who was still there then," Daniel said. "I never questioned Doug about it; in fact I never gave it a thought either."

They took Daniel away. Chip called Amanda and asked to meet with her, Laura, and Brian. As he told them the story, tears came to Laura's eyes. "So sad," she said. "Kelly died of a broken heart because she grieved for Tom, her mother and father. Doug had so much love to give and went crazy at the end trying to give it to a dead woman. It's so strange. The urban legend of the house of blue lights was true; it was just true at a different time. So sad!"

Thursday at 10 a.m. Bud Sawyer walked into Chip's office. Bud was carrying a photo album. The album appeared to be an old album that had seen a lot of use. All the corners and part of the front had been torn.

"Hi detective, thanks for meeting me" "You're welcome and let me introduce Brian Fallon. He is the newspaper reporter that helped me among others to solve this case. I ask him to be here, I hope that is okay." "Not a problem," said Bud.

"What I want to talk to you about detective is of course my father. I want the official version of everything you know. Since we talked the other night I have heard a lot of different things from the news. I know a lot more now than I did when we talked. So can you give me the real story?"

For the next fifteen minutes Chip and Brian told Bud everything they knew about the death and burial of his father in the same casket as Kelly. Bud didn't seem at all surprised at what they told him, however the story did upset him to the point he had to excuse himself a couple of times.

"I'd like to take my father's body home if that is possible," said Bud. "I don't think that will be a problem," said Chip. "No one has claimed him until you and we haven't had time to search for any families members yet." "I can save you a lot of time," Bud said. "I know everyone in my father's family and even have pictures with me if you would like to see them. You see my adopted parents informed me of where I came from. I even grew up knowing my mom."

Bud had pictures of all of Tom's family in the album. He also had a few pictures of Kelly that were taken by Tom's father as well as pictures of the farm. Bud showed a striking resemblance to his father in the pictures, in fact Brian couldn't tell them apart.

"One more thing before I go," said Bud. "What is going to happen to the money you told me Mr. Raines had?" "I don't know," said Chip. "I can find out for you, does it matter?" "Well, since Doug Raines wanted me to have it, I thought I might inquire about that," said Bud. "After all, I think I deserve it and who else is around to get it? All of us in my family went through hell all those years wondering what happened to him." "I understand," said Chip.

Brian's cell phone rang as he walked up the stairs Monday morning. He was looking forward to his coffee and donut and until he had those he wasn't in the mood to talk. However he saw it was Chip and thought he should answer.

"Hello Chip, what can I do for you?" You remember last Thursday when we met with Bud," said Chip. "Sure, you said you were curious about him and was going to run a check on him, so did you get any results?" "As a matter of fact I did," said Chip. "It's like I said, he just seemed so cocky especially about the money. Anyway, I found out he is rich. He owns a huge building in downtown Chicago. He has also been divorced four times and has been arrested twice for wife beating." "Quite a record, I'd say he sounds a lot like his father," said Brian. "I agree," said Chip. "I just thought you'd like to know. Have a good day." "You to Chip, I'll talk to you later."

Chapter 32
Present Day
The Revelation

"Are you Detective Reynolds," asked the young man? "Yes, but please call me Chip. What can I do for you?" "I'm Benson from the student crime lab," he said. "As part of our training we are required to do case studies of past crimes where DNA was used. My assignment was the case you worked on involving the house of blue lights murders."

"Yes, I remember that well," said Chip. "Let's see, this is June and we ended that case last May just before the race so it has been a year. It was one of the most bizarre cases I have done so far in my career. So what's this about," he said.

"Well," said Benson. "I was doing a random check of the DNA from the different people involved in that crime. I was comparing it to different bodies and I don't think you are going to like what I found."

"Well you certainly have my attention," said Chip. "Please continue."

"Well," said Benson. "According to my results, and I checked it twice and my instructor also checked it so I know it's correct. The body in the one grave that you said was a Doug Raines cannot be Doug Raines."

"Is this a joke," said Chip? "If it is it's not very funny. Do you have any idea what this means?" "I know" said Benson "but it is what it is. The DNA from Daniel Raines does not match Doug Raines. Now I understand they were twins and they have to match for that to be possible."

"Okay then," said Chip. "If it's not Doug, who is it?" "We don't know," said Benson. "The DNA from that body does not match any of the other bodies. It is not even close; it stands out like a sore thumb."

"I just can't believe this," said Chip. "That SOB Daniel must have lied about the whole thing, but why would he. And if that isn't Doug, then is he still alive?"

177

"I don't know sir," said Benson, "but can't you just ask this Daniel. Maybe he can tell you." "I'd love to," said Chip "but the guy died 2 weeks ago."

Brian and Laura had just returned from their honeymoon. They had been in Hawaii for 10 days at the expense of Laura's father. He had given them an all expense paid trip, cash to spend, and money for a house down payment for their wedding gift.

Laura had moved in with Brian after the wedding leaving Amanda at her condo. Brian's condo was much too small and they had been looking at houses. They were planning on a family soon and would need the space.

During the past year Amanda had received a promotion due in part to the house of blue lights story she had taken the lead on. She was the new morning anchor on the news and she was shopping for a new Lexus.

As far as her romance, she was still single and between boy friends. Her short relationship with Chip had ended but they still talked and had lunch occasionally.

It was 11:30 a.m. when Brian's cell phone rang. "Brian, this is Chip, how are you." "I'm great," said Brian. "Laura and I just got back from our honeymoon and life is good!" "I'm glad," said Chip. "Say, I need your help. Could we meet for lunch around 12:30 today?" "Sure," said Brian, "what's up?" "I'd rather tell you in person if you don't mind," said Chip. "I'm also going to call Amanda and invite her and if you can have Laura meet us also they would be great. Let's meet at the Spaghetti Factory down the street if that's okay." "Sure," said Brian. "We'll see you there."

Brian was curious. He couldn't think of any reason Chip wanted the three of them to meet him. The only thing they were connected with was the house of blue lights. Since that had been closed for a year now it couldn't be that. Maybe he had a new caper he needed help on.

When Brian and Laura arrived Chip and Amanda were already seated. They had taken a table in the far corner. Chip was facing the front door and Amanda was sitting across from him.

"Hi there guys," said Brian. "It's good to see you both." "Gee you guys look great. Hawaii must have agreed with you," said Amanda. "You both have nice tans and big smiles on your faces." "Yes, I see that," said Chip. "Let's just see if they are still smiling like that after a few years of marriage."

As Chip told the story about what Benson had discovered all the smiles were erased from Laura and Brian's faces. Amanda almost fell out of her chair in shock and about half way fainted. "Are you okay," said Chip. "I guess so," said Amanda, "I just can't believe this."

"What I need guys," said Chip "is your help again. No one is more familiar with this case that you three. I thought if we could brainstorm we might come up with a plan to solve this thing once and for all."

"Who else knows about this," asked Amanda? "A few people at the station," said Chip "but I'm sure news will start leaking out soon. If you guys want to go ahead and break the story that is fine with me," he said.

"Okay," said Amanda, "I'm going to have to skip lunch and get back to the station." "Me too," said Brian. "That's fine," said Chip "but before you go can we plan on meeting later?" "I know," said Laura, "why don't we all meet tonight at our place. That will give me time to gather up all our files. I think we put all that stuff in a tub in the closet. I'll fix a quick dinner and we can get started. You guys show up around six. Is that okay?" "Sounds good," they all said.

"Jack, hold the presses. I have a scoop," said Brian as he stormed into Jack's office. "Hold the presses," said Jack. "Where did you get that at?" "I heard it in those old Superman TV shows from the 50's. Remember when Jimmy Olson, Lois Lane, and Clark Kent would go into the Chief's office and say that?"

"Yes, I remember, Perry White would then yell at them not to call him chief," said Jack. "So, why should I 'hold the presses' Brian?"

"Remember the statement Daniel Raines made about killing

his brother and burying him at the house of blue lights," said Brian. "Remember," said Jack. "That house of blue lights was the biggest story of last year. We hit an all time high on sales that month."

"Well apparently," said Brian, "that body was not Doug Raines. The DNA didn't match his brothers. If you give me a few minutes, I'll write the story. In the mean time you might want to turn on the TV. Amanda is on her way to the station now. It should be on there in the next few minutes." "Okay," said Jack, "get writing and I'll hold the presses for you!"

It was a real quick dinner that Laura prepared or should I say picked up. She said she was so busy getting all the information together she ran out of time. It was ten minutes until six when she got the burgers and fries on the table.

"Looks good honey," said Brian. "I see Amanda and Chip coming up the walk. You got dinner ready just in time."

After dinner the table was cleared and all the fact sheets Laura had gathered were placed in one huge pile. Amanda and Chip had both brought their own files as well. After sorting and putting the files in order of how things had happened Brian said. "I have an idea. Since Laura was so good at this the last time let's let her be the coordinator again." "Sounds great," said Chip, "Laura do you want to start?"

"Okay," she said. "Let's look at what we have. Everything was perfect; all the pieces of the puzzle came together with Daniel's story. So what we have to do is ascertain why he lied about the body being Doug. But, having said that what if he didn't lie?"

"It had to be a lie," said Chip. "The body is not Doug." "That's true," said Laura "but I see no reason for him to lie. What did he have to gain? He was going to prison no matter what. I just can't see a reason to lie here." "I agree," said Brian.

"Okay then," said Amanda. "Let's assume he didn't lie and he did bury his brother. Does it say in the transcript where he buried him or did we just assume it was the same place where the body was?"

"Good point," said Laura. "Chip, do you have the transcript

180

there?" "Yes, here it is. Let's see, it says he buried the body behind the pool somewhere." "That's it," screamed Laura! "Don't you remember the body that we thought was Doug was found in the old pet cemetery? It wasn't behind the pool. It was to the south of the pool which is the side not the back."

"That's right," said Amanda, "and that must mean there is still another body out there." "Oh, no," said Chip, "I don't know if I can do this again. We dug up almost the entire area looking for more bodies but we didn't find anything." "Exactly where did you dig," asked Brian?

"Let's see, I have an aerial view of the property showing that," said Chip. "Here it is. We dug around this area, which is the cemetery, and here, which is between the house and cemetery. We also dug around the garage area and all around the pool. But, I see where we didn't dig. Look at this area here. We only went a few yards behind the pool. We stopped where the hill begins to slope. So Daniel could have buried him there." "That would make sense," said Brian. "If Daniel wanted to hide a body he would take it as far away from the buildings as possible. There would less chance of anyone finding it that way."

"Well, I guess I need to start digging again," said Chip. "Does anyone know what is there now? I haven't been out there in a year. There may be a house sitting right on this spot."

"Okay, let's assume Daniel didn't lie and we find Doug," said Laura. "Now we have to identify the other body. "Let's also assume he did lie," said Amanda "and Doug isn't there." "Good point," said Chip.

"So we have two possibilities," said Brian. "But I think we have to at least look for Doug." "Well," I really don't have a choice but to dig," said Chip. "Let's just hope that if Doug is there we find him. We could miss him or his body could have been chewed up with all that construction."

"Now, no matter whether we find Doug or not we don't know who the other body is," said Amanda. "I'm not sure how we go about finding that out," she said. "We don't have a database with 100% of the populations DNA in it."

181

"What we do have," said Chip "is a database with missing persons in it. If we can get the approximate age of the body we may be able to pin down the time he went missing. We might be able to narrow the search down to something reasonable."

"I think we have to look at another thing," said Brian. "If we identify him we need to find out who killed him."

"Okay," said Laura, "Who is alive that lived, worked there, or knows anything about the place? We can use that list from the Ledbetter guy or contact him again. Just leave it to me I'll find some more people."

"Sounds good," said Chip. "I'll go out to the site tomorrow and see what's there. I want to thank you three for helping me. I owe you again." "Yes you do," squealed Amanda "and you can start tomorrow by taking me with you to the site." "I'd like to go also," said Brian, "you know this thing is going to make headlines again."

"Deal," said Chip. "Let's meet at nine a.m. at the Boy Scout building across Shadeland from the area. We can then take my car up to the site.

Laura had several names to research but narrowed the list down to three. The three of them had worked at the farm around the time Kelly had died. Of the three only one was a long-term employee and had been with Skiles since Madeline had died. Her name was Lucy Gordon and she was Skiles personal secretary. As far as she could tell Lucy was still employed when Skiles died. She might have some valuable information if she was still alive.

The other two had been on the farm about six years before Skiles died. One was Wayne Dillon and the other was Charles Lambert. What Laura didn't know is where on the farm they worked. They could have worked around the house or out in the farm area. Also she didn't know if they were alive. All she knew is those three had at least a questionable status. Everyone else she had found listed as employees or family had passed on.

Chip, Brian, and Amanda with camera crews in tow walked toward what looked like at least a four hundred thousand dollar house sitting where they thought Doug's body might be buried.

Chip didn't know if the department had enough money to pay for a house like that. His boss had already warned him if property had to be destroyed they might have to think about the costs involved.

"Good morning sir," Chip said as the door front door opened. "I have a search warrant here if I need it but I was hoping to get permission to look around. Are you the owner?" "Yes, I'm John Morris, what's this about?"

After a brief explanation of why they were there, Mr. Morris invited them in. He was more than willing to help out anyway he could but he wasn't too keen on having any digging done.

As far as Chip could tell the house sat approximately where the pet cemetery and pool had been located. The front lawn was where the garage had been. Apparently after they found the bodies the plots had been changed. He remembered from the crime scene the first house they were going to build was facing a different direction and was in a different area.

What interested Chip the most was the backyard. There was a deck just off the back of the house and trees a few yards away. Between the deck and trees was mostly yard with a small hill near the end. This area would seem to have been where Daniel might have buried Doug, if in fact he did kill him.

"Brian, can you get your cameraman to get this whole backyard area from the house to the tree line?" "Sure," said Brian. "Are you thinking what I am?" "Most likely," said Chip. "If the body is anywhere this would be the most likely place."

"I think we have enough information Mr. Morris. I want to thank you for your time and letting us poke around," said Chip. "Do you think you will want to dig up my yard," Mr. Morris asked? "I'm not sure yet," Chip said. "We have a few more theories to examine before we make any firm conclusions. If we decide we need to, then the office will get with you to discuss details, payment for property and other costs that might be involved."

"This sure is a beautiful place," Amanda said as they walked toward the park. "I saw a lot of pictures of what this area looked like when it was a farm. This new house looks prettier than the farm house but I think I prefer the simplicity of the old." "The woods are a nice touch no matter which one you prefer," said Brian. "I myself would love to live up here."

"Why don't you buy up here," asked Chip? "Money would be the main reason," said Brian. "I don't think we could swing it on my salary and if we have children, which we plan on doing, Laura will not be able to work for sometime."

"I thought Laura's father was loaded," said Chip. "Well he is pretty well off," said Brian. "But you know that's his money. He did give us a huge amount of money as a wedding gift. We plan to use it for a down payment on a house. We would have to get an extraordinary deal to swing this area."

As they neared the car Chip asked Brian to give Laura a call to see if she had any information yet. After the call he told them she had three leads and she would text them to all of their phones.

"What are you going to do about digging up Mr. Morris's backyard Chip," asked Amanda? "What I am thinking," said Chip "is exactly what I told him. I don't want to do anything until we have more information. If we do find out whom the body is and if there is a connection to Doug we might have a better picture of what we need to do."

"This whole thing is just driving me crazy," said Chip. "Why couldn't this happen two weeks ago when Daniel was alive? Here we are thinking what if he lied, what if he didn't, where is Doug, is Doug really dead? Gee whiz, what a mess! I think I need a drink!"

Amanda was laughing at Chip. She had never seen him so rattled or confused. "Why are you laughing," asked Brian? "I was laughing at Chip," she said. "He is so up tight over this whole thing. I myself think it's great. Just think I may get another promotion!"

Chapter 33
Present Day
Wayne and Diane

It had been three days since the revelation had occurred that Doug was not the body. Laura had located the three people or at least two of them. Charles Lambert had passed away two years ago. Wayne Dillon was still alive and lived in Indianapolis. The third person, Lucy was alive and well in Miami, Florida.

Chip called the Miami police and told them the "farm" story. He asked if they could go to Lucy's and find out what she knew and if she would be willing to make a statement.

Chip was at his desk when the phone rang. "Detective Reynolds," he said, "May I help you?" "This is Lucy Gordon," said the voice on the other end. "I understand you want a statement from me." "Well yes if you have some pertinent information about the case," Chip said.

"I'm not sure whether I can help you or not," she said. "That bozo you sent to talk to me couldn't remember enough of what you told him to give me any clues as to what you wanted. However, I could use some excitement and I'm willing to come to Indianapolis and talk to you." "That would be great," said Chip. "When can you come?" "I'll be there tomorrow; I'll contact you when I get in." Oh, one more thing Chip. This bozo down here did say you were looking for others who had connections to the farm. Have you talked to Diane Cummings? Who is she," asked Chip? "Don't tell me you are a bunch of bozos up there too," she said. "She was Kelly's best friend in college."

"Laura, this is Chip. I have another name for you, Diane Cummings." "That name sounds familiar," she said. "She was Kelly's best friend in college," said Chip. "Oh, wait a minute," said Laura. "I do remember running across her name the first time we went through this. Someone mentioned her but I forgot about her because we solved the case. Where did you get her name," she asked? "I got it from Lucy Gordon who is flying in tomorrow."

"Okay, so when are you going to interview Wayne," Laura asked? "I'm going to do that later today," Chip said.

"Diane Cummings was easy to find. She was still in Indianapolis. She was divorced with three children and had taken her maiden name back. She was still working but was close to retirement.

Wayne Dillon lived on the far west side of Indy. He was fifty-eight and still working. He worked driving a tool truck around town selling his wares to mechanics. He had agreed to be home to meet with Chip. Wayne said he had some pictures Chip might be interested in.

Wayne lived in a modest house in the little town of Avon. He was married with 5 children. All of his children had left home and only he and his wife lived there.

Brian had agreed to go with Chip to interview him. Amanda and Laura had declined. Both of them had other projects they were working on.

Brian rang the doorbell. A short burley bald man answered. "Come on in," said Wayne. "Welcome to my home. Would either of you like something to drink?" "I'll take a soft drink if you have it," said Chip. "Make that two," said Brian.

"Here you go guys I brought one Pepsi and one Coke. Choose your poison. Let's sit here in the living room; I have the pictures here on the end table."

The pictures were of the dog and cat pens, the milk barn, one of the tunnels, the house and the garage. He also had a few pictures of people. One was with him and Doug, one with Charles and himself, and one with Kelly and Doug. The house picture had three people standing in front of it. One was Skiles, one was Lucy, and the other one he didn't know. It was a man but Wayne said he only saw him the one time and it just happen to be the day he was taking pictures. He wasn't' sure of the date, he knew it was late summer 1973 and a few months before Skiles passed away.

"Would you mind if we borrowed these pictures," asked Chip? "No, not all," said Wayne.

"Wayne, I'm sure you are familiar with the bodies we found

last year out on the farm aren't you," asked Chip? "Yes, I watched and read all about them. I also wondered why you didn't contact me then. I was going to come forward but just before I did you guys solved the case or thought you did, until I saw on the news you don't have the identity of that last body."

"Can you tell us anything at all that might help identify the body," asked Brian?

"Well," he said, "you know that unknown guy in the picture with Skiles and Lucy? I saw him drive in that day but he never left. Maybe it's him. I remember the car because it was a bright red corvette. He parked it in front of the storage barn."

"Charles and I were working around the house that day and we walked over and looked at it. The car was still there the next morning and I didn't think that was unusual because that happened all the time. Later that morning I noticed the car was gone. Charles said he saw the car leave but a woman was driving it. Charles said he was too far away to see who it was." "Did you by any chance see the license plate," asked Chip? "I did, he said but I didn't pay any attention to it because it was an Indiana plate."

"Is there anything else you can remember that was going on around that time," asked Chip? "Not really," said Wayne. "Most days were just normal days. In fact that day was just as normal as any other. The reason I remember it was because of the car."

"Did you stay there very long after Mr. Test died," asked Chip. "No, I quit like a week later. I had another job lined up before he died."

"Okay, then thanks for your time," said Chip. "Here is my card and if you can remember anything else, please call me."

"What do you think about the unknown man in the picture Chip?" Brian said as they drove away. "I don't know," he said. "Other than a woman driving the car that morning, I don't see anything there. I don't think it means much. It could just be innocent. I'll have the lab look at the picture of the unknown guy but it's so small and I doubt if I get anywhere with that."

"Brian why don't you call Laura and see if she has any leads on Kelly's best friend in college?" "Okay," Chip, "I can do that now.

"Hi Honey," Brian said, when Laura answered the phone. "Hi," she said. "What's up?" "We just left that Wayne guys house and was wondering if you had any luck with finding Diane." "Yes I did, in fact I already talked to her, and she does not seem to be very cooperative." "What do you mean?" Brian asked. "Well, she said she followed the story a year ago but kept quiet about knowing anything. She said she didn't want to get involved and still didn't."

"I didn't push it any further than that. I just told her that the police might want to talk to her. Tell Chip I'll text him her phone number and work address and he can handle it." "Okay honey, thanks." "Oh, before you go," she said. "What happened with Wayne?"

"The only thing we got from Wayne was a few pictures and a story about a red Corvette. We don't know if it's anything to probe into yet or not. I'll fill you in later tonight."

The next morning Chip went to see Diane. He thought it best to go alone since Laura had said she was uncooperative.

Diane worked for a consulting company near Carmel, just north of Indianapolis. As he entered the building he wasn't sure how to approach her. He couldn't bully her into telling me anything like he had done Daniel. As far as he knew Diane hadn't done anything wrong.

"I'm Detective Reynolds," he said to the receptionist. "I'm here to see Diane Cummings." "Do you have an appointment sir or is this one of those police things where you just walk in?" "No, I don't have an appointment but I did call her. She knows I'm coming," Chip said in a stern tone. He did not appreciate the receptionist's remark.

"This way sir," the receptionist said. She led Chip down a hall way to Diane's office. They passed a couple of other offices on the way. Chip thought they were decorated sort of extravagantly so this must be a pretty solid firm to work for.

Diane's office was no different. The furniture was rich dark leather and the desk was a solid cherry color. Behind her desk was a nice view of the parking lot. That was the only thing negative about the office.

"I told this other lady I didn't have anything to tell," Diane said to Chip. "Well you never know," he said. "Any small piece of information might be of some value. If you add enough small pieces together you sometimes get a big piece."

"How long did you know Kelly?" Chip asked. "We met in college and remained best friends until she died," said Diane.

"When was the last time you spoke or saw her," he asked? "I'm not sure," she said. "I think it was a few weeks before she died. She had been sick and didn't seem herself the last time I had seen her so I was calling to check on her. After she died I was so torn within. I had gotten busy with family and work and never got out to see her. I let her down when she needed me most."

"Did you know Doug Raines?" Chip asked. "Of course, I knew almost everyone except the farm hands. Anyone who worked around the house I knew. During my college years I spent a lot of time swimming in that grand pool."

"Look detective," said Diane. "It's not so much that I don't want to get involved I just don't know anything about this body you can't identify. If I knew something that would help I'd tell you but I don't. You could better serve your investigation somewhere else."

"I understand," said Chip. "Just one more question and I'll go. I understand you and Kelly took a trip to the Bahamas. Was there anything special about that trip or did anything happen there out of the ordinary?" "It was just a couple of girls getting away for a few days," she said. "Skiles had given Kelly two tickets for her graduation and we went. It's that simple."

"Okay," said Chip, "here is my card if you remember anything at all. Thank you for your time."

After Chip left, Diane breathed a huge sigh. She didn't know anything that would help him. She knew a lot about Tom of course and then there was that thing that happened in the Bahamas. But again, she thought to herself there was nothing she knew that was pertinent to the investigation. All she knew was a secret that she had promised to Kelly and she wasn't sharing that.

Chapter 34
Present Day
Bruce

It was Friday morning; Chip had just gotten to the office and was going over his notes. He had given the lab the pictures but found them on his desk this morning with a note. The note said they didn't have enough information or picture quality to identify the unknown guy.

He needed to get with the other three colleagues to go over what they had and do some brainstorming. Laura, Brian, and Amanda had made his job so much easier. If it had not been for those three he was not sure he would ever have solved anything.

Just as he was about to give them a call his phone rang. The man on the phone introduced himself as Bruce Bowser, Lucy Gordon's attorney. Bruce wanted to visit with Chip prior too any conversation he was to have with Lucy. Chip set up an appointment for ten. He had no idea why Lucy had an attorney but he was curious.

Bruce was prompt. It was exactly ten when he arrived. Chip took him to a conference room for their discussion. Bruce was an older man, perhaps in his sixties. He had a lot of hair for an older man but it was white as snow. He was well dressed and groomed.

"So I'm puzzled," said Chip. "Why would Lucy need an attorney?" "We are not sure," he said "that is why I am here. I need to find out what it is you are looking for. If Lucy knows anything and can be implicated in any way then I would be needed. So what I need from you detective is the whole story from beginning to end. I can then make a decision on if I am needed."

For the next hour Chip went over every detail from the discovery of the glass casket to where they were now.

"May I have the name and number of your District Attorney?" Bruce asked. "Sure," said Chip "but why would you need that." "Based on what you have told me," said Bruce I think I need to discuss something with him." "I can see if he is available now if you wish," said Chip. "Sure," said Bruce. "I'll be right back," said

Chip.

"He is on his way Bruce; he said he would be here in about thirty minutes."

During the next thirty minutes before the DA arrived Bruce spent most of the time on the phone with Lucy. When he was finished he asked Chip if he had found Diane. Chip told him he had interviewed her yesterday. Bruce then requested her contact information. He stated that Lucy would like to see her while she was in town.

Paul Langley introduced himself to Bruce. Paul was the district attorney who had worked on the previous case against Daniel Raines. "What can I do for you?" Paul asked Bruce. "My client, Lucy Gordon wants full immunity for her testimony." "Why would she need immunity," Chip asked? "Let's just say this," said Bruce. "Lucy thinks she will be of tremendous help to you in solving this case. During her testimony certain facts may come out that would make one think she had some involvement in what transpired. Believe me my client is not guilty of any heinous crime. However she may be in a gray area when it comes to let's say not coming forth at the time with information."

"Let me understand this," said Paul. "You are hinting that your client may have broken some little law but she is innocent of anything major." "Yes, you could say that," said Bruce.

"How old is Lucy," asked Paul? "She is eighty seven," said Bruce. "If you are thinking she should not be worried about prosecution because she would probably die before any sentence could be carried out, you are wrong. Her mother lived to be a hundred and three and her dad was ninety nine. If you would meet her, you would think she acted and talked like a much younger person."

"Okay, Bruce I'll tell you what I'm willing to do," said Paul. "Let's say something comes out in this testimony that implicates her in some small way. I will guarantee you probation with no time served." "No deal," Bruce said. "It's complete immunity or nothing. Lucy walks as if nothing ever happened. I know you can do this Paul,

---

191

you just want to play hardball and believe me this is not the time. If you want this mystery solved you know and I know Lucy is your only hope."

"Okay," said Paul "but with one stipulation. "If she committed murder the deal is off." "I'll agree to that," said Bruce. "Here is my card, call me when you have the papers and I'll meet you."

"As far as you, detective," said Bruce. "I'll set the meeting up and give you a call as to the time and place. You need to know Lucy wants to control this meeting. That is the way she is. It will be a late morning meeting with lunch to follow and Lucy will pay it for. Let me know what the head count is when I contact you. Good day, gentlemen. It was a pleasure," said Bruce.

As he left the room Chip's phone rang. "Hello, this is detective Reynolds." "This is Mr. Morris." I just received a letter from your office about digging up my back yard. It's a bunch of legal mumbo jumbo so I have to get with my attorney. I hate to throw away money on legal fees and I thought maybe we could just meet and work out a simple agreement. It is not going to matter to me anyway. You see once my wife found out about the body she has been a nervous wreck. My wife has this thing about ghosts and now she is seeing visions and well, let's just say she wants to move.

Are you married detective?" "Yes," said Chip. "Then you know how a wife can be. If they aren't happy, no one is happy. So I am going to call a realtor and put my house on the market."

"I'm sorry about that Mr. Morris," Chip said. "I may however be able to help with the house sale. I know a couple who might be interested if the price is right." "That sounds great," he said. "If I can save a realtor fee, I could take a little less." "Okay, said Chip. I'll have them give you a call."

It was Sunday afternoon, Brian and Laura had been out to see Mr. Morris's house. Laura fell in love with it and said she just had to have it. Mr. Morris gave them his price, which Brian thought was reasonable but it was still a little too much for their budget.

Laura, on the other hand said she knew they could afford it if they had a little more money for the down payment. She said she would ask her father.

Mr. Needham was just about to fall asleep for his Sunday afternoon nap when the phone rang. "Hello Daddy," Laura said. "Did I wake you?" "That's all right," her father said. "I had to get up to answer the phone anyway!" "You are so funny daddy, so funny."

"Okay Laura, what do you want," he asked? "Do I have to want anything to call my daddy," she said. "Laura, every time you call me daddy my wallet starts shaking, my bank account starts sweating, and my banker has a heart attack."

"Well," she said "you remember that down payment money you gave us for our wedding present?" "Do you think you could maybe come up with just a little more?" "What's a little," he said? "I'll tell you what daddy. Why don't I come by, pick you up and take you for a ride? I want to show you this beautiful house." "Okay little girl," he said. I'm hooked, come get me.

Chapter 35
Present Day
Lucy's Story

Lucy was still as spry as she was in her youth. Her mind was sharp and her body was still in great shape. Even though she was now 87 she looked 60.

She had never married although she had many lovers over the years. She found she only needed men occasionally and figured why buy the bull when you get all the free meat you wanted if you were the cow.

Lucy didn't need a man for money either. During her years working on the farm she put aside a lot of money. She had made smart investments and as a result was a millionaire. She thought to herself many times that if Skiles has listened to her she could have brought him back from the brink of bankruptcy. She never thought it was her fault to begin with. Most of the fault was due to an economic turndown, no matter what Skiles thought.

The meeting was to take place at the downtown Radisson hotel. Chip thought it was a little extravagant just for a simple police matter but what did he care? All he wanted was to find out for the last time what the hell had happened. He was tired of the house of blue lights and the never-ending drama.

Brian and Amanda brought a camera crew, with Lucy's permission of course. She said she didn't care since the DA had granted her immunity. Other than the camera guys, the only ones there was Brian, Amanda, Laura, Chip, Diane Cummings, and Lucy's attorney.

Lucy had visited Diane over the weekend and invited her. Lucy wanted Diane to know what happened since she was Kelly's best friend.

"Well let's get this over with," said Lucy, "Does everyone have something to drink and a snack? I'm going to have this donut and a glass of milk," she said, as she picked up a bottle of milk and shook it.

"Okay," said Chip. "But I have a question. Why do you shake the milk?" "Habit," she said. When we were on the farm Skiles had fresh milk. If you have never seen fresh milk it has all the cream at the top. You have to mix it up before you drink it. I know there is not much cream in this but this particular habit is hard to break."

"Don't you guys know anything about farm life?" "Well, that clears that mystery up," said Chip. "I hope you can clear this body one up. I have to assume Lucy that from our phone conversation and the conversation I had with your attorney that you now know as much, and we hope more, about this strange case as we do."

"First," she said let me tell you that Kathryn gave you a hint as to who the body was. Brian and I were talking before you got here Chip. He told me about Kathryn and the toothpaste. He said she had written the words 'Tom' on the floor. If you had paid attention and not jumped to conclusions you would have realized Kathryn was gone by the time these burials were going on at the farm. Therefore she would have no knowledge of Tom being buried in one of those graves. In fact she may not have known Tom was even dead."

"But, Tom was in one of the graves," said Chip.

"Sure he was," Lucy said. "However that was just a stroke of luck on your part that it turned out that way."

"Now, let me get back to where I was before I was interrupted! I was talking about Kathryn. She came back to the farm to visit from time to time and we even saw each other away from the farm. So she did not know about what went on when she was away unless Kelly or I told her."

"On one such visit she and I had a long conversation while sitting on the deck of the pool house. We were up there one afternoon and I had more than the normal two drinks that I allowed myself. Now, you have to remember that I trusted Kathryn with my life. Even if I hadn't been drunk I would have been okay confiding in her. If she liked you and were her friend she would take any secret to the grave with her. Even if that secret was horrible she would keep it if it meant protecting the ones she loved."

195

"But, before I get to the story of what I told her that day let me tell you whom the body is. You remember what I said about Kathryn writing Tom with the toothpaste. The word she was writing wasn't Tom it was Tompkins. She didn't have time to finish it before she died."

"Holy Cow," said Laura. "I remember now. Her daughter told us how proper she was and how much importance she placed on last names. It was right there in front of us. We knew about this guy Tom and we just assumed."

"Who the hell is Tompkins," asked Chip?

"His full name was Curtis Tompkins; he was Kelly's lover in the Bahamas," said Lucy. "Don't tell me we have to go to the Bahamas next," said Chip. "I don't think the department has the funds for that."

"Who Killed Curtis," asked Brian? "Doug Raines did," said Lucy. "Why would he do that and how," asked Chip? "That's the story I'm about to tell you," said Lucy.

"It had been about two months after Kelly and Diane returned from the Bahamas. Kelly had gone to see her physiatrist that day and I'm not sure where else but she didn't come home until late afternoon."

"I was up in my office standing behind Keith's desk looking out the window and I saw this man walking toward the front door. I didn't give it much thought; I figured it was just another visitor. There were a lot of visitors at the farm."

"A few minutes later, Emma came to the office and said Skiles wanted to see me. I grabbed my notebook in case I needed to take notes and went on down. Skiles and this guy were in the piano room. They were just sitting there talking and drinking soft drinks."

"Skiles introduced him as Curtis Tompkins from Atlanta, Georgia. Skiles said he had met Kelly and Diane in the Bahamas."

"Let me interrupt you," said Chip. "I have a picture here of someone. Is this Mr. Tompkins?" "Yes," said Lucy. "I remember standing there that day. Where did you get it?" "An employee named Wayne Dillon gave it to me," said Chip. "Oh I remember him," said Lucy "but I was unaware he had taken that picture."

196

"Sorry to interrupt, please continue," said Chip.

"Well, we sat and talked a few minutes and Skiles told me that Curtis had some business proposals for us. Skiles said in talking with Kelly in the Bahamas that Curtis thought he might be able to help us create what he called a 'profit center.' He told me to spend some time with Curtis to see if we might be interested. He also asked me if I knew where Kelly was because Curtis would like to see her. I told him I didn't know but I'd try to find out."

"Skiles had to leave; he was having a business meeting in Chicago and wouldn't be back for a couple of days. Actually, he had a doctor's appointment with some specialist up there. As you know or as I assume you know by now he was having heart trouble. I'm not too sure you guys know much of anything up here. Well, let me take that back. I guess you know a little. You did solve most of the case and you did locate me."

"Anyway, after the conversation we walked out on the porch and I guess that is when the picture was taken. From there I took Curtis on a short tour of the farm and we ended up at the pool house. We had Emma bring us some lunch, I fixed us some drinks and we talked a couple of hours about business. Then the conversation turned to Kelly. Then we had a few more drinks. Of course I was drinking alcohol and Curtis was drinking cokes."

"Well, who could guess but apparently I was feeling a little frisky that day. I had worn a tight skirt and the friskier I got the higher the skirt seemed to ride up. I also kept putting my hand on Curtis's leg and I guess he thought I was making a pass. The more I rubbed his leg, the friendlier he became. He started talking about what had happened in the Bahamas with Kelly. Well, let me tell you. You take a story like he told. Mix it with a little booze, and your feeling of a little frisky turns into down right horny!"

"Now, in all honesty I must tell you that Curtis was a nice guy. He didn't just lie down and let me take complete control of him. I could tell that he wasn't sure about what was about to happen between him and me. After all he had come a long way to present a business deal and see Kelly. Mixing that and sex with a stranger wasn't his style. So I'll just say that it took me awhile to

---

seduce him. But when I spread my legs wider than the Grand Canyon, the man in him forgot any rational thought he might have had."

Lucy paused for a moment and a smile formed across her face. The room became so quiet you could hear the sounds of the city outside. The smile soon turned into a somber look as a tear dropped from her right eye.

"Are you okay," asked Brian? "Yes, I'm sorry," said Lucy. "Memories are funny; they can also turn quickly into reminders of things you wish you could forget."

"Anyway, after the Grand Canyon thing we made our way to the elevator then upstairs to the bedroom. Now I'm sure you are not interested in all the details so I'll just say---it was great."

"It was getting late and I figured Kelly should be home by now. We went back downstairs and I told Curtis to wait there for me. I found Kelly and took her to the pool house. I told her I had a surprise for her."

"When we walked in and Kelly saw Curtis I could tell she didn't like the surprise. Curtis said it was good to see her and Kelly asked him what he was doing there. He said he had a business proposal for Skiles and he wanted to see her again. Kelly said that was nice and she didn't want to be rude but she wanted to forget about what happened in the Bahamas and he shouldn't have come."

"Well, you could tell Curtis was upset. He didn't know what to say. I also think he was embarrassed. Then Kelly saw lipstick on his shirt and she glanced at me and I guess put two and two together. She then began crying and yelling at Curtis. She told Curtis that she couldn't believe him. She said something about him screwing her on a beach then coming here and screwing me on a pretense of seeing her. Then, bless her heart, she said she got enough of that kind of treatment from Tom. I felt horrible but what was done was done."

"I didn't know what to say, she was blaming Curtis and it was my fault but Kelly was in no mood to hear any explanations. She just kept yelling, and crying and finally just stomped out."

"What I didn't know at the time is Doug had been following Kelly. He had hidden in the stairway and had overheard everything. He had been acting strange anyway ever since Kelly had gotten back from the Bahamas. I don't know if he had missed her or was jealous she had gone or what. I just know he seemed different and was always following her around like a little puppy."

"As soon as the door closed behind Kelly Doug walked into the room. He had this angry hurt weird look on his face and was moving very fast toward the kitchen. He grabbed a knife and came at Curtis. It all happened so fast. Curtis stood up to protect himself but Doug was too fast. Doug was yelling something like you will never hurt my Kelly again as he stabbed him over and over."

"I think Curtis died within a few seconds. Then Doug sat down beside him and starting crying. About that time Kelly came back. When she saw Doug and Curtis she didn't say a word. She just stared for a moment then came over to Doug and said. What have you done Doug?"

"I didn't know what to do. I told Kelly we should call the police. She said no. She said she had to protect Doug he was family. She asked me if I would be willing to help her and keep this a secret."

"It was then I had to make up my mind. Was I going to be loyal to the family or was I going to rat on Doug. I think you know what my choice was."

"It took us until dark to clean up the blood, wash the knife and get Doug to settle down. We explained to Doug that it was an accident. We told him that Curtis had picked a fight with him and he was only protecting himself. Whether he believed it or not we convinced him never to tell a soul."

"We dragged the body to the pet cemetery, found a shovel and dug a hole. We removed most of the clothing and all his personal stuff and buried him. We told Doug that if anyone questioned a new grave he was to say that a couple of cats died."

"Needless to say it was a long night for all of us but morning finally came. We all slept in the pool house that night and were up and gone early before anyone knew."

"The next problem was the corvette he drove, his clothes, and personal stuff. The clothes and personal stuff I took home and later burned in an outside trash burner. I went out to the car, looked inside, and found some papers from a rental company here in Indy. Well, I couldn't take it back there and be seen. I had to think of something else."

"As I was walking away from the car, Kathryn pulled in. I stopped and waited on her. My mind was racing a hundred miles a minute. Then it came to me. I'd take the car somewhere and have Kathryn pick me up and bring me back. I had two places in mind and I'd figure that out as I drove. So I made up a story to tell Kathryn about a guy I had there yesterday. I told her we were drinking and he got to drunk to drive and I had promised to bring his car to him."

"She had no reason not to believe me; people came and went at the farm all the time and a lot of them drank. I was a little concerned that she might ask me about the gloves. I had taken a pair of Playtex gloves from the pool house. I wore them when I went to the car so I wouldn't leave any fingerprints. I had them folded in my right hand while we were talking and I was afraid she would ask me what I was doing wearing gloves. I was all out of stories and had no idea what I'd tell her. However she never mentioned them so maybe she didn't notice."

"We went to my office; I grabbed my purse and stuck the gloves inside. I told her to wait there for fifteen minutes then come pick me up on Monument circle in front of the Test building. I walked out to the car, put the gloves back on, got in, slumped down as far as I could in the seat, hoping none of the farm hands would recognize me, and drove downtown."

"I thought I'd either park in one of the parking garages close to the Test building or maybe in one of the delivery alleys. When I got there, I found an alley off Ohio Street that was deserted. I pulled in, jumped out and walked away. I knew it wouldn't be long before a delivery truck came by and they would call the police."

"It only took a few minutes to walk to the Test building. I went inside, used the restroom, dumped the gloves, and when I came out, Kathryn was there."

"It was about a week later when I had that conversation with Kathryn that I mentioned earlier. She was very upset over it but promised to keep the secret. In fact, if she had lived and told you it was Tompkins in the grave, I'm not sure she would have told you that Doug killed him. Kathryn was very loyal."

"There might be one other thing you can help us with," said Brian. "We don't have a clear picture of what happened to Kelly. After Skiles death there is just no information on the farm or any the events leading up to her death?"

"Do you think there was some foul play involved with Kelly," asked Lucy? "We don't have any reason to believe that," said Chip. "We would just like the entire story so there are no loose ends that come back to bite us." "Okay I can help you with that but first let's do lunch."

All of the attendees went to the lunch Lucy had provided. Lucy had a special treat for everyone. She had brought every person their own Chunky bar. Of course this candy bar was for desert and she told them before lunch to save room for something special.

The main course consisted of grilled chicken, mashed potatoes with gravy, and black eyed peas. Drinks were tea, assorted soft drinks, beer, and mixed drinks if you wanted.

"Okay folks before we go back to the meeting I want to give you the desert, said Lucy. Lucy walked over to a table where she had placed a small attaché case. She picked up the case, brought it back to the lunch table, opened it and passed out the candy bars.

"Now, I know all of you are wondering about this Chunky bar, said Lucy. You may not know this but Skiles had a sweet tooth. He loved these chunky bars. I don't know if it was the raisins, the chocolate or what or maybe the mixture of everything. What I do know is that everyday he would eat at least one small piece. He always bought the largest bar he could find and he kept it in the fridge on the back porch. Then as soon as dinner was over he would go get his piece of candy and eat it. I thought this would be a nice touch to lunch. It is my way of paying tribute to Skiles. After all, if it wasn't for him none of us would be here. Isn't it funny how one person can affect the lives of so many?" "Very well put," said Brian.

"I think it was very thoughtful of you Lucy and I for one appreciate it."

"Okay, if everyone's ready and has their 'chunky' could we get back to the meeting, I'd like to get this wrapped up," said Chip?

Chapter 36
Present Day
Kelly's Story

"I was hoping you wouldn't ask me about Kelly and just let it go that she died of a broken heart," said Lucy. "Are you saying she didn't," asked Chip? "I didn't say that detective and don't worry I don't think there is a body or murder for you to solve in this story." "What do you mean you think," asked Chip. "Just listen, detective, just listen," said Lucy.

"After Skiles death things moved and changed at the farm. There was a group of attorneys that Skiles and I worked with. Kelly and I met with them three days after the funeral. We settled Skiles's will which took us about a month and satisfied the IRS. I don't know what you know about the estate but Skiles owed a lot of money to those tax bozos. It took every dime Skiles had and then some to settle everything."

"We had to start with shutting down the farm. All the farm equipment was sold along with the farm animals. We also had to sell most of the remaining land Skiles owned except for the farm area that later became the nature park and now is a subdivision as I understand it. Of course since we shut down the farm we had to let most of the workers go."

"After all was settled, the only workers left were Doug, Emma, Oakley, and myself. Oakley was the handyman and took care of all the heavy maintenance. Of course Emma did the shopping, laundry, house cleaning, and cooking. Doug took care of the cats and dogs and the light maintenance around the house. I did all the paperwork, payrolls, and bill paying."

"We had it figured down to the penny on what we could afford to spend. There was enough money to maintain the place for a year and then we were going to turn it over to the state as per Skiles's will. I was doing some investments for Doug and Kelly and with the money Skiles had given them there should have been enough to keep them for a lot of years."

"By August of seventy four we were at the stage of status

203

quo just waiting out the rest of the year before we had to vacate the property. During this time we started giving away the cats and dogs. Now I understand Doug may have stayed there as the caretaker after Kelly died, I don't know about that I left right after her funeral."

"It was a hot day in late August. I had seen Kelly earlier that morning and she had been drinking heavily. As you know her mother had stopped making contact and Tom had moved away. She was still playing those silly sad records and even though she still saw Dr. Castle her depression was no better."

"It was just after lunch and I was in my office when Doug came up the stairs with this funny look on his face. He said Kelly was in the pool house and wanted to see me. When I got there she was on the couch naked. She told me her and Doug had been drinking. Now Doug was not a drinker so you can imagine how a couple of drinks affected him. Anyway one thing led to another and Doug had raped her. She was to drunk to make any decisions of what to do so I covered her up, fixed her some food and stayed with her the rest of the day. I don't know where Doug went, I didn't' see him again until the next day."

"That next day Kelly said she wanted to forget about the whole thing. I advised her not to. I said that I thought Doug might be dangerous, after all he had killed Curtis. She said it was just the alcohol and he would not have raped her in normal circumstances."

"Now, I'm getting tired and I think I'll skip all the little details and just tell you that as a result of this rape Kelly got pregnant and about two or three weeks later she had a miscarriage. She refused to go the doctor and I treated her as best I could."

"I'm not sure she ever recovered from that miscarriage. It was so hard to tell with her depression whether she was physically sick or it was just the depression. She stopped eating and slept most of the time."

"She kept getting worse so I called Dr. Castle and asked him if he would come see her. He came the next day and said she should go to the hospital but she refused. Two days later she died."

"Now everybody thinks she died of a broken heart over Tom

204

,her father, and mother. That may be true but she was also distraught over the loss of the child. And who knows she could have been physically hurt from the miscarriage, I'm no doctor."

"Why didn't they do an autopsy," asked Chip? "I think it's because Dr. Castle thought she grieved herself to death. Since he had recently seen her and knew her history he signed the death certificate and no one questioned it."

"Personally I find it ironic that Kelly's depression over all that had happened could have been cured with Madeline's treatment and maybe she would still be alive," said Lucy.

"I don't think I or anyone else here understands what treatment you are talking about," said Brian.

"I'm sorry," said Lucy. "I didn't think before I said that. Of course you didn't know anything about Madeline. I guess I might as well fill you in on that also."

"I was reading your Indianapolis newspaper yesterday when I realized the similarities between the two. There was an article about magnetic therapy curing depression."

"A colleague of mine wrote that," said Brian. "It's called TMS and it uses magnetic stimulation to balance the brain's chemical makeup."

"Very good," said Lucy. "But let me ask you all a question. Didn't any of you ever wonder about the glass casket? Didn't it look weird with terminals on it? Didn't any of you wonder where it came from or why? Well, let me answer those questions for you, of course you didn't because you are all a bunch of bozos!"

"Come to think of it," said Chip, "we were more into the bodies than what a couple of them were in, but I guess it does seem strange."

"Well," said Lucy. "I assume you know and I say that lightly, that Madeline was Skiles's wife. Madeline died just before Skiles hired me. I suppose I had been employed about six months when one day Skiles began talking to me about Madeline. He told me in confidence and didn't want me blabbing the story all over town, which I never did."

"It seems that glass casket was built especially to submerse

Madeline in while they attached all these wires to it. Skiles said they ran electricity through the wires around Madeline to create a magnetic force to change her chemical makeup. It was called something different then but it sounds like almost the same thing they are doing today. I think the only difference is with Madeline they were trying to treat a brain tumor instead of depression."

"So, I just think after all these years medicine has taken a step backwards," said Lucy. "Just think if they could have used that on Kelly and Bonnie for their depression who knows how different things would have been."

"Anyway as I said, I left soon after Kelly died. I wrapped up all the loose ends, paid all the final checks and said my good-byes."

"That's quite a story," said Brian. "I don't see how you carried all that grief with you all these years." "I know these stories have to be told," said Lucy but I was wondering if you could make them as humane as possible and leave my name out of them." "I think we can do that," said Amanda. "I think we can just say a person of interest filled in all the blanks for us but I'm not sure how we are going to sugar coat the murder of Curtis." "Whatever you can do I will be grateful," said Lucy.

As the meeting broke up Laura asked Diane and Lucy to stay for a few minutes. She wanted to talk to them about the farm, Doug, Kelly, and Skiles. She had all the information she and the others needed to close the case but she wanted to hear the personal side. Laura was an emotional person and she was sorry for the way some of their lives had turned out.

Brian and Amanda left to work on their stories and Chip left with a troubled mind and a heavy heart. He had the thankless job of contacting the family of Curtis.

As Chip left the building he noticed it had been raining. As he headed toward the police station he thought to himself, that was all he needed, an overcast day with rain. Talk about making you feel even more sorrowful! How in the world do you tell a family that someone had been brutally murdered for no reason at all? It seemed such a waste of innocent life.

Detective Reynolds was trying to find the words as he walked but all that came to him was something that rarely came to him because he was normally a hard man with few emotions. But there they were as big as life and he couldn't hold them back. Tears, big Crocodile tears!

Six months had passed since the final chapter in the saga of the house of blue lights had been closed. What had started with a glass casket at a housing development eighteen months ago had ended with a complete accounting of who, what, when, and where. The legend had all been wrapped up in a neat little package and tied with a bow.

"You know what's strange Brian," said Laura. "Less than two years ago I didn't know you. I had forgotten about the house of blue lights and was sitting at home jobless and miserable. Now look at me. I'm married, pregnant, and living in a house that used to sit on top of a swimming pool at the house of blue lights."

"And look at me," said Brian. "I found the love of my life, the home of my dreams, and I received a 70 Chevelle as a surprise wedding gift from you. What more could a guy ask for?" "Maybe a better job," said Laura. "I know you enjoyed solving this case but I don't think you liked all the pressure to write about it. Your boss Jack was relentless. No sooner did you find out something he wanted it in print and it will always be that way."

"You are right," said Brian. "I have been thinking about a career change." "What career are you looking at," she said? "I'm not sure," he said. "I haven't told you but your dad has offered me a sweet business deal and I have several other ideas I want to ponder. I have even thought about politics. I think I can do a much better job than most of those bozos in Washington. Whatever I decide I think I'll figure it out soon."

"Let's take a little walk out back," Laura said "there is something I want to talk to you about. Now I know this may sound strange but you remember when we got married I wanted a church wedding?" "Yes, I thought that was nice, and I really liked the minister we had." "Well, since then and when I found out I was pregnant I have been thinking a lot about God. I'd like to attend church next Sunday. What do you think?" "I think that's great, as a matter of fact finding God has always been a goal of mine and it's probably time I made it a priority. There are many times I look around in wonder and awe at all the beauty of this world. I think to myself only God could have made all this come together."

It was a beautiful night. It was now November, the trees were bare and there was crispness in the air. The sky was clear and you could see a million stars.

As they reached the last step from the deck to the yard Laura stopped. "I have something else to ask you," she said. "I hope you don't think I'm crazy but I'd like to name our baby Skiles." There was silence from Brian. "Come on say something," she said. "I'm thinking," said Brian. After a few more seconds he said, "You know I like it. Let's do it!"

They continued their walk out through the yard toward the trees at the back. About half way across Laura stopped again. "I wonder," she said, "if Doug is out here somewhere." "I don't know," said Brian. "I have to assume he is. I'm glad they decided not to dig up the place looking for him." "Me too," she said. "He was a troubled lad. I feel sorry for him even though he did wrong. I feel he deserves to rest in peace."

"You know what would be nice," Laura said? "What," asked Brian? "You see that maple tree where the hill begins. I was thinking about stringing some blue lights from there over to the house." "Are you crazy," he asked? "Come on honey," she said. "If Doug is out there he might enjoy them."

"So let me get this straight," he said. "You want to name our baby Skiles and now string blue lights on the property that became a legend because of Skiles Test and his love for blue lights." "Yes," she said. "I do. I think it would be great as long as you don't bury me here in a glass casket when I die."

There was another moment of silence. Brian then reached down and took Laura's hand and they started walking again. As they reached the maple tree he stopped, turned and looked at her and said. "Blue lights huh? Why not? Why the hell not?"

The End

About the Author

Garry Ledbetter began his working career at age 12 for Skiles Test (The House of Blue Lights). His duties included feeding the cats and dogs, helping milk the cows, baling hay, working in the garden, and cleaning the pool and house areas.

Garry lived with his parents and siblings in one of Mr. Test's tenant houses.

Garry graduated from Lawrence Central High School in 1965. Soon after graduation he joined the U.S. Army. There he served 2 years stateside and 1 year in Vietnam as a Flight Engineer on a Chinook helicopter.

After his military career he continued his education at IUPUI in Indianapolis. His career spans 45 years of employment as a mechanic, management supervisor and an IT manager.

He is retired and living in Indianapolis.